DEATH IN THE WOODS

JO ALLEN

Author Copyright Jo Allen 2021
Cover Art: Mary Jayne Baker
This ebook is licensed for your personal enjoyment and may not be resold or given away.

This story is a work of fiction. The characters are figments of my imagination and any resemblance to anyone living or dead is entirely coincidental.
Some of the locations used are real. Some are invented.

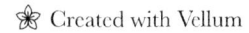

❦ Created with Vellum

FOREWORD

All of the characters in this book are figments of my imagination and bear no resemblance to anyone alive or dead.

The same can't be said for the locations. Many are real but others are not. I've taken several liberties with geography, mainly because I have a superstitious dread of setting a murder in a real building without the express permission of the homeowner, but also because I didn't want to accidentally refer to a real character in a real place or property.

So, for example, you won't find Jude's home village of Wasby on the map; you will find the village of Lazonby but its pub, the Golden Cage, is an invention. Lacy's Caves and the Long Meg stone circle are real but Geri's cottage is not.

Although I've taken these liberties with the details I've tried to remain true to the overwhelming beauty of the Cumbrian landscape. I hope the many fans of the Lake District will understand, and can find it in their hearts to forgive me for these deliberate mistakes.

ONE

It was a day for dying.

Izzy Ecclestone had been hanging around in Cave Wood for hours, smoking the occasional spliff and, as her brain grew hazier, musing on the inevitable end of everything. She'd been sitting for some time in a clearing with her back to a tree, her eyes on a view that was half undergrowth and half sunset, while the shadows of the trees wrapped their stealthy fingers around her soul. Now, as the late summer daylight clung on like an unwanted guest, the time for thinking lapsed and the moment for action was upon her.

Death comes slowly like a soft slipper to a tired foot, she wrote in her notebook, pressing too heavily so that the nib of her mechanical pencil snapped and the sliver of graphite spat into the grass. That was it, a fitting last line to a short life.

Leaving the stub of the cigarette spluttering to extinction on bare earth, she got up and stumbled her way back through the woods towards the stone circle and the oak that the locals called the Sentinel Tree. Around her, the shadows deepened to green on the way to soft, all-consuming black. Sly things moved within them — birds late to roost, perhaps, or bats, or moths with their wingspans as large as the palm of her hand. Still clutching notebook and pencil, she picked her way over-carefully across the soft forest floor, catching her foot from time to time in twisted roots and fallen branches. As she emerged from the woods a little way down the slope the darkness gave way to grey light, but even that would fade away in minutes as night came rolling over the lip of the Pennines and filtered into the valley.

She stopped. From outside the thin margin of the woods, where the undergrowth gave way to a track and eventually to civilisation, someone was watching her.

Many things scared Izzy but ghosts weren't among them. Next to the prospect of a long life in a doomed world the dead had nothing to offer that would hurt her, and none of the many ghosts she'd seen before had seemed remotely threatening. Around her, the woods shivered in a narcotic haze as she stopped and faced down the shrunken figure who confronted her. She lifted a strand of barbed wire with the back of her forearm and squeezed through the gap, oblivious to the pain she should have felt when it snagged the back of her wrist.

At the top of slope, the stone circle of Long Meg and her Daughters stood purple against the skyline. A host of fairy stories floated in Izzy's brain, interweaving like the swirls of smoke she'd inhaled. Here on the cusp between life and death, fantasy and reality, anything was possible. Fascinated, she edged closer to the grey figure. 'Are you Long Meg?'

'No.' It was a woman. Izzy's senses were comfortably blunt but she could see that much, though the darkness and the figure's grey and shapeless clothing showed her little more. 'My name is Raven.'

Izzy's chest contracted in disappointment as a terrible thought came to her, that somehow she'd been drawn over that line into the afterlife without having the courage to take action for herself. She spared a brief thought for the people she'd left behind and how they'd never know what had happened. She'd disappear. They'd search the banks of the River Eden all the way to the sea and never find her body, assuming she'd been washed away by the ever-rolling waves, her soft flesh picked away by the creatures of the deep. In reality she'd be where she always was, a shadow among the shadows, watching as they searched, waiting until it was her time to lure the living through the ever-shifting boundary that kept them apart.

There really was no need to be afraid of the dead. 'Are you a ghost?'

'No.' Raven shuffled forward into what passed for the light. 'Not yet.'

Then if she was no ghost, Izzy herself was not dead. In the centre of the sprawling circle, the skeleton of the Sentinel Tree stood watching, waiting for Izzy to choose her moment and hang from its branches. 'Do you think you will be one day? A ghost, I mean?'

'Oh yes,' said the woman, with confidence. 'We all will. But for me it'll be sooner rather than later.'

'Are you dying?' Anyone she knew would have jumped on her for that, but Izzy was a believer in naming the names of dread things and of speaking the unspeakable. Life was sometimes not worth living and she had the courage to say so. Even without the uninhibiting flow of marijuana through her veins, she'd sensed she was in the presence of a fellow thinker.

'Yes.' Raven's hand fluttered up in front of her almost, Izzy thought, like a soul leaving a body. 'But very slowly.'

I don't know what to say, Izzy's mother might have said in these circumstances, going scarlet with embarrassment, but Izzy wasn't floored. 'Are you scared?'

'Not at all. I've lived a long time. I've been very happy. And it's not a happy world I'm leaving behind. I'll only miss some of the people.' Raven's expression darkened for a moment, before it flared into tranquility. 'And they'll be with me soon enough.'

'I'm ready to die, too. And that's why. The world is such a terrible place. I'm not afraid of death, either. In fact, I positively want to die.' Izzy looked towards the Sentinel Tree, whose shadows had blurred into the dark grey of the grass. 'That's why I'm here. It's what I came here to do.'

'And is it your time?' Raven turned towards the setting sun.

'I don't know what you mean.'

'There's a right time. I don't know when my time will be, only that it isn't quite yet.'

Izzy tried to walk towards her, but her feet seemed unable to meet the ground as easily as usual and she stumbled. Raven held out a thin hand to steady her and the two of them stood for a second looking westward, two scant figures, one old and one young. 'So when will your time be?'

'I don't know. Time chooses you.'

That was very passive. Izzy's dad sometimes used to chide her for that. Her mother, who was kinder, called her timid, but if there was one thing she wanted to prove to them it was that she was capable of taking control of her life, if only in the leaving of it. 'I don't think so. I think you have to choose.' They had their backs to the tree now, but she could still feel it calling her. Such a beautiful shape, such dark, sinister beauty and a promise of peace. 'It's what people do these days.'

'Oh.' Raven laughed. Her voice had been thin but the laugh rang strong. 'I don't think just because something's modern it's necessarily good, do you?'

'I think it's the way we young people fight back. Our parents created an evil world. Our only answer is to leave them behind.' Izzy waited for laughter, but it didn't come. Emboldened, she carried on. 'That's why people are killing themselves. Did you know that? Two people — both around my age, twenty — have killed themselves around here. One of them hanged himself from a tree on Beacon Hill. I didn't know him, but the other was a girl in my village. She jumped off the bridge in Lazonby, in front of a train.' An odd one, because Izzy had known Tania since primary school, and nothing about the girl had ever suggested she might be contemplating taking that final step. In her heart Izzy felt a little cheated. 'Everyone says it was a terrible tragedy, but I think they'll be so much happier away from this world.' Around her, the world swayed a little, flexed in and out as if it was being squeezed. She felt strange.

'Maybe they will,' Raven agreed. She moved a little closer, laid thin fingers on Izzy's arm. 'But it's the people they leave behind. Isn't it?'

Izzy considered. It was true her family would miss her, and of course she felt sorry for them, but there was something so intriguing about death, something so very exciting. For years she'd yearned to know what lay on the other side. Sometimes, in her dreams, she thought she saw into it, this other-worldly place where nothing was ever wrong, where the perpetual sense of calm matched the one she got from smoking weed. 'They'll be sad to start with but they'll realise I won't be sad either. It'll be fine.'

'I have a daughter,' Raven said, suddenly. 'Will you write to her for me?'

Looking down, Izzy saw she was somehow still clutching the notebook and pencil. Blood had trickled from the back of her hands and between her fingers to leave bloody fingermarks smeared on the cover. She looked back at Raven. Two strange people, caught in this half-light. Surely everything happened for a reason. And — it struck her at last — she couldn't hang herself that day. She hadn't brought a rope. 'Can't you do it yourself?'

'My eyes aren't so good any more,' the older woman said, almost apologetically. 'And I have arthritis.' She spread her right hand in front of her to show curled fingers. 'She'll be wondering how I am.'

'You can't phone?'

'I don't have a phone.'

Belatedly, Izzy realised who she was talking to. This must be one of the hippies who'd set up camp in the field between Long Meg and the village of Little Salkeld, cooking on camp fires and, her mother said, doing nothing that could be regarded as useful to anyone. There was something appealing to Izzy about this approach. If you couldn't escape the complexities of modern life, the best way surely was to let it all wash over you.

If she didn't die, she might become a hippy. For the moment that seemed like a noble compromise. 'Why don't you write her a note now? I'll post it.'

'You can write to her for me.' Still holding on to Izzy's arm, Raven drew her out of the lengthening shadows just as they caught up with them. 'Her name is Indigo. Write to her in Oxford. Waldorf College. Tell her I'm not very well and I'd like to see her before I die.'

Izzy tore the top sheet off the notebook and let it fall. She'd have forgotten the poem when she woke in the morning, but that was okay. Poems weren't meant to be permanent and when she needed another one she'd write it. 'I'll do that.'

'Could you do it tonight?'

Bewitched for a moment by a sudden sense of empowerment, Izzy toyed with the idea of offering to phone and solve this strange apparition's problem, but it was late, well after nine, and there would surely be no-one answering the phone on the switchboard of an Oxford college. In the last of the light, she looked down at the clean sheet on the pad and wrote down *Indigo, Waldorf College, Oxford*. In its own way, that qualified as a poem. 'What's her surname?'

'We don't have surnames. Don't worry. It'll find her.'

On impulse, Izzy leaned in and hugged the woman, thinking as she did so of her own grandmother. In her arms Raven was little more than a skeleton bundled up in rags. If this was death, up close, it wasn't the way she imagined it, or the way she read about it in the true crimes and tales of tortured suicides that sent shivers down her spine even as they fascinated her. 'Of course I'll write.'

'Thank you.'

There was a pause and then Raven nodded as if in dismissal. In the brightening moonlight, Izzy passed beneath the bare branches of the mighty Sentinel Tree and headed off down the track towards home.

In the dawn, when the rising sun had repelled the darkness, gathering its full strength and forcing the shadows back into their lairs, Raven made her sleepless way around the edge of the trees and down among them towards the singing River Eden. She shook her head as she turned past a steep outcrop of sandstone striped like a tabby cat, thinking of the strange but appealing child she'd met the night before. So full of life, if only she knew it.

On the far side of the river the rocks were vermilion in the rising sun, but the west-facing woods were still dim. The wind stirred the branches and the branches in their turn set the shadows dancing. It was, she recognised, an unnatural dance, at odds with the light weight of the dappled leaves.

Troubled, Raven stopped. As she'd feared, the worst had happened. A few yards in from the water's edge, a body dangled like a dummy from the branch of a tree.

She stood for a while, staring at it, before she turned and, gathering her skirt around her knees, scrambled as fast as she could back up the hill. And the wind stopped but the heavy weight of death in the trees rumbled on, a solid shadow swinging behind her, back and forth, back and forth.

TWO

'It looks for all the world like a straightforward suicide.' Detective Sergeant Ashleigh O'Halloran turned to her boss — and lover — and crinkled her eyes, partly against the sun and partly in sheer puzzlement. 'One I can understand. But now we have three, and in the space of a couple of months. Does that make it an epidemic?'

Did it? If it didn't it certainly made it more of a puzzle. Jude Satterthwaite, too, frowned at the scene. He'd been dealing with death, whether violent, accidental or self-inflicted, for the better part of two decades, so long he'd become inured to it in a way that shamed him, but he wasn't as hard as he'd thought. These days the death of a youth always struck him a little more close to the heart than it used to. He tried not to think of Mikey, the younger brother around the same age as this most recent corpse, who was the worry that kept him awake at night, the problem he couldn't solve. 'I don't know the definition. But it certainly merits further investigation. Yes.'

'Faye must think it's serious, if she sent you down to deal with it.'

Faye Scanlon, the Detective Superintendent, had an uncanny ear for circumstances that chimed ill. She might be wrong, of course, might have scanned the resources available to her and decided Jude was the one with the least to do — though *least* never meant *not enough*. Or it might be more pragmatic. 'I don't know if it's that. I expect she knows this kind of thing gets people stressed and she wants them to know we're on top of it.'

He'd left his car by the ruins of the old mine by the railway line, where a uniformed police officer had been turning back interested onlookers, and walked the half mile or so to where Ashleigh had been checking over the scene. There was a second uniformed officer on the path in front of them and a CSI team beyond them on the riverside path, picking over the bones of what looked like suicide to make sure that nothing was missed, nothing slipped by.

'Are we on top of it?' Ashleigh asked, in unusual irritation. 'I'm foxed by this one. I don't mind telling you. I don't know what we can bring to it. Three kids killing themselves? Is this really one for the police? If you ask me we should be handing it over to the psychologists.'

Jude looked beyond the uniformed officer and up into the woods where the body of the latest suicide, a young man, had recently been cut down. In the background a mortuary van revved in readiness to take it back along the broken tarmac of the old road, loud even above the rippling of the River Eden a few feet below. 'I'd have thought you were the ideal person to answer that one.' In the year she'd been working with him she was always the one who picked up on the nuances, always the first detective to sense when something wasn't right.

'I'd need to know more. Need to think it through. I worked on the second case, very briefly, but I don't know anything about the first and I didn't have time to look at the case notes before I came out. I'd need to go back and see if there are any connections. As far as I can recall, there aren't.'

'We can go over that later.' Jude had had the luxury of a few minutes to scan through the notes for the previous two deaths before coming out, but no more. There had been nothing in them to suggest anything more sinister than personal tragedy. Two such events were a sad coincidence, perhaps the one triggering the other. Three were potentially more serious. Faye, when she'd detailed him to drop whatever he was doing and get down to Cave Wood as a matter of urgency to manage the impact on the community, had talked about getting professional help as though he was the one who needed it. 'Talk me through this one just now. Then we can see if there are any connections.'

'There's not much I can tell you. There hasn't been time to get a formal ID done yet, but we know who he is from the possessions. He's Charlie Curran. He lives in Penrith, down in Carleton Village. He's twenty-one and he works as a builder.'

Twenty-one. Mikey's age, not the most common demographic for suicide but not one that could be overlooked. Jude worried too much about Mikey. He knew it, and he fought it, but he couldn't stop himself. 'Do his family know?'

'I've got someone going down to talk to them now. And we've assigned them a Family Liaison Officer.' She checked her watch, as if this kind of thing went by the clock.

'Relationships?'

'He lives with his parents and he has a girlfriend, but as far as I know that's a fairly recent relationship. I haven't had time to go into anything in any detail but there's nothing that leaps out as a reason to kill himself.'

'Did he leave a note?'

'Not that we've found.'

Jude took another few seconds to stare at the place where Charlie Curran had died. Suicides raised questions and too many of them were never answered. 'Who found him?'

'Raven.'

Jude, who was familiar with the hippies who'd recently moved in to the Eden Valley, lifted an eyebrow. 'I see.'

'I didn't know they'd set up over here.' He sensed a faint trace of dissatisfaction in Ashleigh's voice and suppressed a smile. Like him, she was beset by the copper's desire to know everything. 'There can't be anything suspicious about that, can there? Not after the last time.'

He shook his head. Raven and her husband Storm attracted the wrong sort of attention for their alternative lifestyle, and a previous association with a series of gruesome murders several months earlier and elsewhere in the county hadn't helped, but the situation had been neither of their making nor their fault. Nevertheless… 'That's two bodies that poor woman has found now.'

'She certainly can't have anything to do with this one. She's so thin now the wind would blow her away. And you know me. Normally I'd be jumping at that, and feeling something.' She fluttered her fingers in the air and rolled her eyes, in a gesture of self-mockery. 'Not this time. No strange feelings, no red flags. As far as Raven is concerned, two and two make four.'

A white suited CSI emerged from the woods, gave them the thumbs up and turned away again. Returning the gesture Jude turned his back, conscious there was only so much he could learn from the scene. There was plenty more casework resting on his desk. This would be a problem of a different sort, a matter of prioritising action in the interests of public confidence even though there was no evidence of crime. 'There's no point in hanging around. I don't see there's a lot more we can do here. Let's go and get a coffee up in Lazonby. You can talk me through what you know of the other two cases and we'll see if anything leaps out this time.'

'I'll be amazed, but yes. I could do with a coffee.'

The path was narrow and he followed her along the river. 'Have you had a chance to speak to Raven?'

'Not yet. Whoever was first on the scene had a quick word, but she was too upset to tell them anything about it. I'm not surprised.'

Raven was a gentle soul, who wished no ill on anyone as far as Jude was aware, though he was too cynical to believe she had no secrets and knew her well enough to think she'd withhold the truth if she thought it was the right thing. Raven might be cowed by the law but she never let it rule her. 'I'd like you to go down and talk to her when she's feeling a little stronger.' There were more junior officers who would normally take on that job, but Ashleigh had the gift of opening up a witness. If Raven was hiding something, she'd know.

'I don't suppose it's a priority,' she said. 'Not with all the other things we have on.'

'No, there's no rush.' He reached his car, parked next to hers in the lane. It was, after all, a question of visibility and reassurance. 'I'll catch up with you in Lazonby.'

He waited for her to head up the lane, sat and checked his messages, and put in a quick call to his deputy. 'Doddsy. Just checking in. It looks like a pretty straightforward suicide to me, I have to say. Something may come up from the CSI people, but there's nothing there that looked out of kilter.'

'Isn't that what Ashleigh said about the first two?' Back in the office, Detective Inspector Chris Dodd, aka Doddsy, sounded as if he had other things on his mind.

'Yes. But the three together merit a closer look. I wouldn't mind running the whole thing past you when we get back.' He closed his eyes for a second and reviewed the resources he could spare. 'Get Chris Marshall to come and sit with us. I suspect that most of what we find out will be down to digging about in the background. If there's anything to find.' Chris had many other things to do, but he was efficient and effective.

'Sure. When will you be back up?'

'Less than an hour. I want to go up to Lazonby. For a coffee.' But there was more to it than that, just the inkling of an idea, a detail to check. 'We'll convene after lunch, maybe, if you've time.' Because Charlie Curran's death, with no evidence of wrongdoing, might stop all the clocks for his family and friends but it slid down a detective's to-do list below any number of actual and potential crimes.

'I'm busy, and I have the newspapers on my back. I fobbed them off, but they'll be back.'

'Thanks for the warning. I'll keep a low profile.'

When he'd checked what he wanted to check at Lazonby, they'd sit down and discuss the case. If no leads came up, it would lie on the file alongside the others. Three deaths. He started the car and steered it up the lane, past the officer stationed at the farm gate that usually blocked it. If it stopped at three, that was one thing. But would it?

The road to Lazonby took him along a network of narrow lanes and high hedges, from behind one of which rose a curl of smoke. Jude had the window down and the woodsmoke tickled his tastebuds. Someone was cooking something. On impulse, he turned off and headed towards the smoke, stopping in a gateway to peer through the gate. A haphazard assembly of canvas tents occupied one corner of a field. You wouldn't be able to see the location of Charlie's death from there, and the path was hidden, too, on the far side of the stone circle in the next field. And it was no short distance from there to Cave Wood, for someone like Raven, shuffling her way towards death at the hands of an illness that was, as far as he was aware, undiagnosed and that he suspected she didn't have the energy to fight, to cover in the darkness of an evening.

It would be interesting to see what Ashleigh got from her later on in the week.

THREE

At Lazonby, Ashleigh parked the car, got out and went into the Co-Op, composing her expression into the blandest she could manage as she did so. The second suicide, a few weeks before, had been that of a local girl and she'd been in and about the place following up. The place would still be reeling from the shock of Tania Baker's death and she'd be the focus of more attention, expected to field questions she couldn't have addressed even if she knew the answers.

She checked her phone as she waited in the queue, aware that the customers in the shop would be watching her, that news of the latest death would already be out there. There were half a dozen messages, most of which could be ignored, but one was more than useful. Her colleague Chris Marshall — possibly prompted by Jude — had sent an admirable summary of both previous suicides, culled from what little was in the files.

She snapped her phone off, managing to ignore the customers leaving the shop, and placed the coffee order.

'More terrible news, Sergeant O'Halloran.' The

woman behind the counter flicked the switches on the coffee machine and delivered the two Americanos that Ashleigh had ordered. 'Two young people taken from us so suddenly. I'm so shocked. We all are.'

Ashleigh took her eyes from the phone, murmured something suitably regretful, and laid a five pound note on the counter.

'It's a wicked world,' the woman went on. 'It's no wonder the kids don't want to live in it, with what we're doing to it. House prices and politics and global warming? What kind of future is that? Do we know who it was?'

'Not yet. The identity has still to be confirmed.'

'And it was suicide, wasn't it? And one of those hippies up by Long Meg found him, they say? They're a strange lot, aren't they? Filling people's heads with a lot of nonsense, no doubt.' She slapped the change down on the counter. 'But I dare say they mean well.'

'We're treating the death as unexplained.' With relief, Ashleigh saw Jude's Mercedes pull up outside. 'I'd better go.'

'You make sure you do something to stop this happening any more.'

As if she could. Ashleigh carried the two coffees outside to where Jude had got out of the car and was leaning on the door with an air of studied carelessness, looking like a sharp-suited businessman snatching a break before a meeting. It might have fooled any passers-by, but everyone who worked with him recognised that the casual outlook was a mask. He was always on the watch, always looking for the crucial detail everyone else had missed.

'Here you go.' She handed him one of the two disposable cups. 'Coffee.'

'Excellent. Thanks.' He smiled at her as he took it. 'I need something to sharpen my brain.'

'Chris has sent me a note about the other suicides.' Ashleigh sipped her coffee and found it as good as it was welcome.

'Right. Do you want to talk me through them?'

'One of them was here.' Ashleigh stopped, out of habit, as a young woman came past, a stamped envelope in her hand, and thrust it into the post box. She'd seen her on the way into the village, a spindly figure distinctive in black, standing in one of the embayments of the solid old bridge over the river and staring down into the swirling waters. Ashleigh had slowed the car and looked twice, as a precaution, but her concern had been misplaced and the girl had jogged off with a sprightly step. 'But you know that, don't you, or we'd have been back at the office by now?'

'I had a quick look through the files before I came out, but that was all I had time for. And I think we deserve a coffee. Let's amble down along the railway, shall we?'

'Do we have time?'

'It'll take us twenty minutes. Call it a coffee break.' He set off with a long stride. 'Begin at the beginning.'

She followed, phone in hand, scanning the case notes and reading them out. Chris Marshall had many talents but his capacity for swift communication of key information was particularly useful. 'In May, Connor Turnbull, a forestry worker from Stainton, took his own life. He was twenty-three and single. He hanged himself in a small wood within sight of his home. He left no note, but had struggled with mental health issues as a teenager. There were no marks on the body indicating any sign of violence. No-one was surprised.' When you stripped a young life down to the bare bones it seemed simple and easy. Connor Turnbull's past must surely have been more complicated than that.

'No-one saw him the evening he died?'

She consulted the notes. 'No. He went out in the evening, spoke to a neighbour, who thought he was going to the pub. He was drinking in Penrith later that night, on his own, and CCTV shows him walking past the station. That's all. Verdict — suicide. There was no reason to think otherwise. As far as I know there still isn't. It was very straightforward.'

'Okay.' Jude turned left onto a road out of the village, up the hill and broadly alongside the railway. Like a spaniel on the trail, Ashleigh thought as she struggled to keep up with him. 'What about the next one?' He slowed to allow her to catch up and they took a more leisurely pace as the road levelled out. 'It was up here, wasn't it?'

'Yes. Up at the bridge. Here.' They were the better part of three quarters of a mile from where they'd left the cars and it would have been quicker to drive, but Jude was scanning the scene just as Ashleigh herself had done a bare three weeks earlier, when Doddsy had sent her down to oversee what was going on. 'It was a young woman, Tania Baker. She was nineteen. She lived here in Lazonby, up at the top of the village, in a flat two doors along from her parents. She used to work in a shop in Carlisle but was made redundant about six months ago and was unemployed. Her financial situation was precarious but not desperate. Her parents kept an eye out for her and they were as astonished as they were devastated at what happened. She left no note, and she had no history of mental health issues.' Unlike Connor Turnbull, Tania's death had taken everyone by surprise.

'And what happened?'

'She was in the village at about eight o'clock on a Wednesday evening, where she stopped and chatted to a couple of people. Her behaviour seemed normal. No-one saw her go up Fiddler's Lane. Here.' They'd almost reached the bridge which crossed the railway line and they stopped to stare down on the bare tracks of the Settle-Carlisle line, gleaming away as they narrowed into the distance. 'The last train leaves Carlisle just before twenty past eight and gets to Langwathby at about quarter to nine.'

Jude placed both hands on the sandstone parapet of the bridge and frowned along the railway line. 'It doesn't stop here in Lazonby?'

'Not that one. I think we can assume Tania would have known that, so she'd known it wouldn't have been slowing down. As the train came under the bridge she dropped from this side onto the track in front of it. There was nothing the driver could do except shut his eyes.'

They were silent. Down on the railway line, a ragged bouquet of flowers, long dead and with its cellophane wrapping in tatters, as a memorial to a life lost. For a moment they stared at it.

'Okay,' Jude said, after a moment's contemplation. He strode up to the bridge, took out his phone and snapped a series of quick shots in both directions. 'So no-one saw her.'

'No-one saw her after she'd walked off the main street and up Fiddler's Lane. No.'

'And no-one saw her jump.'

'Only the train driver. He didn't see anyone on the bridge as he approached.'

'But Tania was there and he didn't see her. Okay. So if we want to look at this in a different way…maybe someone else was with her who he also didn't see. So it's theoretically possible she wasn't alone on the bridge.'

Ashleigh stared down at the track. 'Theoretically, yes. But aren't you overthinking it? It's theoretically possible most suicides weren't alone when they died, although almost all of them will have been. There's nothing in this case to suggest she wasn't.'

'You're probably right. And there's nothing to suggest she didn't jump. It's just my suspicious mind.'

Sometimes Ashleigh struggled not to laugh at Jude. There could have been no other career for him but the police, no other way of life for someone with as keen a sense of justice and so sharp a determination to see that evil never went unpunished. It had come at a cost for him — these things always did — but it had turned out all right. The girlfriend who'd found his sense of fair play too much to handle when it had forced a choice between his friends and his job was firmly in the past, and Ashleigh had stepped neatly into her place. 'The CSI people went over it pretty thoroughly.' Perhaps, under time pressure, they hadn't spent as long on it as they might have done if there had been a suggestion of foul play, but they'd been thorough enough.

'I don't doubt it. Nevertheless, I think I'd like to revisit that one, just on the off chance. Perhaps go back and talk to the train driver. He's our only witness.'

'Do we have the time?' It wasn't that she disbelieved him, but nor could Ashleigh bring herself to give full credibility to what he was suggesting. It was suicide. 'Do we have the resources?'

He was silent for a few seconds. 'I suppose the answer to that is that if I seriously thought it was suspicious we'd find the time and the resources. But no. I don't think that. I just think it bears another look. A call to the driver will take you ten minutes. And someone — Chris or Aditi, maybe — can go through the files and double-check that nothing stands out. For example, statistically it probably isn't unusual to find three suicides in two months in this area, overall, but maybe it is in this age group. If that's the case, it makes me wonder. Could they have known each other? Can you can find the time to check that out?'

Ashleigh finished her coffee, cold now, and crushed the cardboard cup between her fingers. 'If I put off doing something else. Or you could come round tonight and we could discuss it over supper. Or actually, as Lisa's in tonight we can discuss it after supper. In private.'

'I can manage that. I don't have anything else on.'

Jude never compromised. Work was everything and nothing got in the way of it, so that even this half-hearted recognition of the relationship they were in felt very slightly risky in office hours, but that didn't bother Ashleigh, cut from the same cloth. 'Excellent. Then let's head back. I think we've stretched the coffee break to its limit.'

'It's a gorgeous day,' said Ashleigh, with regret, 'but I don't suppose we can play hooky much longer.' Being out in the sunshine when there was work to be done in the office always did feel like skiving off, even if what they were doing had some bearing on the case.

If it did. Jude must think so, or he wouldn't have wasted time looking. She stepped aside to allow a jogger to get past them, a young man barely in his twenties. As they reached the end of Fiddler's Lane, a police car drove past in the direction of Great Salkeld and the young officer in the passenger seat, Tyrone Garner, raised a hand in recognition.

Jude was frowning after him long after the car had crossed the solid sandstone bridge and even if she hadn't known him so well Ashleigh would have had a clear guess about what he was thinking. Tyrone; the young woman in black who'd been posting the letter; the jogger who was even then puffing his way over the bridge from which

Tania Baker had fallen to her death... All fitted the age and the demographic of three recent suicides. They weren't the only ones. 'Mikey will be okay.'

'I'm glad you're so comfortable about it.'

'There's no reason why he shouldn't be. You know yourself. People always feel these things personally, because they're local to them. You're no different. There must be thousands of young people of that age, locally. They'll survive. And so will Mikey.' They'd reached her car by then and she tossed her cup into a nearby bin.

'It won't stop people worrying. It never does.' He shook his head as if he was impatient with himself. 'Kid brothers are more trouble than your own kids, if you ask me. I'll need to have a word with him. Since his dad won't.'

Jude and Mikey's father had walked out on the family years before. Ashleigh had never met him, though she knew he haunted the bars of Penrith on a regular basis. 'Would he, if you asked?'

'I doubt it. And if he did Mikey wouldn't listen to him. I'll do it myself, and I might make something useful out of it. Mikey's a mine of information. I don't think he goes looking for it. Just absorbs it. But if there's some chat around these suicides he'll have heard it.'

FOUR

Becca Reid, finishing off with the patient she visited twice a week at the Eden's End nursing home, checked her watch and found she had time on her hands. That happened rarely enough for her to be surprised by it. Picking up her bag, she headed back up through the thickly-carpeted lobby and through the lounge, where a knot of the home's staff clustered around the tea trolley.

'Becca might know,' Ellie Jack, the head nurse, tossed her a quick — and not altogether friendly — glance. 'She used to go out with that policeman. Didn't you, Becca?'

Becca's lip curled, as it always did when she thought of Jude Satterthwaite. This time it was less in irritation at the way things had gone so badly wrong between them that it still troubled her years on, and more amusement at the way Ellie sniffed and tossed her head when she mentioned him. The previous year, a killer had crept through the corridors of Eden's End and laid a hand on a woman already dying, and Ellie's view on the matter had been very much that things were best left to lie.

But Ellie, for all her resistance to the investigation and her callous approach to the dying, wasn't the killer. That was one of the many things Becca had learned from her years with Jude. Because someone could have committed a crime, or any other misdemeanour, didn't mean they had, and therefore it was wise to keep an open mind and refrain from prejudgement. A useful lesson. 'Yes, but that was years ago. I don't see him that often these days.' And when they did meet their conversation was brief and sterile unless Ashleigh O'Halloran was present, in which case it became forced.

'Yes but you'll know how these things work. Someone said they had the police all over the place down at Lacy's Caves this morning. That's not standard for suicide. Is it?'

Someone else drifted over, and Becca found herself somehow at the centre of a group of staff, with the elderly residents at the margins, all looking at her as if she was up to speed not just with police procedure in general but with the details of this specific case. 'I don't know. I imagine they have to look at these things. Just to be on the safe side.'

'Three suicides in a couple of months isn't normal, is it?'

What was normal? Suicide was more common that many people realised, something that cropped up in Becca's work from time to time. And it was indiscriminate. It affected the popular and the apparently fulfilled as much as the friendless and obviously lonely, snatched away those who couldn't cope with the pressures of wealth as well as those who struggled to make ends meet. She wouldn't be surprised to find the numbers were nothing outside the normal, but there was no question there was something about this latest clutch of local losses that chilled the community's heart. They were young. That must be it. 'I don't know.'

'I've read about copycat suicides before.' One of the carers perched herself on the arm of a chair and flicked a sidelong look at a colleague who, Becca remembered, had a teenage daughter of her own. 'No-one knows why they happen. It could be anyone next. We all need to watch our kids.'

For God's sake, Becca chided the woman, in her head. *Is this helping anyone?* 'I'm pretty sure it'll turn out to be coincidence.'

'Somebody get the teas,' Ellie said, tiring of the conversation. 'I don't have time to stand around gossiping. I'm a busy woman.'

'I'm on my way.' Her colleague jumped down from the chair and turned away. 'We don't want you giving us hassle because the tea's cold, do we, Leslie, my heart?' She dimpled a cheerful smile at the elderly man sitting in the corner and began rattling the tea cups. 'Ellie, give Leslie his tea and biscuits on your way past, would you?'

'I'll take it over.' Becca had spotted what no-one else had — that the old man's cheek was damp with grief and another thin tear was trickling down his cheek to join those he'd already shed. Ellie, who tended to the brisk and businesslike, didn't always respond to other people's emotion as gently as she might have done, but Becca was a pushover for tears. That must be why something within her soul responded so painfully to the loss of three young people, why her heart ached for their parents. If she'd had children — if she'd only stayed with Jude long enough for that to become a reality, rather than letting his work and his absurdly rigid conscience come between them — she'd have been watching over their beds every night after the recent news. As they grew older she'd have talked to them, listened to them, supported them, done everything she could to protect them. If, by chance, she'd met one of the three young people the community had lost and seen some sign of their inner pain, she might have been the one to say something that changed their histories and saved their lives.

But she didn't know them, and no-one who did had seen anything amiss. *If ifs and ands were pot and pans*, her mother used to say, *there'd be no need for tinkers*. Just now Becca had to focus on the living. At least she could do something for them, no matter how small. She picked up the cup and saucer in her free hand and carried them over. 'Here you go, Mr Chester. I've brought you your tea. Let me get you a biscuit.'

She put the cup and saucer down on the table next to him, dropped her bag on the floor and went back to the trolley for a biscuit. Two for him and one for her, because she'd been on the go since eight and hadn't had lunch. 'Chocolate ones, today. I've picked the right time to call.' Without waiting for an invitation, she slid onto the chair next to his and lowered her voice. 'Are you all right?'

'It's a wicked world,' Leslie Chester said. He straightened his back, took the tissue that Becca automatically offered him, and dabbed at his eyes before thrusting the tissue deep into the pocket of his old, oversized jacket.

'It's all of that.' She sighed. On the television in the corner of the room one of the daytime TV shows was running a series of outtakes involving animals doing hilarious things. In the act of dishing out the coffee, the woman in charge of the tea trolley couldn't stop herself spluttering with laughter as a goat bounded onto an unstable stepping stone and tipped into the water. Whatever had triggered Leslie's distress, it couldn't be that. 'Do you want to talk about it?'

He put his head on one side for a moment. Leslie was of that generation to whom tears were a weakness, but it seemed he was too old to fight against them. 'A very sad, mad world,' he repeated.

Sensing a part of his life story coming her way, Becca made herself comfortable. It was bound to be something to do with the conversation at the tea trolley. 'Yes.'

'I had a son,' Leslie said, twisting his fingers in distress, 'a long time ago.'

Even before the tears renewed and the next of them trickled down onto the front of his navy blue cable-knit sweater, Becca knew where the story was going. This was how the world went round, nothing new under the sun. Someone's personal tragedy in this generation was a repeat of someone else's from the generation before. All it took was a snatch of a song or a clip on the news to bring it out. 'What happened to him?'

'He died.' Leslie's fingers went to the inside pocket of his jacket and he felt about in it, unable to see through his own tears. He pulled out a small brown envelope. 'Here.'

Becca took it. The thin paper was fragile under her fingers as she slid open the flap and drew out a photograph. In the sad, faded images from perhaps forty years before, a teenager in flared jeans and a mullet hairdo pushed a younger girl on a swing that was too small for her. The copper colours of the trees in the background, even though they were fading to sepia, told her it had been taken in autumn, and in the background she recognised the familiar shape of the Pennines and the conical peak of Dufton Pike. 'Your children?'

'Yes.' His finger jabbed at the image and he folded his lips tightly together in a vain effort to stop them quivering. 'This is Nicholas.'

'How old was he?'

'Sixteen.' The finger quivered. 'This is the last picture I have of him.'

Sixteen. Becca's heart quivered. It was too young. No-one should ever lose a child, let alone have to live on for forty years or more without them. 'What happened to him?'

After all those decades, Leslie was struggling to find the words. Although he was in his eighties, Becca's occasional dealings with him had shown her he was an educated and articulate man, someone who had embraced growing old and been determined to make the most of it. But in the face of death, as she knew too well, the most determined people could crumble.

'It was an accident.' Leslie regained the stiff upper lip his upbringing must have taught him and the words came out clearly. 'He fell.'

'Fell?' asked Becca, caught in the dilemma between allowing him to talk and probing too deeply into his unhappiness. 'On the hills?'

'On the railway.' He dabbed at his eyes. 'Up at Eden Lacy. He was playing on the tracks up on the viaduct and a train came and he jumped out of the way and fell into the river.' He looked down at the picture again. 'A proper daredevil, they said at school. Always trying to prove something.'

The viaduct at Eden Lacy was just a couple of miles from Lazonby, where Tania had met her death, and within sight of Cave Wood where everyone said the police had been that morning. It was no wonder he was distressed. 'Oh, Leslie. I'm so sorry.'

'If I'd known it would happen,' he said dolefully, 'I'd have talked to him more. Told him I loved him.

For a second Becca closed her eyes. Having a child — she would love to have a child — was so precious. Too often parents failed to communicate their love to their children or the children, for whatever reason, were unable to accept it. 'This must have brought it all back.'

'Aye.' He took the picture back from her and slid it carefully back into the inside pocket of his jacket. She had the impression he didn't normally keep it there, that it was something he'd dug out of a folder or a drawer and chosen, for today, to keep close to his heart. 'Those poor kids. Three of them, they said.'

'And their poor parents.'

'Their parents should have looked out for them a bit better,' he said, sharply.

He reached for his cup of tea and Becca sensed the moment of confidence was over. She wasn't going to judge the grieving families, but nor was she going to take issue with the harshness of his opinion. Unbidden, the image of Jude Satterthwaite swept once more into her head. If there was one thing harder than bringing up your own child it had to be dealing with the dysfunctionality of someone else's. Jude's relationship with his brother was fragile at best but whatever she thought about his dedication to his job, his dedication to Mikey was as justifiable as it was admirable.

But the task might be impossible. Mikey was just twenty-one and yet to mature, still seething with resentment at the break-up of his family and blaming everyone else for the pain of it. If there was one person he wouldn't listen to it was his father and if there was a second it was surely Jude, whose determination to look after him he deeply resented.

David Satterthwaite was the one really at fault, but Becca didn't know him well enough to remind him of his responsibilities and would never have presumed to do so if she did. In any case, he shouldn't need prompting. But she got on well enough with Mikey, despite more than ten years' difference in their ages. Maybe she should try and talk to him herself.

Best not to interfere without speaking to Jude first. She shook her head as she left Leslie and the rest of Eden's End behind her. And on the way out, noticing the television had flicked to the news, she changed the channel to something less brutal so that at least she could spare Leslie Chester an ill-timed camera shot of the viaduct where young Nicholas had died, all those years before.

FIVE

'Well.' Lisa, Ashleigh's friend and flatmate, pushed her chair back and sighed in satisfaction. 'That was pretty damn good. We'll make a cook of you yet, Ash. Maybe.'

'That's harsh.' Jude got on well with Lisa, who was intense, sensible and outspoken. Two of those qualities he valued and the third he could cope with. He sat back and smiled, replete. 'She's learning all the time. And for the record, I did the cooking.'

'I might have known she'd let you do the work.' Lisa reached for his plate, then Ashleigh's and piled them on top of one another, forks to the left of the plate, knives to the right. 'I'll finish clearing up later. Right now I'm going to leave you lovebirds alone together. I'm doing a school talk to a bunch of sixth formers tomorrow and the school have asked me to tone it down.'

'Tone it down?' Ashleigh jeered. 'What on earth was in it?'

Lisa rolled her eyes. 'Yeah, I know. It's a careers talk, to help them with their subject choices. It's not easy trying to sell the best job in the world when too many people only think about the dirt.'

Archaeology, to Jude's mind, was as dry as the dust Lisa spent much of her summers digging in. 'So how were you trying to corrupt these kids? Sex drugs and rock and roll? Spicing it up a little?'

'No, though I could do a pretty good talk on hallucinogenic plants if called on.' Lisa picked the plates up and carried them over to the dishwasher. 'I always go as gory as I can with these talks, to try and keep the kids — sorry, young people — interested. Crime and punishment, a bit about how we excavate the graves, some examples of the more unusual deaths and so on. Bog bodies, executions, human sacrifices, the lot. They love it. I do this one at the beginning of every school year but today the head emailed me to say she thinks too much graphic detail probably isn't wise at this point in time, so could I please revisit my usual talk. And so. I shall describe in detail the graves where we've found various people who've died peacefully of old age, explain how we can tell their diet from the isotopic make up of their teeth, show them a few slides of pollen grains, and my audience of snowflakes can doze quietly away.'

Even as he laughed at Lisa's self-deprecation, Jude thought once more of the cluster of suicides. In his experience most young people were more resilient than they looked when it came to the darker side of history. It was their own present, the immediacy of their own problems, with which they struggled. That said, he could see where the head teacher was coming from. 'There's a bit of concern about this, then?'

'You'd probably know that better than me.'

'People talk to me about it a particular way.' They were direct, demanding he do something about it. The mystery of what went on in people's minds — and what they thought he could achieve in healing it — was beyond him. 'I was wondering what the general buzz was.'

She considered. 'I do hear a bit of talk. I spend most of my time up in Carlisle, of course, and I don't do a lot of school work this early in the academic year, but I'm sensing a bit of concern among the staff. Three suicides is a lot.'

None of the suicides had been of school age, but nor were they much older. When Jude nodded his agreement, Lisa's expression sobered further. 'If I'm honest I think the adults are more concerned about it than the kids.'

Jude thought of Mikey again, knowing he was falling into the same trap. He looked across at Ashleigh to see if she'd picked up his concern, but she'd been frowning at her phone rather than listening to the conversation.

'That's a message,' she said. 'I'd better deal with it, I suppose. In case it's something important.' She jumped up from the table and shouldered her way through the door, the phone clamped to her ear. 'No. It's not a good time to talk. Jude's here. What do you want?' Her voice faded into the distance as she snapped the living room door closed.

When Ashleigh, normally so calm and together, got flustered, there was only one cause. Resisting the temptation to comment, Jude got up and joined Lisa at the sink, reaching for a cloth to wipe the crumbs from the table.

'Well, now.' Lisa shifted the pot from the cooker to the sink. Her forthrightness always overwhelmed any attempts she might make at discretion. She'd been Ashleigh's friend too long to care, or so it seemed, and time had bomb-proofed their relationship so no slip of the tongue or moment of irritation could damage it. 'I think we know who that was.'

He did. He opened the washing machine and tossed the dirty dishcloth into it.

Lisa wasn't letting go. 'You realise you have a rival?'

'I don't think so.' Scott, the ex-husband who was on the phone, might still be a part of Ashleigh's life but the core of that relationship was firmly in her past. 'He calls her and she answers. That's fine. I talk to Becca all the time.' But even as he spoke the thought niggled at him. He'd never really got over Becca, and there were moments when he believed he was still in love with her. 'Ash gets on well with her exes.'

'Is that what she told you? Ha! And you believed her?'

'Why wouldn't I?'

'You're supposed to be a detective.'

'Yes, not a psychologist.' It occurred to him, periodically, that being a psychologist would be a distinct advantage in the job and it was never truer than at that moment.

'She doesn't have that many exes. Scott was the one and only, until you came along. Apart from the meaningless ones at school.' Lisa turned the tap on too fiercely, so that the water splashed over the worktop and onto the window. 'Not that I'm warning you about her.'

'Thanks,' he said, amused.

She missed, or ignored, the sarcasm. 'It's not her you've a problem with. It's Scott. I've known that man for years and he never gives up. He also likes to have the last word. So you can take it from me. He doesn't like the fact she ditched him, even though he knows it was his fault. He's trying to get her back. You need to do something about it. Because he won't change his ways and she'll get hurt.'

'I'm pretty certain she knows exactly what he's up to. She's a grown woman and I don't own her.'

'No, of course you don't. But I thought I'd let you know. Because he's not doing it for her. He's doing it because he can't bear rejection. For her sake if not yours, you need to do something to stop her getting sucked back into a toxic relationship with someone who—'

'I can look out for myself, thanks.' Ashleigh had come back into the room while their backs were turned, and was thrusting the phone back into the pocket of her jeans in obvious irritation. 'I don't need you nannying me. We all know you don't like Scott.'

'Right now you're in a relationship with someone else.'

'You sound like my bloody mother, only she liked him.'

'Yes, well he can be very charming when he wants, I'll admit that. But he's toxic, as well. And controlling. You don't need that in your life.'

'Thanks for the life advice, but I don't need it. I try to be civil with him, that's all. Now just leave it. I thought you had work to do.'

'Lisa can be an interfering cow,' Ashleigh murmured in Jude's ear, much later on in the darkness. Scott had unsettled her, as he always did. 'I hope you know better than to listen to anything she says.'

Beside her, he lay still for a moment, and she imagined his smile. 'You know me. I listen to everyone. Then I decide what to believe.'

She thought she could trust him not to take Lisa literally. After all, there was no need to. 'I've told you how it is. He's only up here for the summer, and he's working. He didn't come because of me. I see him because we're grown ups and it wouldn't be civilised not to.'

'Indeed.'

Was she protesting too much? She shifted a little closer to him as if nearness to her current partner could cancel out thoughts of her ex. Living with Scott had been impossible, forcing her to walk an unmanageable tightrope between being herself, keeping her independence, and allowing him the role he'd wanted to play in her life. It might have lasted if he'd been able to keep his charm on a tight rein instead of unleashing it at every skimpily-dressed young woman who'd rolled up at the yacht-hire business where he'd worked for the summers they'd been married. Good-looking, happy-go-lucky Scott, bare-chested on the deck of a yacht, was a holiday temptation any woman might have fallen for and the sunshine and the wine had too often proved his undoing. Hers, too, in the final reckoning. 'You know I won't go back to him.'

'Lisa certainly hopes not.'

Jude was hard to read in the daylight when she could see his face, so much harder in the darkness. Downstairs Lisa, an incurable insomniac, was still rattling about, though it was way past midnight. 'What does she know?'

'Well, who knows? But I'd guess she cares about you, just the way I do.'

It would hardly be unreasonable of Jude to be jealous. Ashleigh was almost put out that he wasn't, or at least that he hid it so well, but she couldn't stop herself rattling on. 'How many times do I have to tell you? He's only up here for the summer and I only see him for old times' sake. And when I say I see him, I mean it's an occasional cup of coffee. No more.'

'Not even a cake?'

'You can come along and see, if you want.' She was annoyed with herself. If she didn't believe what she was saying, why would he?

Jude slid an arm around her, an affectionate squeeze. 'No. I trust you.'

That almost annoyed her more. At heart, what was the value of a relationship if it didn't involve total commitment? There was a part of her that would have welcomed a show of jealousy. After all, she was jealous of Becca Reid and the hold the woman still had over Jude, even though Becca had been the one to end their relationship. But of course, she never said so because to do so would make her seem as mean-spirited and possessive as Scott himself. 'Just as well.' She turned towards him. 'And I do love you.'

'And I love you, too.'

But neither of them, she knew, was telling the truth.

SIX

It felt much longer than two days since Raven had found the body of the young man hanging in the woods. Two days since she'd scrambled up the slope to the camp in the early morning light, with her frail heart hammering inside her rib cage and her blood pulsing round her body so violently she thought it would break her; since she'd cried when the police had arrived and panicked in a way that defied her usual serenity. Gripped by the horror of what she'd seen, she'd been unable to talk to them about it and Storm had eventually chased the abashed police constable away.

Raven had known the police would be back and was almost relieved when a car crawled along the lane beside the field, slowed and pulled over, blocking the gateway. In a moment the door opened and Ashleigh O'Halloran's generous figure presented itself as a silhouette against the sun. The detective was the kind of woman you always looked at twice and even Storm, who for forty years had had eyes for Raven and Raven only, stopped fiddling about at whatever he was pretending to do and stared at her as she came across the field, picking her way through a skin of mud that the overnight rain had formed across the grass. 'Look who it is.'

'Make her a cup of tea,' Raven suggested. Storm's attentiveness was touching and she valued every minute she spent with him, but she sensed he was suffering an underlying distress that matched her own.

'I told them you weren't to be upset. The boy did it himself. There's nothing you can say to help them. I'll tell her to go away.'

'It's routine. They have to do these things. It won't take long. And I like her.'

He harrumphed a bit at that, but he did as he was bid and forged his way through the sun and shadows of the field to where Ashleigh was standing with the sun behind her. They shook hands and then he headed off to the brazier, apparently to rustle up the requested cup of tea, and she paused for a second to survey the camp.

The police who'd been popping up around Cave Wood in the previous forty-eight hours had kept drifting into the field and, after a brief look, out again. After this procession of clumsy would-be interviewers, Raven was especially relieved when she saw who they'd sent. In the past she'd had secrets and Ashleigh had proved the most uncomfortable interviewer, capable of shifting questions around and capturing her goodwill as if it were a butterfly in a net. Once entrapped, it had been too easy to tell her everything, and Raven's attempts to conceal the truth had failed. Now her conscience was clear and she found Ashleigh the only detective she was comfortable talking to.

In an ideal world, Raven said to herself as she watched Ashleigh taking in the field, looking across to the low and fractured hedge that separated the camp from Long Meg and the woods beyond, there would be no interviews and the police would leave them to get on with their blameless lives. But this world wasn't perfect and too many of the local people, failing to understand just how straightforward their philosophy was, misinterpreted simplicity as shiftiness and ended by blaming them for everything that went wrong. Vandalism and petty theft brought the police to their field on too regular a basis, a couple of times a year, and the constables had yet to go back to the courts with any evidence against them.

But this was the second time in a year the detectives were around the camp, investigating a suspicious death. As her life drew to a close, Raven felt its problems and its cynicism weighing ever more heavily upon her. She pulled her shapeless knitted shawl around herself and shivered.

The sun was out. Storm had found a couple of chairs and a wobbly wooden table from somewhere, and she felt strong enough to sit outside their tent in the sun. He'd found her a small table, too, and she sat there with the mug of tea he'd brewed for her at her elbow, shuffling a stained pack of tarot cards in her hand.

She drew three cards from the pack and set them out face down on the table, lacking the energy for a longer, more complicated reading. These days when she read the cards, the deck was kind to her. When Death came up, as it so often did, it was always coupled with a positive card, as if to reassure her there was nothing to fear from the future. At worst it would be nothing. At best it would be a simple existence on the far side of a margin from which she could look back and watch Storm grieving for her until it was time for him to join her.

With a frown, she remembered the conversation with the girl in the woods. There was a right time to pass on and she was approaching hers. Age was irrelevant — she was only sixty — and what mattered was where you fitted into the plan the universe had for you. When she'd talked to the girl she'd known it wasn't the right time for her, and when she'd stumbled upon the boy's body — a young man, she supposed she ought to call him, but he'd looked so much like a boy — she'd known it wasn't the right time for him, either. The balance of nature had been upset, affronted.

The girl had been there again the next day, loitering around the edges of Cave Wood, but she hadn't gone in. That was something, at least, but still Raven's stomach churned with unaccustomed anxiety and foreboding, in case the girl hadn't listened to her.

Just out of earshot, Storm broke into Ashleigh's contemplation and nodded her in Raven's direction. For a moment, Raven saw the camp through the detective's cynical eyes — half a dozen townies taking a break from the rat race for a few weeks over the summer, and herself and Storm, tattered and isolated, in a corner. *I'm like an animal waiting to die*, she thought.

'Look who's here,' said Storm, finally leading Ashleigh O'Halloran across the field towards her.

'Good morning, Raven,' said the sergeant, with a broad smile.

Raven dipped her head. Ashleigh O'Halloran, she suspected, didn't deal with them the way she dealt with others, and certainly not the way the younger, less empathetic officers did. She spared them the focus on detail that Raven's free spirit had long ago lost the knack of remembering. Nevertheless, under that smile Raven found a curdling of unaccustomed shame at her own inadequacies. 'Hello, Sergeant. Do sit down.'

Ashleigh sat, her back to the sun, and looked down at the table where Raven had turned up the first of the cards. The Queen of Cups smiled up at them. 'I should have brought you some biscuits or something, shouldn't I?'

Raven smiled back at her, unsure what to say. It didn't matter; she'd only have to answer questions.

'I'm sorry to bother you again,' Ashleigh went on. 'I just want to have a quick word about what happened up in Cave Wood. It shouldn't take long. Ticking boxes, form filling. Sometimes I think it's all we ever do. But there are procedures and this is one of them. I'd just like you to talk me through what you saw. Then I can leave you in peace. I can see you're busy.'

Nodding, Raven saw that Ashleigh was looking at the cards with interest. 'They teach me serenity,' she said, forced by that interest into defending something she really shouldn't need to.

'I know.' Ashleigh looked down at the cards. 'Not a bad card to turn up, that one.'

'You know it?'

'Oh, yes. I read the cards myself.' Ashleigh waved a hand to one side. 'I probably shouldn't have told you. I don't imagine it sounds particularly professional. But I thought you might understand.'

It made her that much more empathetic. Encouraged, Raven turned the second card upwards. 'The Ace of Swords,' she said, though the detective surely had sharp enough eyesight to be able to see that for herself.

'Another good one,' said the woman, as if she was being tested on the subject. 'Lots of positive energy there.' But she paused as if she, like Raven, interpreted the sword in the card as double-edged, cutting for ill as well as for good.

'Yes.' They hesitated, while Raven decided whether to draw the next card or leave it for later, and in the end decided against it. Tempting though it was to confide, the gap between her world and Ashleigh's was too wide to bridge. To indicate the reading was temporarily suspended, she laid the remainder of the pack face down upon the table. 'There's not much to tell. I don't sleep very well these days, and I woke up when it was light. I don't know what time it was.' Because who needed a watch when the the sun would tell the time for them, without numbers? 'I got up and went for a walk along by the river and into the woods.'

'Did you see anyone?'

Raven shook her head. There had been no-one to see, in the pearly pink dawn — only the dew on the grass, the birds clattering in the trees and the precious glimpse of a red squirrel scampering from branch to branch. 'I expect you'll think I'm foolish.' She felt herself going pink. Good-natured and sympathetic though she was, this smart and intuitive police officer made her feel naive and foolish. 'I had a funny feeling about things.'

'I know how that is.' Ashleigh O'Halloran didn't write down anything about a funny feeling, only (Raven tried not to look too obviously) the bit about the woods. 'Any reason?'

'I was worried. But not about him. The night before, when I'd been walking in the woods, I met a young girl. Twenty, maybe. No more.' The police always liked facts, and this was the nearest she could get. 'I spoke to her. She talked a lot about death and dying.'

Ashleigh's expression stilled for a moment, but Raven sensed a curl of concern beneath. 'Okay. Did she say her name?'

'No. But she was small — only a little taller than I am, and very thin. A waif of a girl. I was worried about her.'

'Did she say anything,' asked Ashleigh, looking down at the upturned deck of cards, 'about wanting to die? Or about anyone else wanting to die?'

'I don't remember exactly. Maybe not those words,

exactly, but she said there had been two young people who'd passed away too young.' Gossip passed Raven by. Now she wished it hadn't, and she might have been better equipped to speak to the girl and maybe save a life. 'Everything about her was sad. She talked about what a terrible world we live in.' And how could you disagree with that?

'How did the conversation end?'

'I told your constable. I wanted to get her out of the woods but I didn't know what to do. I thought I'd ask her for help, so I asked her to write a letter to my daughter for me and she agreed. We walked back up towards the camp and she went back up the lane. That was just when it was getting dark. And when I woke up I could feel death.' Most mornings she felt it, but it was her own, approaching serenely for when she was ready. The day of her grim discovery had been different and the sense of doom had been dark and unwelcome.

'Just feel it? You didn't hear anything or see anything?'

Raven offered the detective an indulgent smile. She couldn't offer evidence, which was what the police wanted, so they would have to accept what she could give them. And in any case, she'd been right. 'No. I was sure it would be the girl. I'd been thinking about her. So I went down to the woods where I'd first seen her, and then on down to the river. That's where I found him.' She stilled, thinking about it. 'I went back up to the camp as fast as I could. Then Storm went down to the farm and they called the police.'

Ashleigh looked across at the modern tents, with a half frown. 'You didn't ask—?'

Raven shook her head. 'They don't wake up early. We knew the farmer would be up.' What else would the police want to know? 'I didn't touch anything when I found him. I just left him as he was.' Though she'd ached to loosen the rope and cradle the young man in her arms, as if by so doing she could ease his passing, she hadn't. The police, with their procedures and their questions, had stolen away some of her innocence.

'Did you know him?'

Raven shook her head.

'And the girl.' Ashleigh wore quickly, her brow crinkling into a frown. 'Would you know her if you saw her again?'

Did Ashleigh, like Raven herself, sense the need to heal the living before troubling the dead? 'I think I would.'

'Excellent.' Ashleigh reached out for the mug of tea Storm had delivered to her and which must surely be cold by now, but she sipped at it without showing anything other than enjoyment. 'I'll get this typed up and send someone down with it for you to sign, if that's all right. I might have some more questions later on. But nothing more just now.'

For all her otherworldliness, Raven wasn't simple. She could have initialled the woman's notes — they were clear enough — and been done with it, but there must be something else going on. Perhaps it was the girl. Perhaps she was missing, or in trouble. But her courage failed her, and she didn't ask.

SEVEN

In summer, when the Lakes were heaving with tourists and only the early bird captured a parking place, Jude headed east on his days off. Up in the Pennines, even in peak holiday season, you could walk for miles without seeing anyone, a perfect opportunity for reflection. There was plenty for him to think about — Mikey, mainly, though Ashleigh's inability to let go of Scott and his own failure to cut himself free of Becca troubled him too.

His and Ashleigh's situations with regard to their exes were, he thought, different. He and Becca hadn't been married, and their relationship had never been as toxic as everything suggested Ashleigh's marriage to the possessive Scott had become. He never actively sought out Becca's company, nor she his, but she lived opposite his mother and so they regularly met.

It had been four years, he reminded himself as he drove round the series of hairpin bends that twisted down the western edge of the Pennines and into the low-lying haze that smudged one of the best views in England. Four years since he'd suspected Mikey of involvement with soft drugs and challenged him, ending by marching him down to the police station at Hunter Lane to hand them over. It had been an act of good faith, but it had come back to bite him in ways he'd never expected. Sometimes he thought if he had his time over again he'd have waited to find out where the drugs had come from — but that would have brought him a greater dilemma and one he still wasn't sure he'd have been able to handle. Justice had been done in the end and the dealer, Adam Fleetwood, had earned himself a six-year prison sentence for drug dealing, for resisting arrest, and for actual bodily harm when one of the arresting officers had sustained a broken collarbone. It was unfortunate for everyone that Adam had once been a close friend of Jude's.

Adam was out now, half his sentence served; he was fully rehabilitated and a valued part of the local community, but Jude retained a deep cynicism about the respectable face Adam presented to the world. He'd known the man long enough to recognise his determination for revenge on his former friend. Adam rented a flat almost opposite Jude's house and sat in the living room or the tiny front garden, ever obvious. He was responsible for low-level harassment, a steady drip-drip of unsubstantiated anonymous complaints that trickled in to the Professional Standards Department until their patience with Jude wore thin, even though everyone knew, even if they couldn't prove, the source of the complaints. And there had been Adam's calculated wooing and winning of Becca. That had been a short-term relationship and was over, now, or seemed to be. It would be good to know which of them had finished it and why, but Jude didn't ask and no-one told him; whenever he saw Becca she was her usual thoughtful self and

Adam persisted with that smiling facade and its underlying menace.

On impulse, he pulled the car over in a lay-by and reached for his phone, dialling his brother's number. It rang and rang and rang, and finally switched to voicemail. 'Mikey. I was trying to haul you out for a walk, you lazy sod. You might even have enjoyed it. But if you fancy a pint later on, give me a shout.'

He started the car again and pulled out, moving slowly along the winding road and settling in behind a lumber lorry. There was a reason he was going over old ground years on, fruitlessly, and that reason was Mikey, who hadn't replied to his older brother's message that morning, his suggestion that they head up to the hills for a walk or at the very least off to some pub for a bite of lunch. The death in Cave Wood, coming so soon after two other apparent suicides, had set Jude's conscience jangling. Mikey was the same age as those who'd found modern life too hard to live and might just have been prodded towards ending it. His refusal to acknowledge Jude's messages and texts was both routine and understandable, a rejection of an older brother's attempt to do the job of a father. It was yet another olive branch offered, yet another resounding silence in reply, but the worm of worry still gnawed at him.

He took the scenic route, intending to wind through the villages of Kirkoswald and Lazonby, but at Glassonby he turned off and headed up towards Long Meg. A walk down past the scene of the latest suicide was unlikely to tell him anything he didn't already know, but it was action of some kind.

Up in the gateway to the New Agers' field, Ashleigh's car was parked. He hesitated for a moment, then turned the car and retraced his route to the Little Salkeld road. It was as well he'd split with Becca; there was every chance the relationship wouldn't have survived Ashleigh's arrival in his workplace.

At that thought he allowed himself a wry smile. No-one could be sure how they'd react in an alternate set of circumstances. Would he have found Ashleigh so irresistible if it wasn't for the empty space Becca had left in his life and in his bed? And earlier? How would he have acted if he'd known it was Adam supplying Mikey with drugs? Would he have been so robust if he'd known how Becca would respond? He'd never know.

Parking the car where he'd left it on the day after Charlie Curran's suicide, he flipped Ashleigh a quick text. *Just down by the old mine if you've time to come down when you've finished.* Then he got out of the car, stretching in the sunshine. The riverside path was busy at the best of times and the local tragedy had attracted more interest. His Mercedes wasn't the only car parked down at the mine, and there had been more vehicles up by Long Meg and her Daughters. Word got around. He could hardly criticise people for being ghoulish when he was there himself, looking to see what there was to see.

'Afternoon.' He nodded to a man with a dog, received an acknowledgement in reply and set off along the river where a young woman was sitting with her back to a tree, flicking away at her phone. Ever suspicious, Jude took a second look to see what that was all about, and the girl returned his interest, scrambling to her feet and coming toward him. There was a faint scent of marijuana on the air, so faint he was able to pretend to himself, without qualms, that it was only his imagination and so he could ignore it. If he'd learned one lesson from Mikey's experiences, that was it.

'Hi,' the girl said, brightly. She stuck her phone in her pocket but kept her forefinger on it, as if she was afraid of being disconnected from it. 'I think I know you. Aren't you Mikey Satterthwaite's brother?'

Usually people who said *I know you* followed it up with *you're the detective*. Jude allowed himself a smile and made a note to tell Mikey, if he ever managed to catch up with him. 'That's me. And what about you? Are you a friend of his?'

'Izzy Ecclestone. I know him from uni. We locals have to stick together up in the big city.'

Mikey, who had just graduated from Newcastle University, was twenty-one but this girl, with her wraith-like figure and her pale face, barely looked eighteen. 'Nice to meet you, Izzy.' The name meant nothing to him. Mikey never mentioned his university friends.

She fidgeted. The phone in her pocket buzzed with a notification and the finger on it twitched, but she managed not to allow it to distract her. 'You're a detective, aren't you?'

'That's me.' They stepped off the path to allow a woman with a Labrador to pass them.

'Then you'll know. This is where that boy killed himself, isn't it?'

'Up in the woods, yes.' That much was public knowledge.

'And there were the others, weren't there? Do you know about them?'

How did you deal with that? Jude opted for the straightforward lie. 'I'm not up on the details. But if it's any comfort I don't think there's anything to worry about.'

'I'm not. But my mam and dad are on my back about it all the time.' Izzy tossed her head and a stray ray of sunlight bounced off the array of silver studs in her earlobe. She jerked her head back towards the woods. 'Why do you think he did it?'

'I've no idea.'

'All these young people killing themselves. It's interesting, isn't it? I was reading a blog about it this morning. It's quite exciting, in a way, that it's happening here.' Her bright-eyed stare dropped away from him, as if she remembered who he was and that she shouldn't have been talking so carelessly to him. Izzy might be fascinated by death, but it appeared she still had some sensitivity. 'I suppose I'd better go. My mam will be going mental. I didn't tell her where I was going. I never do.' She was digging the phone out her pocket as she spoke, curling her fingers around it as she jogged the first few steps down the path. 'Tell Mikey I'm asking for him,' she said, over her shoulder.

All across the Eden Valley, parents would be going mental, as she'd put it, when their teenage children did what teenage children always did, and went out without telling them where they were going and when they'd be back. Jude watched Izzy disappear around the turn in the path and frowned. There had been a fevered look about her, a dangerous intensity. Maybe that was down to the marijuana he'd rather not know for certain she'd been smoking, but even so it could lead to dangerous thinking. It might be worth asking Mikey if he could shed any light on her.

The woman with the Labrador had barely gone twenty yards down the path before she turned and strode back towards him, an obvious change of plan that left the dog gambolling on ahead of her, as if it expected to be followed not led. 'Excuse me. Did I hear you say you're a detective?'

'In the day job, yes. But I'm an ordinary human being on my days off.' He smiled at her, telegraphing as politely as he could that he wasn't going to chat about it. He was well enough known in the neighbourhood, to the point of acquiring local notoriety that wasn't entirely in his favour, but most people left him to his own devices when he wasn't on official business.

The deflectionary tactic failed him. He could guess from the way she stared at him, from the flick of the fingers that summoned the Labrador to heel, that she wasn't used to being trifled with. 'Good. Then you can tell me whether I should worry about my son and what to do about it if I should.'

He stuck his hands in his pockets and looked at her. This question was going to keep coming at him from every concerned parent even if there were no more unexpected deaths, and he'd need an answer for it in future. Just then, he didn't have one. 'I don't think I know your son.'

'You don't need to.' She shook her head at him with a scowl. 'What matters is, he's nineteen and in the Co-Op this morning someone was telling me there's an epidemic of teenage suicides in the area. Is that right?'

'We treat them as unexplained deaths,' Jude corrected her. That was the official line and the one that the newspapers, sticking to the required guidelines, were reporting. Everyone locally would know the deaths were suicide and the bush telegraph would no doubt have embroidered the stories well beyond any hope of accuracy, but he wasn't going to join in.

'But they're suicides, yes?'

'That's for the coroner to decide.'

'And has there been an inquest?'

'Only for the first one.'

'And was that suicide?'

Jude sighed. 'Yes.'

The dog, bored, ran off in fruitless pursuit of something unseen, completed a figure of eight movement around two trees and flopped down on the path at his owner's feet, panting. The woman ignored it. 'So should I worry about Josh?'

There was a catch in her voice and at this first sign of vulnerability, Jude's initial irritation softened. 'I honestly don't know. Do you worry about him anyway?'

'Oh, of course I do. He's like all kids of that age. A bright enough boy, but he never tells me anything important. And he spends far too much time on his computer.'

'Don't they all?' Jude turned towards his car. Ashleigh hadn't replied to his text so either she hadn't received it or else she'd headed straight back to the office. He hoped it wasn't because something else had come up, and if it had then the something else wasn't the untimely death of someone else's child. His time was his own so it might be worth drifting on up to the New Agers' camp to see if she was still there. 'I can't advise you. You can only do what you think is best.'

'It's hard enough being a parent as it is,' she said, aggrieved, 'never mind with all this going on.'

They were almost back at his car by then. He clicked the door unlocked from a distance. 'Enjoy your walk.'

'I'm heading back up the road myself.' Regardless of his reluctance, she fell into step beside him. 'I don't mean to sound brisk. I do apologise for that. But Josh is all I have, so I have to look out for him. Without being a control freak, of course.'

'Of course,' he agreed, placing a mental bet on the fact that it was exactly what she was.

'His father's worse than useless for that.' She snapped her fingers and the dog drifted to heel. 'Is it three teenage suicides there have been? I'm not a local here. I'm up for the summer. We arrived last week. All that talk in the shop freaked me out, but you'll know. So you can just tell me and save the hassle of looking up the facts in the local rag.'

'There have been three incidents,' Jude said, 'and I can tell you there's no evidence they're in any way connected.'

'These things can become self-fulfilling. Can't they?'

'I think it's been known.'

She sighed. They reached the Mercedes and she clicked the lock on the Range Rover parked next to it. 'I'd better introduce myself, I suppose. My name's Geri. Geri Foster. I'm up here for the summer to spend a bit of time with my mum. And you are?'

He couldn't decide whether her directness amused or annoyed him. 'My name's Satterthwaite.'

'A detective, you said. Rank?'

'DCI.'

'Senior, then. So it's more serious than you're letting on.'

She opened the boot of the Range Rover and the dog jumped in. Jude got into the Mercedes and negotiated the narrow track up into Little Salkeld and Geri Foster followed him, up into the village, out again and down the dead end that led to Long Meg. Jude parked in the field, where the skeleton of a long-dead oak tree commanded the centre of the stone circle. Two older trees, living but contorted with time and weather, grew a short distance away. Geri pulled up beside him. He got out; she did the same.

'Looks like we're going to the same place,' she said to him.

'I doubt it.' She was irritating him, now, not least because she clearly knew he wasn't giving her the whole story and seemed to think she was entitled to it. He turned his back on her and strode off.

Ashleigh's car was still in the gateway to the New

Agers' field and he could see her, standing talking to Storm outside one of the tents. He paused at the gate just as the dog bounded up to it. When he opened the gate the dog dashed through and Geri caught him up and came through beside him. 'I think we are. But there's nothing serious going on in Cave Wood, of course, or so you say. So what's so important up here?'

'I thought I'd check in with one of my colleagues.'

'Just routine, eh?' She was regarding him keenly.

'It's not even routine. I was passing.'

Ashleigh looked up as the dog bounced past, jumping up at Storm and almost knocking him flying. Storm's gaze went past Jude to Geri and the nod he gave her was that of a conspirator. He turned his attention to the dog. 'Whoa, Burma. Down, girl. No need to get excited.'

'Indigo?' Raven's voice emerged from inside the tent, pitifully thin and shot through with incredulity. 'Is that you, Moppet? Is it? Really.'

'Yep.' Brushing the dog aside, Geri lifted the flap of the tent and disappeared inside. 'It's okay, Mum. You're not hallucinating. I came as soon as I got your message. How are you doing?' The tent flap dropped shut behind her.

'That's my daughter,' Storm said, by way of explanation, but the shiftiness of his stance gave him away as the worst sort of conspirator. He turned his attention to the dog, petting it until it dropped down at his feet. Something was going on.

Jude recalled the notes of Raven's initial, barely coherent interview. Geri Foster must be the woman summoned by Izzy Ecclestone's note. On the other side of Storm, Ashleigh nodded briefly, as if she'd made the same connection. 'That'll be nice for you both, to see her.'

'Aye.' Storm was till looking Jude up and down. He'd

always been jittery around authority. 'Are you up here on business? Don't tell me there's anything else—'

'No. I'm on a day off, but I was just passing and I saw Ashleigh's car so I thought I'd stop by and see what the chat is.'

'There's none up here,' Storm said with a sigh. His gaze was still on the tent but he reached down to give the enthusiastic Burma a casual caress.

'I'm finished here,' Ashleigh said. 'Thanks for your time, Storm. I know it's been a pain for you, but hopefully that's an end of it. We'll leave you in peace.'

Jude, who liked Storm, raised a hand to him in salute and they drifted off out of the field, stepping along the lane towards Long Meg and out of earshot of the camp.

'You're suppose to be having a day off,' said Ashleigh, checking her phone for messages. 'Can't you keep away?'

'From the job, easily. From you…' He smiled at her. 'Not so easy.'

'Go on with you.' She returned the smile. 'He didn't buy that stuff about you just passing, you know. No-one just passes here. I spoke to Raven and I think she's okay about what happened, even though she's so physically frail, but she didn't have anything concrete to say. Nothing that sheds light on Charlie Curran, anyway, though she did say something that worried me.'

'Oh?' They paused in the centre of the stone circle. It was late afternoon. The sun drifted out from behind a cloud and Long Meg's grasping shadow, dominating those of her daughters, reached towards them. Inside the circle, the spindly shadow of the dead tree stretched out towards the east.

'She saw a girl hanging around in the woods the night before Charlie died and they talked. The girl talked a lot about dying. Raven asked her to send a letter to her daughter for her, because she wanted to get her out of the woods. I think she went down there in the morning half expecting to find her dead, but she found poor Charlie Curran instead.'

Jude digested that. In the daylight the stone circle and the woods round it were attractive and unthreatening, but it was too easy to see how dusk might bring shadows to a vulnerable mind. 'I think I know who she meant. There was a young woman in black on the riverside path just now. Mikey's age, maybe, or a bit younger. I spoke to her.'

'What did you think?' Ashleigh's brow puckered into a frown. Her concern for the local youth would be as great as his.

'I don't think a preoccupation with death is that unusual in teenagers, is it? It's a question of where it leads. In most cases, that's nowhere.'

'True. But Raven was worried about her. She might be just the sort of person who'd be influenced by a series of suicides, mightn't she? Perhaps we should try and identify her.'

'No need. She's a friend of Mikey's or so she said. I can get someone to have a quiet word with her parents if you think it'll help.' Mentally, Jude added another thing to his to do list and allowed himself a wry smile. 'If I'd thought I'd have asked her to give Mikey a message from me. He ignores me, but he might listen to someone else.'

Ashleigh's look was sympathetic, but she didn't pursue it. They both knew there was nothing constructive she could say. 'So the woman who arrived at the same time as you is Storm and Raven's daughter, then? It looks like Izzy did send the letter Raven asked her to.'

'It certainly does. I bumped into her down by the river earlier. Anyone less like Storm and Raven is hard to imagine. She introduced herself as Geri Foster, though I doubt Geri is her real name.'

'Raven called her Indigo.'

'I heard. Who'd have thought it? Those two unworldly hippies produce a daughter who drives around the countryside in her Range Rover, walking the Labrador?' On first glance Geri Foster was everything her parents weren't, the archetype of conventional affluence and with an acquired sense of self-belief that was totally lacking in the wary New Agers. 'She said she's up here for the rest of the summer.'

'I imagine she's planning to spend as much time as she can with her mother.'

'Looks like it. And she says she's up with her son.'

They paused, contemplating the steady approach of certain death which would take Raven, gently, when the time was right. There was a rough contrast with the ambush of its rogue counterpart, suicide. Eventually Ashleigh broke the spell by turning back towards her car. 'I'd better get back to the office. And you should get back home and do something restful with what's left of the day.'

'I've just been for a long walk up at Nenthead. That was very restful.'

'I bet you weren't really relaxing though. You were thinking about work, or you wouldn't have been here.'

'Fair point.' Through the hedge, Jude saw Geri Foster deep in conversation with her father. The physical resemblance between them was clear — a strong jawline, an identical stance with upright shoulders. Facially it was impossible to tell whether there was a relationship because Geri, he suspected, had indulged in some subtle plastic surgery. 'Any chance of catching up later?'

'I'm not planning to work late, so yes.'

'Pop round to my place when you're done.'

'I will do.'

They kissed quickly and parted, and he made his slow way down to his car, pausing before he got in to fire off one more optimistic text to Mikey. *Fancy a pint?* But there was no answer, and he hadn't expected one.

EIGHT

'Don't mind me,' Faye Scanlon said, drifting into the office where Jude had finally got round to pulling together the team who'd been keeping tabs on what they had come to refer to among themselves, though never in public, as the Eden Valley suicides. Suicide wasn't usually a priority and there were always other, more pressing investigations under way. A week had passed since Charlie Curran's death and there had been no further incidents, though Jude, keeping his ear to the ground, hadn't noticed any quietening of the local concerns. Faye's presence, despite the casual disclaimer that had accompanied it, was significant, indicating either that something was up, or else she had some idea as to how he might better do his job. Though he respected her, and over time had come to like her, Jude nevertheless nursed an instinctive resentment against her interference.

It was Faye's style. She interfered with everything, a woman who wasn't good at delegation and somehow maintained the capacity for keeping hold of every detail on almost every case run by the officers under her command.

Her micromanagement was an occupational hazard for them all. 'Sure. I don't imagine we'll be very long.'

Chris Marshall, the youngest of them, got up to fetch his senior officer a chair and resumed his seat in front of his laptop and a pile of notes. It was a shared office and Doddsy, Jude's friend and deputy, wasn't on the team but nevertheless seemed to be giving them more than half an ear. Ashleigh shuffled her chair up to put as great a distance as possible between herself and Faye, and Tammy Garner, the CSI who'd been in charge of all three suicide scenes, gave up trying to make space for herself in the very cramped circle around Jude's desk and chose to perch on the corner of Doddsy's desk instead. The room was warm.

'Ashleigh.' When Faye was around Jude had to make a conscious effort to keep control of his own cases. 'Do you want to start off? I don't imagine we'll be long. I don't think there's much new to say.'

'Not much at all. As you asked, I went down to the New Agers' camp at Little Salkeld to talk to Raven.' That was for Faye's benefit.

'You got some sense out of her?' Chris had little time for Storm and Raven and their tenuous grasp of the modern world.

'She gave me her version of events, which is all I needed.' Quickly, Ashleigh outlined Raven's statement. 'She was concerned about the other girl, Izzy Ecclestone, who was around the day I went there, though I didn't see her. But I don't think her concern was misplaced. I asked around a bit at the farm. Izzy's local, from Lazonby, and they know her. They think she's a bit strange — *fey* was the word they used for her. She comes up often and they'll keep an eye open for her. But they didn't know Charlie and they'd never seen him up there. And that's about all I learned from them.'

'Okay.' Jude ticked that off his list, but there was something that suggested more to come. He'd hoped the meeting could be wrapped up in fifteen minutes and everyone sent swiftly on their way, leaving Faye and himself to decide on any next steps. He couldn't see them agreeing to do anything more dynamic than take up a watching brief. 'Tammy. I know you've got other things to do.' Tammy was always the elusive one, always rushing from crime scene to crime scene. The hasty convening of this meeting had been dictated by her availability. 'Anything to report?'

'Nothing significant. Or I should say, nothing that's worth looking at again. At none of the three sites were there any signs of external involvements. Connor Turnbull and Charlie Curran died by hanging, Tania Baker was hit by a train. In the hangings the ropes were different.'

'Connor's came from his parents' garage,' supplied Chris, ever ready with the details. 'Charlie had bought his the week previously, at an agricultural suppliers on the industrial estate, presumably for the purpose.'

'They used different knots. I couldn't see anything to connect them.' She looked around the group for questions, but none was forthcoming.

Jude crossed Tammy's name off the list, too. There was nothing so far that he didn't know, nothing to surprise him, and yet the situation troubled him. It was cumulative. You could roll a die and get a six and the odds of doing so were always the same, but it you rolled that same die twenty times and scored six every time then a pattern emerged that begged questions. Was a series of three events enough to make a pattern? 'Okay. So let's talk numbers. How abnormal is this?'

He looked, as everyone did, to Chris, present at the team because of his unquestionable thoroughness in tracking down information and his instinctive knack of reaching straight to the right place for it. 'Suicides aren't that common in that age group. Teen suicides are low, about five per hundred thousand in a year and it's ten per hundred thousand for ages twenty to twenty four.'

Jude took a moment to reflect that ten per hundred thousand was, in its own way, a painfully high number. 'We've had three in a couple of months. In an area with a total population of what…fifty thousand?'

'Depending on how you define the area. The district council population is just over that, yeah. But if you limit it to the area where they all lived it's much less than that.'

'So we might expect ten per hundred thousand in the year, in the district. Five, in other words. And we've had three of those in the last couple of months, all in the same age group. What other suicides have we had this year?' He turned his pen over in his fingers. Suicides never normally made it up the chain to his level, but he'd attended his fair share earlier in his career.

'There were three others recorded locally. One was associated with mental illness, one with relationship breakdown and one with business failure.' Chris checked his notes. 'None of the people knew each other, and all were significantly older than the most recent three. The big difference is that we know why those three did it, but none of the later three gave any specific reason and for two of those it was a complete surprise.'

Jude saw Ashleigh doodle a huge question mark on her pad. Her mind must be following the same track as his. He looked up at Faye and saw that her face bore an expression of deep thought. Tammy was shaking her head. Chris, alone, tramped on through the facts without stopping to interpret them.

'Okay.' Jude sighed. 'Three young people, two of them

with no known reason to take their own lives, killing themselves within a small area and a small time period. No evidence of any external involvement.'

'There is one thing.' Ashleigh looked at him, apologetically. 'Maybe it's not significant. As you suggested, I called the driver of the train that hit Tania Baker. He's been off work ever since the incident and didn't really want to talk about it, but he did say one thing that concerned me a little. He doesn't think about what happened but he thought as he came under the bridge that he saw a shadow. And then he shut his eyes. That was all.'

There was silence around the table. Everyone knew shadows could play tricks and a fleeting glimpse in the arc of a falling body, a flash of a second that could be too-easily distorted by nightmares, was anything but reliable.

'He never mentioned it his initial interview, I suppose?' asked Jude.

'No. He said it comes back to him at night.'

'And he's been off work ever since. Hmm.' Faye was unimpressed. 'Don't get me wrong. I've every sympathy with the poor man's trauma. But he doesn't sound like a reliable witness.'

Tania Baker had died in the evening light, as the train had flashed under the bridge outside Lazonby. Jude thought again of the dead tree at Long Meg, its shadows stretching out like welcoming arms. But Faye was right. He moved the conversation on, looking to Chris. 'Tammy's covered the crime scenes and they're clearly separate. I know you've been digging about online. Have you found anything to connect our victims?'

Faye flicked an eyebrow at his choice of language as Chris turned away from his laptop and back to the sheaf of notes he'd dug out. 'They may have known one another. You know what this place is like. Two of them had been at the Community College, but not in the same year, and Charlie was at the Grammar School. They probably knew of each other, at least. In this place everybody does, or so it seems. I haven't had a chance to look much into their social media but I haven't yet come across anything that suggests they socialised together.'

All four of them — Faye, Tammy, Chris and Ashleigh — were looking at Jude as if he had all the answers. Even Doddsy, on the other side of the room, had given up trying to concentrate on what he was supposed to be doing and was listening in. Jude thought again of the idea of a rolling die. If he rolled twenty sixes on the trot he'd be checking to see if it was loaded. 'I distrust coincidence.' There was a tiny ripple around the room, as if they'd all been expecting him to say exactly that. 'I'd like to look a little more closely at this.'

Faye coughed. 'This is a delicate matter. We have a responsibility to ensure suicide doesn't breed suicide, as far as we can. I'm sure we've all thought some form of copycat incident might already be taking place. It's a known phenomenon, the Werther Effect. Within a particular demographic group, suicide can sometimes trigger repeat incidents if it becomes seen as glamorous or fashionable. Don't forget that. I've already had to remind a couple of the local press about their responsibilities.'

Faye naturally distrusted the media and had had her run-ins with them in the past, but when it came to crime the local press were reliably good at sticking to the guidelines and not sensationalising. What Jude had seen of the local reports had been properly restrained and avoided any speculation or unnecessary detail, but Faye had a point.

'I'm not suggesting we go in heavily,' he said, as if his boss needed reassurance. 'The last thing I want to do is set any more panic running locally than there already is.' He understood exactly where she was coming from. There was nothing to suggest a single crime had been committed, let alone three of them. If it was nothing more than a tragic series of coincidences — if the die was honest and that run of three rolls was unusual but still possibly pure chance — then an overt investigation would do nothing except heighten the tension, generate hysteria and increase the risk of further deaths. But if it wasn't — if the die was loaded — more deaths might follow. 'Chris. I'd like you to be discreet. Have another look and see if you can find any connections between them. Anything at all.'

He looked to Faye and she inclined her head, judging him with her silence. 'It's not a priority,' he added, in case that mollified her and stopped her thinking he was over-keen to pursue the sensational at the risk of the mundane, 'and if nothing comes up we'll let it drop. But it's for everyone's peace of mind. Okay?' Silence around the table. 'Then that's all.'

They pushed their chairs back and shuffled out of the room but Faye hung back. When Ashleigh had closed the door behind her, she pulled her chair forward until she was facing him. 'I'm not entirely convinced by your theories, Jude, I have to say. But on this occasion I'm prepared to pander to your peace of mind and let you have a closer look.'

Faye, at her worst, could be patronising, but he'd learned to handle it. All she ever needed was a little validation. 'I may be wrong. But it seems to me there's a serious problem here and whatever it is, we need to know what's causing it.' The image of Izzy Ecclestone swam again into his head, the prime candidate for a copycat suicide. Mikey, when he'd finally deigned to return one of Jude's many calls, had been surprisingly positive in his response, agreeing to meet up for a pint even though he must know it would come with a pep talk attached, and he'd also offered to look up Izzy and see if he could find anything. This enthusiasm had made a refreshing change and had gone some way, at least, to offering Jude reassurance but Izzy — and every other troubled young person in the area — remained a worry.

'I totally accept that. But I don't see any evidence of crime. And there's what Ashleigh said about Izzy Ecclestone.'

'That has no evidential weight at all, and you know it.'

Right again, but both of them knew that Ashleigh's instinct was usually true. The task was to find enough evidence to back them up and that was the problem. Faye would be thinking about resources, costs and personnel. 'Aside from that. I don't like the way the numbers stack up.'

'Three. And one of them had serious issues.'

'I think that's enough to raise a red flag.'

'Possibly, but there's an explanation other than crime, and there are alternative options for exploring it. Which is something I wanted to talk to you about. I had a phone call this morning from someone who thinks, like you, that there's something about this cluster of suicides we should all be very concerned about. However, her concern comes from rather a different direction than yours. She's a psychiatrist.'

So that was where Faye's sudden grasp of psychological theory had come from. 'Is that where you found out about the Werther Effect?

'Exactly. As it happens, Jude, I do think we need to be doing more about this, but treating it as a potential crime might do more harm than good. We need to work with the relevant educational and social services to resolve matters. Dr Wood — the psychiatrist — has offered to advise us on the matter and to liaise with those agencies. So while I'm quite happy for you to put Chris on to looking more closely into the background, and while I do think there might be some value in understanding how these young people communicate, if they do, I don't want to see these three cases treated as potential crimes. Can you work with that?'

'I think so.'

'Good. I believe Dr Wood has reasons of her own for wanting to help. I'll email you her details and you can arrange to meet her and see what she says.'

And that, Jude realised, meant that whether Faye thought the deaths were crime or not, she'd identified them as a serious problem.

NINE

'Dr Wood? I'm DCI Jude Satterthwaite. Thanks for making the time to see me.'

Vanessa Wood had seen Jude Satterthwaite's name in the newspapers from time to time and, she vaguely remembered, seen the man himself giving the occasional press conference on the television. A chief inspector, no less. Faye Scanlon had sent a senior detective down to see her. So much the better. It meant they were taking her seriously.

She prided herself on being an instant judge of character. Her first assessment of him was that he was young for the post, which immediately indicated he must be highly thought of. As she shook his hand, she met his thoughtful grey eyes. In front of the cameras he came across as stiff and awkward; in the flesh he was much more at ease, more obviously in control. 'It's no trouble. I have some very severe concerns about these recent incidents, and as I told Superintendent Scanlon, it's important we get to grips with it before we lose any more young people.'

He nodded, and as he did so his eyes flicked around the

room as if he was judging her. Perhaps he resented, or suspected, her intervention.

She pulled herself up. She was overthinking it. Just because she liked to make instant judgements and test out their accuracy didn't mean it was necessary; she was aware of her own weakness, knew how easily pride and vanity could lead her to overstretch herself. In her job she had to be very careful how she handled people, and in most cases she was. It was all the more important when the issue at hand was neither her actions nor her motives, but the deaths that were beginning to cut a swathe through the youth in the local community.

And would continue to do so. Bearing that in mind, it would be unwise to indulge an irrational, instant dislike of a senior police officer. She forced a smile. 'Sit down. I'll get coffee.'

Jude Satterthwaite made himself comfortable while Vanessa flicked buttons on the coffee machine. Her consulting room, wedged into an attic in one of the taller buildings in Penrith's Market Square, was large and bright, like an artist's studio. The sash windows looked down on the bustling town centre and, if you stood on your tiptoes (she was tall, five feet ten) you could just about catch a glimpse of the fells beyond.

To make it as welcoming as possible for her clients she'd possibly gone a little overboard, with a squashy sofa and a couple of armchairs, with regular fresh flowers and the Nespresso coffee machine. The effect on the detective appeared to be gratifyingly confusing; he sank into the low sofa as though he'd never get up.

'I try not to make the place too intimidating,' she explained, handing him a coffee while the machine hissed and whistled happily away with a second for herself. 'It may not feel terribly professional to you, but I'd struggle to squeeze us into my office, which is the alternative.' And anyway the office was barely more than a cupboard and couldn't fit more than her desk and a single chair. That, along with the reception area where her part-time secretary camped out for the three days a week when she saw clients, and a bathroom, constituted her workplace.

The second coffee cup filled, she passed a plate of foil-wrapped teacakes to the chief inspector, which he declined. The formalities dispensed with, she sat down in her own chair and crossed her ankles. 'I don't know how much Superintendent Scanlon told you about our conversation.'

'Not a lot,' said Satterthwaite, curling his hand around the coffee mug and looking at her. Again she stared back. She knew such a direct gaze was nothing more than a tool of his trade but she couldn't help taking it as a challenge. This was her territory and he had to know she was in charge.

It was an extraordinary lapse in her professionalism. With an effort, she forced her gaze away. You got nothing out of people if you antagonised them and her purpose was to help the police. She swung into her practised smile. 'I'll summarise. You probably know that copycat suicides are widely documented.'

He nodded, but he listened.

'The Werther Syndrome, as it's known, is named for the first recorded instance, following the publication of a novel by Goethe in the eighteenth century. At the end of the novel, the protagonist commits suicide. The book stimulated a flurry of copycat suicides. Since then there have been multiple cases where a notable suicide has been copied by others. In recent times suicides by celebrities are particular triggers. Social media has been a considerable new player in this.'

'And in plenty of other areas, too,' he agreed. 'It's a

shame we can't police it a bit more than we do. Budgets don't allow it.'

'Indeed. You may not know that I work a lot with younger people, in particular those who have issues of depression and suicidal impulses. One of them was Connor Turnbull. He had multiple problems, including the loss of his mother when he was a child. It caused him deep-rooted mental health issues which, in the end, we couldn't address. I won't go into them with you, because although it's case closed, for me confidentiality continues after his death. We still have his father to consider.' She paused to think of Connor, a lost soul who could too easily be led along the wrong route and persuaded there was a simple solution to his many problems. And she noticed that the detective flinched slightly at the mention of a lost parent, as if he had issues of his own. 'I had no real concerns after the first of the deaths, other than that one always considers such a thing as a professional failure. The second one, did, however, trigger an alarm with me though I knew nothing about the case.'

'Any reason?'

'None. Call it instinct, if you will, or just something learned from experience. But then we had the third.'

He nodded again, as if she'd affirmed his own thinking, and again Vanessa had to fight her irritation 'Copycat suicides, by definition, are generally the same method, no?' he asked. He tried to sit forward but the softness of the sofa defeated him and he sank back again.

'In most cases. It may be that the young woman who jumped from the bridge struggled to hang herself for whatever reason. Perhaps she couldn't get hold of a rope.'

'We're looking into that.'

'Of course, it may that's a complete outlier.'

'Yes. I'm interested that you suspect something so early.

Statistically, would you say the numbers constitute an epidemic?'

'That's open for debate. If I had to answer I'd say no, but I'm afraid the signs are there. I was sufficiently concerned to raise the issue with the social services department with the local council and, at their suggestion, take it up with your superintendent.'

'She says you've offered to help. Is that right?'

'It is. I'm semi-retired and work out of these premises three days a week. I've committed myself to being available for the whole of the two days I don't work, and at any other time I might be required, to help out for as long as this crisis lasts. Free of charge, of course. I've already spent several days making myself available to any student who wants to speak to me. The schools are just back, of course, which makes it easier to access that age group. I stay late in the evenings here in case anyone else wants to come in and talk to me. That's had a reasonable response. Mostly it's people seeking reassurance, but with that and the school, there's the occasional character who does need help. I do my best to intervene or refer them on.'

'Okay. And do you feel you can contribute to our…investigation?'

'There's no need to downplay it,' said Vanessa, amused. 'I'm aware of how potentially serious this is. The reason I wanted to see you is because something about the case particularly bothers me and Superintendent Scanlon thought I should raise it with you directly. It's about the reporting guidelines.'

'Don't worry,' Satterthwaite said, a smile lurking on his lips. 'Nobody's more tightlipped than we are when it comes to telling the public as little a possible. Has there been something in the press? If there has, I've missed it. The papers are always sniffing out a story but they're usually pretty good about reporting with care when we ask them to. Otherwise they won't get any information from us at all.'

'I'm sure you're far too busy to spend much of your leisure time on the internet, but I make a point of keeping up with social media.'

'Knowing your enemy, eh?'

He was right about that. 'I think it's useful to know the kind of things that are influencing young minds.' Young minds. She almost laughed at herself.

'Facebook?' DCI Satterthwaite asked, setting his coffee cup down on the floor. 'Twitter? Instagram? I don't go to those places, I'm afraid. Except in the line of duty, and even then I mostly leave it to others.'

'Two of the young people who died were members of a local Facebook group. A couple of other youngsters also mentioned it. There's been what I consider some inappropriate comment in there — unnecessary detail about the deaths and some associated gossip, as well.'

He got out a notebook and jotted something down. 'Interesting. I'll follow up.'

'I'm a member of that group, though I only keep a watching brief. I contacted the group admins and asked for the relevant posts to be removed, which they were.'

'What sort of inappropriate detail?'

'There were some comments on how quickly the person would have died. Not that they needed information on that from the coroner's report or anything like that. It came straight from Wikipedia, as a far as I could tell, but I was concerned to see the more difficult details were left out. The deaths were presented as being painless and almost desirable. We should never encourage anyone to believe suicide is the easy way to escape our problems, even though there may sometimes be an element of truth in it.'

Jude Satterthwaite tapped a finger on his knee. 'There's nothing illegal in that, I'm afraid.'

'No. Not at all.' As if she didn't know that. 'But it did indicate to me that there's someone locally who enjoys stirring up trouble and that kind of thing — the glorification of suicide, presenting it as a simple solution — is a classic stimulus in suicide epidemics.'

'Did you note who it was?'

'I took a note of the name — someone called Four Hats Jose, so I would imagine that's a fake identity, given the profile picture was a generic view of the Langdales and the account was recently created. It concerns me there's someone with potential personality issues, possibly a personality disorder, who's taking pleasure from this, and this sense of power might have fatal consequences.'

'All right,' Jude said, after a moment of thought. 'I see the difficulty. But—'

'There's more.' She took pleasure in cutting across him. 'I follow a number of local blogs. After the posts were deleted a new blog appeared. I found it through a link to the same FB group. It's called Eden Whispers, which I think has a deliberately sinister sound to it, and it's locally based, very chatty. The first article was on running routes around Penrith. The second covered local music events. The third was about history. Nothing new, nothing that hadn't been culled from the local paper or a book or elsewhere on the internet. But the fourth post was different.'

She had her iPad on the arm of the chair in which she was sitting and flicked it on, touched the screen a few times with rapid fingers and turned it round towards him. He leaned forward and read it from across the room. The blog was entitled: *The Eden Valley Suicides* and was accompanied by a series of photographs — the wood at Stainton, a bunch of fresh flowers on the track at Lazonby.

'The language of the blog mimics that of the deleted comments in the FB page, some of it word for word. It invites comments from readers and actively responds to them. Again, the blog is anonymous. I emailed the blogger, via the contact link on the website, and asked that they be more careful in how they expressed themselves. I sent them a link to the Samaritans' guidelines on the media representation of suicide. When I had no reply after twenty four hours I emailed again. After a second day I posted a comment on the blog. It was deleted and when I tried to comment again I found I'd been blocked.'

'You're suggesting it's deliberate?'

'I wouldn't go so far as that. It may be a twisted idea of fun, and I may come across as a bit of a killjoy. But it's irresponsible and if it goes on it could cost lives. I hope the work I've been doing in the schools and in the community generally will go some way towards countering the damage that's unquestionably being done.'

'That's really interesting,' he said, stroking his chin and sounding as if he meant it.

'Will you be able to identify the blogger?'

'Theoretically, yes. But I'm afraid there there are plenty of obstacles.'

Money, mainly. Vanessa had thought it through, at length. It was hardly surprising to find him getting his excuses in early. These days, so everyone said, it wasn't about what you could do but what you could afford to do and the look on the detective's face bore witness to just that. 'There is one other thing.'

'Yes?'

'You're obviously looking at recent events. But I think perhaps you should look further back.'

His attention sharpened at that. She'd thought he was

listening to her before, but there was a perceptible change. 'Okay. Anything specific?'

'At the beginning of last year I lost another patient. Another young woman. Her name was Clara Beaton and she took an overdose. That's all. It may be nothing. I can't recall the details, but you might want to look at it.'

'I'll do that. Thank you.'

'I can assure you,' she said, as though there was some doubt, 'I'm fully committed to helping our young people. No parent should have to mourn a child.'

She took a look at her watch just overtly enough to telegraph her message and Jude Satterthwaite, taking the hint, got to his feet and took his leave.

When he'd gone she watched him disappear round the corner of the Market Square she stood there for a moment, watching the pigeons clattering about on the rooftops, and thinking about Nick.

TEN

'I'm sorry about this evening,' Jude said as he and Ashleigh trooped round the M&S food hall together. Their meeting was prearranged, even though they were filling separate baskets. They'd planned on spending the evening together but a text from Mikey had popped up in Jude's messages just as he was leaving Vanessa Wood's office, suggesting they meet for a drink. Even without such unexpected enthusiasm, this kind of opportunity came too rarely to be ignored; with some reluctance from both, their date had been pushed back to another day, or another.

Understanding, or so Jude hoped, that Mikey had to be his priority, Ashleigh appeared sanguine about the cancellation. 'Can't be helped.' She hauled down a bag of stir-fry mix and tossed it on top of the fruit and veg in the bottom of her basket. 'It'll make a nice change to cancel something else to meet him, rather than cancelling meeting him because of work.'

Evenings with Mikey were rare enough, and Jude did cancel them too often. He'd still have preferred to spend the time with Ashleigh. 'You know I wouldn't cancel—'

'— if you didn't think it as important. I know. But it's not like you to be so worried about him.'

'I worry about him all the time.'

'Yes, but for other reasons. He's not the type to harm himself.'

Jude considered, briefly. Ashleigh had met Mikey only a couple of times but she was rarely wrong about people and that gave him some encouragement. Mikey's issues were his casual attitude to life in general, his broken-down relationship with his father, and his inability to find anything more remunerative than bar work to keep him going. That offered a degree of reassurance. On the other hand, there had been nothing to suggest that two of the three suicides had any intention of taking their own lives. And now Vanessa had thrown another spanner in the works, another suicide, potentially linked. 'I don't talk to him often enough to know what he thinks about a whole shedload of stuff.' All the important things. When in the mood Mikey would chatter on about football and music and the local gossip, in which he professed no interest yet had the knack of acquiring and remembering with ease, but he never talked about anything that mattered. When pressed, he became as surly and reluctant as a teenager.

Ashleigh stopped in the middle of the veg aisle and looked at him. 'Okay. I don't have kids or a kid brother, but I think I understand. This has really got to you—'

'No more than anyone else.' Often Ashleigh's intuitive reading of his mind amused him, but at that moment she'd fingered his weak spot. He tossed a packet of tenderstem broccoli into his basket and moved on.

'That's rather my point. It's getting to everyone. We need to keep it in proportion, because that's how hysteria works. If it's bugging you, the calmest person I know, it's a measure of how much others are affected. We need to keep cool heads.'

She had a point. There had been a couple — in their late forties, he guessed, the age group to have teenage children — sitting in the cafe and as he and Ashleigh had passed they'd overheard them talking about the latest goings on in Cave Wood. If those in charge couldn't pretend to keep calm, how could anyone else? Nevertheless, something inside him tightened like a violin string slowly winding to a higher pitch. It was about risk. It was about chances you didn't dare take and people you couldn't afford to lose. 'I'm perfectly cool.'

'You think I believe that? Of course it's worrying. Of course it's stressful.' She looked around and even though there was no-one within ten feet, she lowered her voice. 'I know you think there may be something sinister about it, Jude, but even if that's the case, it's hardly likely to be targeted at Mikey.'

Was that right? He thought for a moment of the enemies he'd acquired along the road to his present position. A lot of clever people were in prison and some of them had influential friends. Others had served their time but would never forgive. Inevitably his mind flipped to his former best friend, Adam Fleetwood — but surely Adam wouldn't stoop so low as to draw so many people to their deaths for the sake of vengeance?

He dismissed the thought immediately. 'You need to meet Dr Vanessa Wood. I'd be interested to know what you think of her.'

'The psychiatrist Faye was talking about? How did you get on?'

'I'm glad I popped in to see her rather than call her. I thought she was impressive and determined to help.'

Vanessa, direct to the point of confrontation, had obviously not liked him.

'And of course she poured scorn on your theories about a crime.'

Ashleigh was in a niggly mood that evening, as though she wasn't entirely happy with herself and her behaviour. He saw her scowling at her reflection in the glass front of one of the cabinets and for once it irritated rather than amused him. 'I didn't put my theories to her. I was there to listen to what she had to say, not interrogate her.' Just as well; she'd have been a difficult interviewee.

They'd reached the checkouts by then and discretion silenced them, but Ashleigh was back on the subject as soon as they were out in the car park. 'So what did Dr Wood say?'

'She's concerned, though she didn't put it much stronger than that. But she thinks there's someone who's behaving in a way that I would call criminally irresponsible and which she attributes to a personality disorder.' As she opened the boot and loaded the carrier bags into it, he outlined Vanessa's thoughts.

'Hmm.' For some reason Ashleigh seemed strangely unimpressed. 'And do you find that convincing?'

'I'll have a look at the blogs when I've seen Mikey. But she talks a good game. And although she didn't mention it, Faye told me she has her own personal reasons for wanting to help.'

'Do you think she lost someone to suicide?'

'Faye didn't say, but it's possible.'

'I wonder—?' Ashleigh began, then stopped herself and slammed the boot shut. 'Really, don't worry about Mikey. He hero-worships you. He'll come to you when he needs help.'

'He didn't come to me before.'

'He was much younger then, and you were the authority figure. It was his rebellion. He must know now that you did the right thing, or he wouldn't be speaking to you at all. Maybe if he wants to talk to you, that's what he wants to talk about. And that's a good thing.'

'You reckon?'

'Yes.' She turned away from the car, then flung her arms around him in the middle of the car park. 'I'm sorry I was a bit short with you. I've got things on my mind, too.'

He held her tightly against him and decided against asking what they were. If she wanted to, she'd tell him. 'Don't worry. It happens to us all.'

'You get off and catch up with Mikey.' She stepped away from him. 'I'll see you tomorrow.'

'I'll see you then.'

He stood and watched her as she slid into the car with the elegance taught by a private school education, then got back in the car and drove up Wordsworth Street to drop off the shopping before he headed out to Wasby to pick up his brother.

'Are you going to do a dine and dash on me, like you usually do?' Mikey asked, with what might have been forced cheerfulness, as he came loping down the path of Linda Satterthwaite's cottage and got into the passenger seat of the Mercedes. 'Because if you are, I'd better make sure I've got enough cash for a taxi home.'

'I'm not on call today, so I'll get you home.'

'Makes a nice change.'

Jude turned the Mercedes in the lane, taking a moment to steal a glance at Becca's cottage as he did so, but there was no sign of her — only a line of washing rippling in a gentle breeze and the inquiring presence of her cat, Holmes, bounding up onto the wall by the side of the road just a little too late to get the fuss he took as his due. Jude turned the car up out of the village and onto the Askham road. 'Where shall we go? Askham? Or Pooley Bridge?'

It was a pleasant evening, with the sun and clouds playing chasing games across the fells. Mikey was in an amiable mood. 'Pooley Bridge. We can sit out by the river.' This contribution to sociability complete, he turned his attention to his phone.

'Any plans for the immediate future?' Jude said, after a few moments of companionable silence had taken them through the village of Askham and up onto the lower slopes of the fell beyond.

'Nah.' Mikey checked his phone again, sighed and looked down at it. 'Get a job, I suppose. A proper one.' He'd graduated a couple of months before and was working shifts in one of the local pubs. Like Jude, he had a strong affinity to the area and a reluctance to leave it. 'I dunno what, though. See if something comes up. Media. Comms. Anything, really.'

The road climbed up along the side of Askham Fell and crept down again into the deep trough filled by Ullswater. Jude pulled the car up in the main street and by common consent they made their way to the pub with a lakeside beer garden. Here, taking advantage of seniority, he made himself comfortable and sent Mikey for the drinks. A pint of Coke was all he could risk as the driver, and he found himself looking longingly at the glass of Eden Gold in his younger brother's hand.

'Come on then, bro.' Mikey slid him a sidelong look as he sat down, stretching his legs out into what was left of the sun. 'I know we're going to have the pep talk. Let's get it over with. But I'm okay. Honest I am.'

Jude breathed deeply and took a moment before answering. With Mikey, in the past, he'd never quite known whether an opening like that was a trap or not and, though his brother was maturing, there were occasional flashbacks to the angry teenager. Fair enough; there was plenty for him to be angry about. 'I can't help worrying about you.'

'Why?' At last Mikey met his gaze — grey-eyed, like Jude himself, with his own variations from the template of their absent father. 'Because of these suicides? Do you know something I don't?'

In the silence Jude raised his glass. 'Of course. But that's not particularly the reason I'm worrying.'

'Like, you'll know for certain they killed themselves. I mean, we all know that even if no-one's saying it. Do you know why they did it?'

'No.' Jude looked down towards the river. Two youngsters, maybe ten or eleven years old, were busy with a futile attempt to dam the wide, shallow river. If they were ten years older, their parents would be having sleepless nights on their account, that was for sure.

'There's a lot you need to worry about.' Mikey blew the froth off his pint. 'Not you particularly. People in general. But you don't need to worry about me. Okay?'

'Who should I be worrying about?'

Mikey drank, and only after that did he reply. 'Remember what we talked about the other day?'

'I asked you if you knew Izzy Ecclestone.'

'Yeah. She's a good kid, Izzy. I looked her up. Because you asked.' Unusually, Mikey had gone pink. 'Met her in town. Had a coffee, that sort of stuff. A chat. What you'd call information gathering.'

'I'll make a policeman of you yet. What did she say?'

'She didn't say anything, much. She never does.' Mikey's sigh was that of a man much older than twenty-one. 'We just had a chat about stuff. I can see why you're worried, though.'

'It wasn't so much me that was worried.' Jude thought of Raven, following Izzy down into the woods like the shadow of a shadow, keeping watch over her, luring her out of the darkness by begging a favour from the girl's kind heart. They couldn't know for certain whether Izzy had intended to harm herself that night but if she had, either her nerve had failed her or Raven's intervention had changed her mind. 'Someone saw her and was concerned.'

'Yeah. She said. She couldn't quite remember what happened. You know.' Shifting in his seat, Mikey gave all the signs of realising he was about to say the wrong thing. 'She was a bit confused.'

'I imagine she'd been smoking something,' said Jude, to help him out. 'I know these things go on. Let's be grown up about them.'

'Yeah, it's just me you come down on—'

'You weren't even seventeen and you were my responsibility.'

'I was Dad's responsibility, not yours. And he was nowhere.'

They glared at one another for a second, while the summer drinkers around them laughed and a dog ran past, wet from the river, shaking itself and spraying them with water. It was enough of a distraction. Jude remembered himself. 'And was Izzy all right?'

Mikey sat on his silent dignity for a moment longer, then relaxed. 'I wish I knew. She's a sweet kid, but she's easily influenced. She's studying French and history. Reads a lot of Beaudelaire. He's a French poet who wrote a lot about death. She was quoting him at me over coffee. *The true voyagers are only those who leave. They never turn aside from their fatality*, or something.'

Jude waited. Sometimes Mikey took a while to get to the point.

'She's fascinated by these suicides' said Mikey, after a restorative sip of his pint. 'She knows every detail of them, though God knows where she's got it from or whether she's right. You'd know all about that.'

Jude merely nodded.

'Anyway, she just went on about it. How she's been fascinated by death ever since she was a kid. She hangs about in the woods to watch owls hunting, though she says she hardly ever sees them catch anything. She watches crows on dead lambs. Weird stuff. She goes up to Cave Wood most days when she's at home. She loves the dead tree up in the field by Long Meg.'

Jude thought of the tree, its clean, dead limbs bleached white against the green of the woods. 'I can understand that. I like it, too.'

'Yeah, so do I. It's a cool beast, isn't it? I bet it's been dead longer than I've been alive and it'll probably still be standing there when I'm gone, unless a storm brings it down. But I've never fantasised about hanging myself on it, and I bet you never have, either.'

'Is that what she said?' Jude's heart dipped. He couldn't worry about every troubled youngster in the district.

'Yep. In so many words.' Mikey lifted his chin in defiance. 'Don't look at me like that. I didn't just leave it. I couldn't. After she'd gone I called her mum and told her about it.'

Jude looked at him. Maybe, after all, Mikey was learning something. Maybe he finally appreciated that Jude's decision those four years before had been the only one open to him. 'Careful, Mikey. You're turning into me.'

'Yeah. Except I told her I was going to do it first.'

'What did she say?'

'*I can't stop you.*' Mikey drank again, deeply. 'But I didn't think she was too upset. She didn't storm off or anything. And with a bit of luck I'll see her again.'

'You did the right thing.'

'I know. And I kind of think she wanted me to. Like sometimes when I was a kid and I asked to do stuff that everyone else was doing, and Mum would say no. And I was a bit relieved because I didn't really want to but I felt I had to go along with it, even if I knew if I did it I might get into trouble. That sort of stuff.'

And then, distracted by divorce and years of ill-health, Linda Satterthwaite had given up the unequal struggle and there had been no-one to haul Mikey back from the edge of trouble until after he'd overstepped it. The simmering resentment which had hovered within him for years might, at last, be cooling as Mikey began to see things through an adult's eyes. 'What did her mum say?'

'Thanked me and said she'd have a chat with her and keep an eye on her. And I will too, of course.' Mikey turned his eyes towards the river, where the big dog had found a small one and the two were charging into the shallow water in pursuit of a pair of unconcerned ducks. 'Shame I missed your hike up in the Pennines. But I'm going walking at the weekend. Helvellyn, probably.'

The subject was closed. They chatted about walking and Mikey's plans and all sorts of other nonsense for a while, had another drink and then headed back to Wasby.

'We'll catch up again soon, hey?' Jude pulled up outside the cottage. A light flicked on in Becca's living room opposite.

'Yeah, why not?' Mikey's phone tinged with a notification and he glanced down at it. 'Ah, shit. Not again.'

'What?' Jude heard the note of sharpness in his own

voice. 'Has something happened?' If it had he wouldn't have heard about it because he wasn't on call.

'I doubt it.' Mikey unclipped his seatbelt. 'Just a WhatsApp notification. My mates are all freaked out.' Like everyone else. 'If someone isn't in touch every ten minutes there's someone on the group wondering where they are and whether they've topped themselves. That's the third one today. It's always the same. No charge on their phone, or no signal. I had someone getting stressed about me the other day and all that happened was that I went out and didn't take my phone.' He slid out of his seat. 'See you.'

Jude watched him up the path and in through the door as if he were a child, then sat there for a moment longer wondering just how far Mikey's new-found maturity had overtaken his teenage suggestibility. Just because things were wrong didn't mean Mikey wouldn't do them. He'd admitted that himself. That made it all the more important that someone kept him on the straight and narrow.

He got out of the car and headed up Becca's front path. Holmes, the cat, shot out from underneath the low-spreading foliage of a rhododendron and bolted up the path just as the front door opened and Becca appeared on the step. 'Jude. I was hoping to catch you.'

He stopped. Becca continued down the path and Holmes executed a neat U-turn before taking up his position at Jude's feet, rubbing up around his shins. It was a declaration of loyalty usually guaranteed to rub Becca up the wrong way but today she didn't seem remotely bothered when Jude, for something to do, picked the cat up. 'I was hoping for a word with you too.'

'It's about Mikey.'

'Yep,' he said, as noncommittal as he could,

'Not that there's anything to worry about. Of course

there isn't. I just wondered if you wanted me to keep half an eye on him. Things being what they are around here.'

Holmes' ecstatic purring drowned out the beating of Jude's heart. It was as well. He shouldn't be reacting like that when all Becca wanted to to talk to him about was a good deed. He shouldn't be reacting like that at all. He was already in a relationship, for God's sake. His grip on Holmes tightened. It wasn't the first time. 'That's what I was hoping to see you about.'

'You don't think there's any real risk, do you?'

'To Mikey? No.' But he thought of Adam Fleetwood nevertheless. 'None at all. I just thought—'

'Better safe than sorry?'

'I know I shouldn't worry about him. But I can't help it.'

'No. But you always will, won't you?'

'I don't want to worry you, and he isn't your responsibility. But I wondered if you could keep an eye on him. Let me know if he says anything.'

'Don't worry. I'll have a chat with him.'

There was a chance Mikey might even be flattered at so many people making their concern for him obvious. 'Thanks.' In Jude's arms, Holmes wriggled in protest.

'I'm fond of him, and it costs me nothing.' She took a step towards him. 'Don't squeeze poor old Holmes so hard. He doesn't like it.'

'Sorry.' Jude loosened his grip and Holmes jumped down and began to weave round their legs, circling Becca's, then Jude's, then Becca's again, as if he were binding them together. 'I'd better go.'

'You know if there's anything I can ever do, just ask.'

'Same.' Jude backed down the path and Holmes sat down in the middle of it, unconcerned and began to wash his face. 'Brilliant. Thanks.'

'See you.'

'See you.' He reached the Mercedes with relief, got in and slammed the door. When he looked back to raise a hand in farewell, Becca was already on her way up the path.

Back home in Wordsworth Street, having negotiated the psychological obstacle of Adam Fleetwood, deliberately visible in his living room and giving him an obvious and ironic wave, Jude settled down to his laptop. There was little he could do. The case still remained one of apparently unconnected suicides and he'd come up with nothing to support his theory — if it even merited that description — that there might be a criminal element to it, but he couldn't let it go. *The probability of rolling a six twenty consecutive times* he read, is *one in 3 quadrillion, 656 trillion, 158 billion, 440 million, 62 thousand and 976.*

Numbers he could manage, but these numbers were beyond him. Three consecutive sixes came in at odds of just over 200 — nothing major, but Vanessa had mentioned a fourth suicide and four would take it to one in over a thousand. Of course the numbers didn't translate to the human problem that was in front of him, but one thing caught him. Every additional consecutive event dramatically reduced the odds of whatever happened being a normal occurrence.

He messaged Mikey. *Did you find your pal?* And it was a chilling two minutes before the answer came back. *Yeah. He turned up*.

Jude stared and stared at the numbers in front of him, and then he turned elsewhere on the internet and began to look at Eden Whispers.

ELEVEN

'Well, this is brewing up into a nasty one, and no mistake,' said Tammy, briskly.

Doddsy had stopped on the edge of the clearing in Cave Wood. Jude's greatest fear — and Doddsy's own, and Faye's, and that of every parent in the district — had come to nightmare fruition; the body of a young woman dangled from the branch of an oak tree in front of him. The branch was about ten feet from the ground and the rope short; the young woman's feet brushed the long grass and brambles as she swayed slightly in a stiff breeze. Blonde hair hung loose on her shoulders. Thank God, her face was turned away from him. A prayer framed itself inside his head and went drifting off up to heaven, too late to save anything except, possibly, her soul.

At Tammy's appearance, he turned his back on the grim scene, but he said nothing. He'd stopped at the line of blue tape that Tyrone Garner, the young police officer who was first on the scene had strung from tree to tree like a garland. Doddsy, who was more than twice Tyrone's age and in love with him, shivered a little.

Tammy followed his gaze, allowed herself the tiniest shrug and began pulling her forensic gloves on. 'I don't imagine this is going to be anything other than a suicide, just like the others. But that's not the point any more, is it? We're all getting a bit jumpy now.'

'It's not surprising.' Doddsy stepped back for fear of being accused of contaminating the scene, even though he was well outside it and knew exactly what to do. His relationship with Tammy, once close, had chilled once he'd started dating her son and these days he never quite knew how she was going to respond to him. Today she seemed more melancholy than terse. And why not? At the end of the day they both cared for the young man, both had his best interests at heart.

Just like Jude and Mikey, Doddsy reminded himself. Just like everyone who knew there were kids in the area killing themselves for no obvious reason. Just like every parent whose child was back late or out early and not answering messages, just like every young person who knew their mates were ridden with angst like teens and young adults always were and who, for the first time, saw something sinister in it.

'Your lads need to get on top of it, Doddsy.'

He judged that to be a joke. Tammy knew they were doing everything they could, even though it must look as though they were falling short. And they were. Someone else had died. 'Yeah. I'll refer the matter up to my boss.'

Tammy pulled the hood of her forensic suit up over her short hair and stepped inside the tape. 'I'll get on.'

Doddsy stared at the scene for another second, then strayed away from it, back the way he'd come. A woman's bicycle, its pale purple paintwork gleaming with dew in the early morning light, stood propped against the base of a tree just by the path. The scene looked for all the world like an arty photograph of a summer heaven, except that Tyrone had taped the bicycle off, too, and it was waiting for Tammy or one of her colleagues to check for anything incriminating about its position before it was carted off for further examination.

In his heart Doddsy knew there would be nothing. It would be exactly what it looked like — a suicide — but there were many triggers. Somewhere, there was an answer. He strode up the path, thinking of how the girl's soft, sad footsteps must have passed that way before him, back up past Long Meg and her Daughters and along the lane to the New Agers' camp. Their numbers blossomed in summer but now, with the return of the schools ten days or so before, they'd gone, except for a couple of middle aged women with a camper van. Ashleigh had run a routine check on them after Charlie's death and they'd been absent when it had happened, photographing the Milky Way over Tewet Tarn and Castlerigg and producing some better-than-amateur images to prove it.

Now, he could see, they were packing their belongings. They'd be out of the place as soon as the interview process was over and only Storm and Raven, too long out of the world ever to want to go back into it, would be left to stick it out through the winter. When it was really cold there was always someone who'd offer them shelter, but both of them grew anxious indoors and preferred to take their chances. This might be one of the reasons why Raven was fading, shivering even in the September sun as she sat outside on her rickety chair, a blanket wrapped around her and a chipped mug of tea in her hand. As always, Storm hovered anxiously at her shoulder. There was a way between the primitive and the ultra-modern, and in Doddsy's view, cutting yourself off from the benefits of the modern world along with its negativity wasn't it.

But he knew from experience there was nothing to be done for people so determined to live their lives their own way.

Before going into the field he stopped and checked his watch. It was almost seven thirty. Jude, who was on the verge of being a workaholic, would probably be in the office by now and although Doddsy had resisted calling him too early, it was legitimate to let him know. He called and got no answer, so let it go to voicemail. 'Jude. There's been another suicide up in Cave Wood.' That was the second in the same place. Was that significant? 'A young woman, late teens, early twenties maybe. No ID yet but we'll get to it. Raven found her this morning.' And could that be significant, too?

He waited for a second in case Jude had merely missed the call, but there was no reply. He must be driving. Thrusting the phone into his pocket, he opened the gate to the field. A short distance from Storm and Raven was a woman — head held high, blonde, shoulder-length hair corralled by an Alice band, stout walking boots stained with dried mud. She was swinging a dog leash in her hand and the Labrador to which it must have belonged was gambolling at the far end of the field.

Doddsy made his way over to the New Agers and read their different expressions — Storm's of stoical resignation, Raven's melancholy, the woman's challenging. He recognised her from Jude's description as Geri Foster, Storm and Raven's daughter.

'DI Dodd,' he said, as if they didn't already know. 'I'm here to talk to you about what happened down in the woods.'

'We don't know anything about it,' called one of the camper van women from across the field. 'Raven found the poor girl.'

'It's bloody shocking,' added the other. 'You should be doing something about it.'

Doddsy allowed himself a smile at the last remark, ringing as it did with middle-class disgust. No doubt he'd find out the speaker was a retired teacher or a banker, a lawyer or a civil engineer who was getting back to nature for the summer. However frustrating he found Storm and Raven's obstinate refusal to play by the rules of the world in which they lived, at least they were true to themselves. He respected them for that. He got out his notebook.

'I'm pretty sure my mother doesn't want to talk about what she found.' Geri Foster's voice was laced through with impatience.

'You found her too,' Raven said, with unexpected empowerment, but she said it into the mug of tea as though she hoped no-one would hear her.

'I bumped into you on the path by the girl's bike. You were the one who insisted on going down there. God knows why. You should be resting.'

'Yes, but it was because—'

'Okay.' Doddsy cleared his throat and addressed himself to Geri, who seemed the one he was most likely to get some sense out of. 'Geri Foster, is that right? Were you with your mum when she found the body? Can you talk me through what happened?'

'How did you know who I am?' she demanded. 'I suppose your boss told you. We met.'

Geri was the type who was once seen and never forgotten, even for someone not trained to observe. 'That's right.' He gave her a genial smile, sensing she was already on the defensive.

'Nice to know you're all on the ball.' She swung the dog lead in her hand. 'There's not a lot to tell. I came up here to walk the dog.'

'You're an early riser?'

'Oh God, yes. I always have been. It's my upbringing.' The look she tossed to her parents verged on contempt. 'We always got up with the dawn and I've never been able to reset my body clock. Josh — my son — was up and about before sunrise, I think, to go for a run. He keeps abnormal hours, too. I'm supposed to be working while I'm up here, but I knew Mum and Dad would be up and about so I thought I'd bring Burma up here for a walk and pop in and see them.'

'Where are you staying?'

'Over at Eden Lacy.' She gave him an address, and gestured across the river. 'It's a holiday home, really. I bought it a few years back. I'm here most summers but this time I came as soon as Mum asked me to come up.'

Storm, Doddsy noticed, was looking at his feet.

'It was very good of you.' Raven lifted her head from her mug. 'But you didn't have to.'

'Mum. I'm talking to DI Dodd. The sooner he goes, the sooner you can forget about it.' She turned her attention back to Doddsy. 'I came along here about a quarter to six, I think it was, and I could see Mum down on the path. I didn't come into the field. I went down past Long Meg and she was looking at this bicycle.'

'It wasn't there last night,' Raven whispered. 'I went to look.'

Went to look. Doddsy starred that in his notes, but carried on. Strictly speaking he should be interviewing each of them separately but Storm and Raven's serene refusal to acknowledge the rules sent all procedure and formality out of the window. 'Why did you do that?'

'Ever since that poor young man died last week I've been down every evening to make sure there was no-one else. I worry about the girl I saw there last week, the one in black. She comes here on a bicycle, you know, and I thought it might be hers. It's the same colour.' She shook herself. Storm twitched the blanket over her knees.

'What time did you go down there last night?' Doddsy asked, though asking Storm and Raven the time was pointless, since neither of them wore a watch or cared what day of the week it was.

'Before dark. When I saw there was no-one about I came back up. The sun had just set.'

That would have put it just before eight o'clock. The bike, Doddsy had noticed, had had lights on it. 'And this morning?'

'I woke up so I got up,' said Raven, as though everything were that simple.

'I came along here at six. Just before, in fact. Five to, it must have been, because I thought about waiting in the car for the six o'clock news and decided not to bother. It was only just starting to get light. I parked up at Long Meg and then I saw Mum and went down to join her.'

'I'd seen the bicycle,' Raven said with another shiver, 'and I just knew the worst had happened. Then Indigo came along—'

'That's me,' Geri said, with an over-obvious sigh. 'She calls me Indigo.'

Both her parents turned to her. 'It's because it's your name!' Storm said, in exasperation.

She shrugged again. 'I changed my name, Inspector. However. To go on with the story. I found Mum standing next to the bicycle.'

'I hadn't touched it,' Raven said, as if proud of having remembered this detail of procedure.

'And I didn't touch it either. Mum was all wound up, so I put Burma back on the lead and tied her up to a tree so we wouldn't disturb anything, and we went in through the gap in the trees where the bike was parked. It's not so much a path — more of a sort of animal track. Badgers, maybe? Anyway, it was getting light by then, so we followed it. And we found the poor girl. We came straight back out and I called for help, obviously. And that's all there is. Your lot were quick getting here, I'll say that for you.'

'It's not quite all there is.' Raven didn't meet Doddsy's eye. 'I did get up last night. After dark. I couldn't sleep. I thought I saw lights in the woods.'

'Lights?' Doddsy questioned.

'You never told me that.' Aggrieved, Geri shifted her way in front of Doddsy, to the point at which he had to intervene. 'Mrs Foster. If you don't mind—'

'It's Ms Foster. If *you* don't mind.'

'Ms Foster. If you don't mind, may I carry on questioning your mother?' Jude would have stopped Geri with a look and Faye Scanlon with a sharp word, but Doddsy knew no way other than courtesy and in the end it always worked. It did so again, though not seamlessly. Geri harrumphed a little before she stepped back.

'I wasn't quite sure. I was very tired, yet somehow I couldn't sleep. We go to bed with the sun, as you know. I don't know how long it was. Maybe an hour?' She shook her head, all doubt. 'I got up and came out of the tent. Such a beautiful, clear night! I stood in the middle of the stone circle to feed off its energy, and I looked up at the stars. Then I thought I saw lights in the woods. Two of them. But I wasn't sure. I thought I must be imagining it.'

'Well, of course you were imagining it! Honestly, Mum.'

Raven dashed a tear from her eye. 'Maybe. I wish I hadn't gone back to bed. That poor girl. It wasn't her time.'

'And what would you have done?' demanded her daughter.

'I might have been able to save her.'

'Some people can't be saved, you know? Some don't deserve it. You need to look after yourself.'

'That's enough, Indigo!' It took a lot to rouse Storm to anger. Raven was shaking; he placed a large, calloused hand on her thin shoulder.

'Thanks very much,' Doddsy said to her, as gently as he could to make up for the treatment she was receiving from her daughter. 'I'm going to get a note typed up and brought back over for you to sign. You too, Ms Foster, if that's okay.'

'Oh, of course.' Geri fidgeted a little, looked at her watch. 'God, that's after eight o'clock. I'd better get back. Some of us have work to do, you know. Just because I'm not in an office doesn't mean I can afford to waste time hanging around. Mum and Dad will give you my number.'

'But Indigo, we don't know—'

'Oh, fine.' Geri turned back, gave Doddsy her contact details with bad grace, then whistled for Burma and the two of them loped off back through the field and out of sight.

Raven and Storm exchanged glances, Storm gave Doddsy a helpless look, and Doddsy, feeling as discombobulated as he always did when dealing with these innocents, turned his attention to the women in the camper van.

TWELVE

'She had no phone on her,' Doddsy said, to his audience of Jude, Ashleigh and Chris as they clustered around the table in the conference room that had become their dedicated meeting space, an incident room for a slow-burning investigation with no evidence of crime. 'It's probably in the river. The water's quite low, and I've had people looking for it, but nothing so far.'

'Low, maybe. The flow can be quite swift there. It could be well away by now.' Jude looked up at the photographs on the board, at the array of young people who should have been in the news for all the right reasons, the things they'd achieved or hoped to achieve. There was a new face up there — Clara Beaton, a young woman who'd been unable to take the pressure of university, dropped out and died of hypothermia at the start of the previous year, after overdosing on vodka and painkillers in Cave Wood.

Cave Wood. Jude had no belief in the spirit world, but he wasn't so foolish as to think everyone else was so hard-headed. It wasn't hard to see how the place might exert a draw on a certain type of mind. Even Raven had talked about its energy.

But Clara Beaton was a closed case, death by misadventure, a suicide attempt signed off by the brutal cold of a winter's night. Juliet Kennedy's death, which might be suicide, was complex, open and attracting unwelcome attention. The national media hadn't picked it up, or if they had they were acting responsibly and staying silent. Now, in an an attempt to dampen down the rising tide of concern throughout the district, the local news outlets were giving this latest victim no more than a name and half a column inch. *The body found in Cave Wood has been identified as 16 year old Juliet Kennedy, who was known to suffer from a heart condition. Police say the death remains unexplained.*

It hadn't taken two days waiting for the post mortem to know the underlying heart condition hadn't killed her. Hanging had killed her. Now they had the official confirmation, the statements from her family and friends, the results from Tammy's investigation and everything available to them except the forensic tests on the bike, and he didn't expect anything startling from that. There was no evidence to suggest anyone other than the dead girl had been involved. He sat back and waited to see what everyone else had to say.

'What do we think?' Ashleigh shook her head. 'Social media too much for her? Or something she read there that upset her? And if so, is that criminal?'

'If we find the phone, the sim card will be pretty useless,' said Doddsy, with a sigh, 'and the way kids work these days, there's every chance she'd be using WhatsApp and it'll all be encrypted anyway. But it would be good if we can find it and follow it up.'

Even before Doddsy had finished allowing his optimistic nature to assert itself, Jude was shaking his head.

Accessing the messages on Juliet Kennedy's phone was possible but it wasn't simple. There was a case that would have to be made for it, forms to be filled in, resources allocated. 'Sorry. I don't think I could get it past Faye.'

'Surely with four deaths—'

'Five,' Jude corrected him, 'if we include Clara Beaton.' Which he was inclined to think they should, and so it made a difference. The odds on rolling the same number on a die five times running were, he knew, one in over seven thousand seven hundred. It might be an irrelevance to the case, but it kept him to the point. Every time it happened it increased the chances of a connection. 'I've requested a report of caller usage for Juliet's phone, and for the others.' That would tell them who the dead young people had called, and who had called them, but no more. 'But unless and until we can demonstrate a crime has been committed, or might be committed, there's nothing we can do.'

'But the blogs—'

'I've already had the conversation with Faye about Eden Whispers.' Jude did the maths in his head. God forbid it happened, but where would a sixth death take them? Odds of almost fifty thousand to one. Impossible. 'She reckons there's nothing explicit enough. Not that we can identify it as a crime.'

'If it's encouraging or assisting suicide, we don't need to prove they knew who they were targeting, or that they were targeting anyone.'

'I know that.' But the blog had nevertheless been delicately vague. He'd spent the evening reading it after he'd left Mikey, the very day that Juliet had strung herself from the oak tree in Cave Wood. Three recent blog posts had caught his notice — the one on the Eden Valley suicides, another on the growth of the social media menace with links to websites which contained, in his view, questionable content, and a third on famous suicides, almost exactly echoing the Werther Effect that Vanessa had talked about.

'I had a look at that, too.' Ashleigh made a face. 'Grim stuff. but I can't say I saw anything illegal in it.'

'No. That's the problem. If there was something a bit more explicit, we might have a case for going after them, if I could persuade Faye there's a direct link.' That was unlikely, because although he believed in the connection himself it wouldn't be quantifiable. And besides, making that particular crime stick was complicated and relied on a higher authority than his own. 'Catch 22. We don't have the resources unless I can justify them and I can't justify them until we know what's going on with this blog. There may be other things we can look at, but unless I can prove one of those kids read it and was influenced by it, I can't act to stop it.'

'It's pretty nuanced, isn't it?' said Ashleigh, with a sigh. 'Nothing that says *go out and do it*, but a lot of stuff about the positive side of death.'

The comments on the blog had been worryingly enthusiastic, too, but none of the names of its followers matched those of the dead. 'It's interesting to take the time to compare it with the press guidelines for reporting suicides. It's in breach of almost every single one.'

'I looked at those, too. Almost as if someone had been through it and ticked them all off.'

'In which case the person behind the blog may be familiar with them. A journalist, perhaps.' Chris made himself a note. 'I can follow that one up, if you like. But the guidelines are there on the internet for anyone to download.'

'Yes.' Jude ran through the contents of the blog in his mind. 'The article on the suicides was interesting, because it gave a lot of information on each death and it was mainly accurate.'

'Stuff we haven't given out?'

'Yes, though nothing they couldn't have picked up locally. There wasn't anything on the forensics or CSI or anything.' That was a relief, because if there had been they'd have been looking at a leak from inside the force, a serious matter. Faye would have thrown resources at that one, all right. He smiled at the irony. 'We've obviously been careful to limit what we say and to whom, but all of the stuff will be talked about in the immediate area of each death. So that implies that if the person isn't a newspaper person they'll have an extremely good local network.'

'And there's a post up about Juliet,' added Ashleigh. 'Nothing much in it, but it went up in double quick time. And it includes a list of youth suicides over the last five years.'

'Give me an hour on Twitter.' Chris was scribbling down all sorts of things now, a veritable mind map of possibilities. 'I'll find out what people have been saying. It may be as simple as that.'

'I doubt you'll be able to track whoever it is down, but it's worth a try.' Jude remembered Vanessa's irritation with it, her conviction that this was the kind of approach which could do real harm. His own fear was that every death made another one more likely. 'Reference to other deaths implies someone local.' The names would have been cherry-picked and the details tweaked to build a narrative of inevitable, impending doom. Clara Beaton's death, for example, would be listed as the suicide she seemed to have intended rather than the misadventure which had been the coroner's conclusion. 'What else have you come up with? I'm sure you'll have all the information we need on Juliet Kennedy.'

'There isn't much to find.' Chris was the go-to man on this sort of thing, someone who charmed strangers with a phone call and pulled the rug from beneath their feet in cross-checking what they'd told him. 'She lived in Lazonby, and went to school at the community college in Penrith. Bright girl. Not an A* student, but popular. Until recently there was no indication of any problem, but she'd been to Dr Wood's drop-in sessions and expressed anxiety about what was happening.'

Jude sat back and sighed. 'Ash, I know you've been sounding people out locally. I don't suppose you've tracked down the local know-it-all-blogger with a background in media and a finger in every pie?'

'I wish. Everyone has an opinion and no-one really knows anything. The most interesting thing is that I spoke to Izzy Ecclestone.'

'Is that right?' Chris sat up, interested, and tapped his pen rapidly in the palm of his hand.

'Yes. Raven was right about the bicycle. It was hers. She'd been telling Juliet about the hanging in the woods and about the dead oak. She calls it the Sentinel Tree.'

'When was this?'

'The day after Charlie died. She and Izzy knew each other, although Juliet was a couple of years younger and still at school, and they'd been chatting about it in the village.'

'Did Izzy encourage Juliet in any way, do you think?'

'I don't think so. My impression is that Izzy's fascination with death — and it's an obvious one, nothing she tries to hide — is entirely personal. She's at that age where they only think about themselves, and I almost felt she regarded Juliet's approach as encroaching on her territory. Not that she put it like that, of course.'

Jude nodded. It chimed in with his impressions. 'Juliet

had been along to one of Dr Wood's drop-in sessions at the school.' He'd called Vanessa with the news that morning and she hadn't been happy, as if his failure to stop it was somehow his fault. 'Not often. Obviously Dr Wood wouldn't tell me what was said, on grounds of patient confidentiality, but she did say Juliet had displayed early signs of a morbid fascination with death. Her view was that they stemmed almost entirely from anxiety about the current situation, and she'd arranged for a second conversation next week.'

'That's interesting. Izzy certainly wasn't under the impression that Juliet actually intended to take her own life. She said they parted reasonably cheerfully, and Juliet had asked if she could borrow her bike at some point because her own had a problem with the brakes. Izzy told her she'd leave it round the side of the house and she could take it any time she wanted, as long as she put it back. The bike was there on Friday evening and gone the next morning. She never saw Juliet come and take it.'

'I don't suppose it matters. Juliet must have cycled up to Long Meg, left the bike and then done the deed in the trees.' Jude turned to the whiteboard with its Ordnance Survey map, squinted at the route Juliet must have taken, over the Eden Bridge. From there she could have cycled almost unseen through a network of country lanes and up the hill to Cave Wood.

'The pathology report said the body had been there for some hours. Juliet was last seen in the village at about seven and Raven said the bike wasn't there the previous evening. The earliest time of death would be about nine, but it could have been later.' Doddsy checked the map, too, as if there was anything to be learned from it. 'And there's something odd about that, too. Remember Raven says she saw two lights in the woods.'

'That could be anything.' Chris tapped his fingers on his and. 'Someone taking the dog out. Teenagers going up there for a dare. Especially now.'

There was a footpath along the river, but you couldn't see it from Long Meg. The idea of a night time dog walker, so far from the path, was, Jude thought, implausible; the teenager theory was more credible. 'Maybe. It had a bit of a reputation as a haunt for underage drinking when I was younger. But I'd like to look at it more closely, because it fits the time frame for Juliet's death, and it's in the right place. One light would be simple. Two, not so much.'

'That perplexes me, too,' said Ashleigh. 'Two lights. One might be Juliet's phone, but if that ended up in the river she'd still have had to make her way back to the tree. What was the other?'

'I wondered about the bike light,' Doddsy said, 'but the same problem applies. The light was still on the bike. That means she'd have had to put it back on the bike and walk back down in the dark—'

'In which case, why bother?'

'Exactly. Or there was someone else with her.'

It was almost too attractive, almost too easy a piece of evidence to suit Jude's theory of murder. He challenged it, before one of them could. 'Raven could be wrong.'

'Very possible.' Ashleigh reviewed Raven's statement on her iPad. 'She admits she was half asleep.'

Jude pondered on it. There had been no sign of anyone else having been on the scene, and the only footmarks were Raven's delicate ones, tiptoeing down the path with the light tread of the dying, and Geri's more determined prints, striding on ahead. Both overlaid the tyre tracks from the bicycle and neither approached the trail that Juliet had blazed on the way to her death. 'Let's not forget that, though. Two lights.'

There was silence for a moment. Creasing his brow in thought, Jude lifted the cup of coffee he'd allowed to go cold. 'Okay. And now I want to think again about anything that might connect any two or more of any of these deaths. I know we've talked about this before, but Juliet's death bring us into new territory. I can see some obvious similarities between her death and Charlie Curran's, and I want to know if there are any more, or if we can make an association between Juliet and any of the others.'

'The Beaton case looks to me like an outlier,' said Doddsy. 'At one level it's noteworthy that Dr Wood mentioned it, but that's probably just her being thorough. It's more interesting that Eden Whispers picked it up.'

The list on Eden Whispers had, as far as Jude could see, included every death of a young person that could be conceivably dressed up as suicide, even those for which the coroner had returned a verdict of accidental death. 'Yes. But they cast their net very wide.'

'We'll start with the obvious weak link. Raven.' As if expecting argument. Chris folded his lips into a stubborn line. He'd never trusted the New Agers, even before he'd first come across them when Raven had found a body at her feet. She'd been guiltless then, but the faint distrust still seemed to linger at the back of his mind.

Aware that his own predisposition lay in the opposite direction, Jude fought hard against a subconscious assumption of innocence. 'Yes. Although as she and Storm happen to live in that field, I'm inclined to think that's not a critical factor. She found them because she's in the habit of going for an early morning walk in the woods. The question might be more why two of them died in the same place.'

'Raven's surely physically incapable of harming anyone,' Ashleigh pointed out, 'and there's no evidence that she was anywhere near any of the other suicides. In fact I think we can prove easily enough that she wasn't.'

'She isn't incapable of talking them into it, though. Isn't that what the psychiatrist implied? She talked to Izzy Ecclestone in the woods the night Charlie Curran died, and she told us they talked about dying.'

'She persuaded Izzy not to kill herself.'

'Izzy was vague about exactly what was said. And who's to say Raven didn't go down and talk to Charlie Curran, or to Juliet Kennedy?'

Jude rubbed his chin and thought once again of Mikey. The more he looked at these cases, the more he saw that some of these young people had shown no previous disposition to any kind of mental health issues, then the more he worried about his brother and his perennial insistence that he was fine. 'She could have done,' he conceded. 'But remember, Dr Wood thinks there's some dangerous level of trolling going on online, and I can't believe Raven knows how to switch a computer on, let alone use it.'

'She may not. But you can bet your life some of those fair-weather summertime hippies do. Maybe they showed her. Or did it for her.'

'We can ask them.' They'd deny it if they had anything to hide, but least it might give more weight to any request to Faye to look at the Eden Whispers blog. 'Anything else? Let's talk about Geri, shall we? Because she was in the area when both Charlie and Juliet died.'

His enthusiasm renewed, Chris turned back to his keyboard. 'I ran a check on her, just as a precaution. Because of being on two suicide scenes, even if she only turned up on the first one after the event. She's an interesting character.'

'I'll say. She seems the exact opposite of her parents.

Ran away from the circus to join a bank, or the equivalent.'

'Her given name is Indigo Sunset Sky.' Chris read aloud from his notes. 'Jesus. What a thing to do to a kid. I'm surprised she's sane. She changed it as soon as she was old enough.'

'The Geri is after Geri Halliwell, then, I assume.' That would fit. Jude could think of nothing less New Age than naming yourself after a Spice Girl.

'Yeah, I guess so. Here we go. Born in Keswick. She's thirty-eight. Father's name is given as Storm, Kevin Foster in brackets. Mother's name is Raven, aka Sarah Twist.'

Storm and Raven must have hated having to give up their independence for the moment the system held them in its grasp, locking the child into it with a name and a National Health Service number, the first of many chains in which life would bind her. 'Keswick, eh? They move around a bit here. Never very far, though. I think Storm is a Londoner, though I'm sure I've heard he has local connections, but I've no idea where Raven comes from.' Raven had an old person's voice, a frail echo of what it might once have been, without any accent but that which she'd picked up from the river and the trees and the birds above.

Chris swiped on through his notes. 'The kid stuck it out until she was sixteen, then ran away and got a job waitressing. She's a bright girl. Formidably so, by the look of it. She won herself a place at Oxford and talked them into giving her a bursary on the strength of her unusual background. She got an upper second in mathematics, qualified as an actuary and later went into academia. She now lives in Oxford, where she lectures in mathematics and business at Waldorf College.'

'She has a son,' Jude observed. 'I think she said his

name was Josh. I bumped into her down by the river a couple of days after Charlie died. She spoke to me because she was concerned about him.'

'That needn't mean anything. One way or another.'

'No. It needn't.' Geri hadn't shown any reticence about the local suicides — the opposite — but crime was bluff and double-bluff. The smart operator could look you in the eye and invite you to investigate them, taking the chance you'd assume their innocence on the back of it. Jude never fell for that one. 'Raven wrote to her — or rather, got Izzy Ecclestone to write to her — the days after Charlie died, so she came straight up.'

'That's what she said.' Ashleigh was shaking her head over that. 'Is that right, though? If Izzy posted a note to her on the day after, she'd have received it on the Thursday and even assuming she dropped everything to come up here, she couldn't have made it any earlier than late on Thursday. The timing fits, because she was there on the Friday, wasn't she? That was that time I was talking to Raven about it. You saw her. That was two days later. So it's possible. But don't you think it's odd she went to her house and took the dog for a walk and only then went up to see her dying mother?'

Jude reflected on Geri Foster. He wouldn't be at all surprised to find she was a liar; her approach had seemed defined by her own self-interest. Her attitude to her parents, frustration mixed in with a shot of resentment, suggested she hadn't appreciated her unworldly upbringing. 'Anything else about her? You said she was an academic, which is presumably how she can afford to spend the whole summer up here.'

'She's one of those who dips her toes in commercial waters as well.' Chris consulted his notes again. 'According to this, she has a few non-exec directorships. Some earn her a substantial amount. Those tend to be down south, in the City. There are a few others in this neck of the woods that she seems to do *pro bono*. I'm guessing that's a nod to her local upbringing, or a sop to her social conscience or something.'

'It looks like it. Is there anything interesting locally?'

'Nothing obvious. She's involved in a charitable trust down in Kendal that's all about restoring marginal farmland to a natural state. And she's on the board of a drugs rehabilitation charity, here in Penrith.'

'Right.' Jude kept his personal and professional lives separate, a rule he rarely broke. When he'd begun the process that had landed Adam Fleetwood in jail he'd unwillingly but inevitably switched Adam from a friend to a felon. 'And the name of that charity?'

'Drug Rehabilitation Eden.'

He dared to look up and found Doddsy, who knew everything, and Ashleigh, who guessed everything, looking at him. He wasn't so foolish as to think the whole thing could have been planned to spite him. He genuinely didn't believe Adam was capable of killing, unless it was in the heat of a fight-or-flight panic. Yet now his former friend, however tenuously, was one of the many strands in the web that wrapped around the young people of the Eden Valley — and one of those threads led to the answer.

He pulled himself up. The connection rang too closely with that fleeting thought he'd had, the fear for Mikey, but it was implausible if not impossible. But how implausible did things have to be before you could discount them?

'Interesting,' he said, keeping his tone as neutral as possible. 'Anything else?'

'She audits the annual charitable fundraising drive run by one of the local papers. That's all.'

'Local papers?' Ashleigh was the quickest off the mark,

something that suggested to Jude that she didn't really trust Geri Foster either. She wouldn't have a sound reason for it, wouldn't be able to place any evidence on the table, but she'd be right. 'What were we saying about someone with networking skills?'

'Indeed. Do you fancy going down and talking to her?'

'I can do it if you like, but not today. I've a pile of things a mile high to do before I even think about something that isn't urgent.'

'It's probably best done informally anyway. I might take a run down there after work and have a chat with Storm. He may be able to shed some light on what's going on, even if he doesn't realise it.' Under his shaggy, unkempt exterior Storm had a sharp businessman's brain and though his knowledge of how business worked was way out of date, Jude usually managed a productive conversation with him. 'Okay. Let's wrap up. We've all got other things to think about.'

'I don't think Storm was telling the truth,' said Ashleigh, as he was leaving. 'Just a sense. But you might want to ask him about Geri and how long she's been here.'

'I'd had the same thought myself.' He turned his back on the room and headed out. The meeting had provided him with plenty of food for thought.

THIRTEEN

'You don't need to keep checking up on me.'

It was always difficult to tell over the phone whether Mikey was genuinely aggrieved. Taking a moment to assess it, Jude reminded himself to tread carefully. Their relationship had improved rapidly over the past couple of weeks, but that didn't mean the change was permanent. In the past such thaws had frozen again very quickly when Jude had trespassed too far on his brother's goodwill. Sometimes Mikey reminded him of Holmes, setting and changing his own boundaries without warning. 'It wasn't that. I just wondered if you'd heard anything on the grapevine.'

'You're the policeman, not me.'

'Yes, and you're the one with the knack of getting people to talk to them.'

'It's because they feel sorry for me. Do you think they'd tell me if they thought I was going to tell you?'

'Maybe.' Privately, Jude thought exactly that. Before he'd divided the community by sending one of its more popular and charismatic young men to jail (or so the local narrative went) he'd been reasonably popular himself, someone people would have a quiet word with when they were concerned about something. Now half the population seemed to have decided anything they said to him would be held against them at some point in the future, but they still talked to Mikey, leaving him to decide what to pass on and what to keep to himself. That suggested to Jude that he, not his brother, was the problem. He could handle that. The only thing he really regretted about the Adam Fleetwood affair was the damage to his relationship with Mikey, and even that was finally healing.

And there was Becca. More than ever, he regretted the way it had cost him Becca.

'Well, yeah. Maybe. But I haven't heard anything. I didn't know the latest kid.' A pause. 'Bummer for you, though, Jude. Are you okay about it?'

'I'd rather we could have stopped it, if that's what you mean.'

'You can't stop it, though. No-one expects you to. These aren't criminal matters. That's what this psychiatrist the Council have brought in says.'

'You've spoken to her?'

'There's no need to panic. No. She had a piece in the paper today. All very woolly and offering help to anyone who feels they need to talk.'

Jude snatched at the moment. 'Mikey. If you ever—'

'It's okay.' Mikey laughed. 'Look, I'm going to go now. Things to do. Places to go. People to see. That stuff. See you.' The line went dead.

Jude sat for a while, watching as the sun began to slip sideways towards the bank of cloud which lay behind Wan Fell in the west. He'd called Mikey from his car up at Long Meg, before going to speak to Storm. If he'd managed to keep him on the line any longer he'd have asked if he'd

DEATH IN THE WOODS

heard anything about Geri through his continuing — and contentious — association with Adam, but Mikey had the knack of sensing and avoiding difficult questions. And he probably wasn't the best source of information. The person who would be bound to know, and who might conceivably speak to him about it, was Becca.

Maybe. If it wasn't too difficult, if he could find an excuse to talk to her, he'd ask her. He got out of the car in the fading light and looked down towards Long Meg, past the shadows of the dead oak stretching out its long, twigless branches in defiance of gravity. No doubt Izzy Ecclestone would be back before long, dancing around it as she tried to summon enough courage to find out whether there was life after death, but there was nothing he could do about that. Her parents knew the score and she was their responsibility. She wouldn't have her bicycle, so if she wanted to hang around Long Meg in the dark she'd have a four-mile walk, long enough to changer her mind if she was looking for reasons not to make mistakes, exactly as Mikey had confessed to doing.

Geri's car was parked just off the track which bisected the stone circle; it was both the reason for his momentary hesitation and the prompt for his call to Mikey. Locking the Mercedes, he strolled towards the New Agers' field. The scent of cooking drifted across towards him. He detected meat, and onion, and some kind of herb he couldn't identify. The camper van had gone, leaving a burned circle where the occupants had lit a fire, and the grass had already sprung back on the pale squares where the camp's summer families had pitched their tents. He wondered what they really thought. A holiday? A glimpse at a life they yearned to live? A recharging of the batteries for themselves and their children? The views of the youngsters would be interesting, too. Did they enjoy the wholesome upbringing their parents sought for them, or did they long to be online, gaming with their friends?

One thing was for sure. Whatever your parents did for you, you wanted the opposite. Proof of that was a few yards in front of him in the shape of Geri Foster, standing with her hands plunged into the pockets of her lightweight Barbour jacket, tapping a booted foot on the ground impatiently as she talked to — or rather, he thought, lectured — her mother.

Raven and Storm's tent had always sat a little way from the others, as if in a deliberate move to give her a little peace as she eased her way to the shadows. Now it looked furtive, crouched in a corner. Beside it, Storm was unpegging washing from a sagging line and dropping it into a tatty wicker basket. Looking up he saw Jude and abandoned the basket, striding across towards him. 'Not you again. Don't tell me there's more bad news.'

Such churlishness was untypical. Storm was a gentle man, whose main concern was negotiating life without causing trouble to, or being troubled by, anyone. Geri's nagging presence could hardly be soothing, and Raven's illness must be a drain on his physical and mental resources. 'No, but I wanted to ask you something.'

'I don't think there's anything I can tell you.'

'Storm.' Jude liked him, so he softened his tone more than he might have done with someone else. 'Let's just cut out the middle man, shall we, and save me a lot of effort? Ashleigh reckons you haven't been entirely truthful and it'll save everybody a whole load of effort if you just tell me what's going on.'

For a moment Storm looked at him, then turned swiftly towards Raven and then back. 'It's nothing you can do anything about.'

It was an implicit admission of a lie. Jude waited.

'It's Raven,' Storm went on, moving closer so his voice didn't drift along the field to where his wife and daughter were engaged in an unevenly-matched verbal tussle. 'She's dying.'

'I thought so. I'm sorry.'

'I've known it for a while. I think she knows it too. Well, we're all dying, aren't we, if you want to think of it like that?'

Jude didn't think like that. He was too often in contact with people whose lives had been suddenly and violently, sometimes deliberately, cut short. They hadn't been dying. They'd been busy living. 'I suppose so.'

'Right. She's never admitted it. But when she met that girl in the woods she asked her to get in touch with Indigo. That said to me that she thinks she hasn't got much longer. Because we'd talked about it. They don't get on. Indigo intimidates her. You can see.'

'Your daughter was here all the time,' Jude said, 'wasn't she?'

Storm put his head to one side, thoughtfully. 'Yes.'

'How long has she been here?'

'There's no point in asking me about time. A couple of weeks, maybe? You'll have to ask her.'

'Why so secretive?' asked Jude. It was falling into place; nothing sinister, but a domestic difficulty that loomed too large in Storm and Raven's small world.

'I asked her to. I asked her to come up a while back. She has a house here, comes up, visits, goes away again. I wanted her back nearby, in case something happens.'

The *something* referred to Raven. Jude knew she didn't like doctors, knew she preferred to let time and nature run her down, so there was every chance she'd had no diagnosis, but he could guess. His own mother had suffered a bout of breast cancer, caught early, and had survived it. The modern world wasn't altogether destructive. 'I understand. But why didn't you tell Raven?'

Storm's face settled to a mutinous expression. 'We talked about Indigo coming and Raven didn't want to worry her. But it would have been Indigo who suffered for it if she wasn't here when her mum needed her. I don't always see eye to eye with the girl, God knows, but I had to think about that. So she's been up here for a while, planning to spend the summer here. But it wasn't the right moment to tell Raven.'

'Until she asked Izzy to write a letter?'

'Sometimes fate deals with things for you. Yes. She didn't want Indigo to come. She just wanted to get the girl away from the woods. She asked me to write another letter and tell her to stay away, but I just told her Indigo left the minute she got the note. When you saw her, she'd decided it was time to tell her she was here.'

Jude digested that. In the past Storm hadn't always been honest with him, but the man was a poor liar and his anxious expression had given way to one of calm, as if the lie had blown away and he was free of it. 'Simple as that, eh?'

'Is it important?'

'I don't think so. I'm just trying to see things clearly, and the more honest people are with me the easier it is.' And if, as seemed to be the case, this lie was tied to Raven's protection, then who was he to argue with it?

'You can speak to Indigo about the dates. She'll know them.'

'I'll do that, then.'

'Indigo!' Storm raised his voice and the two women stopped their discussion and turned. 'Someone here wants to talk to you.'

Geri said something to her mother and turned sharply

away, not waiting for an answer. 'I was heading home anyway.' She hadn't brought the dog with her this time. 'Bye, Dad. I'll pop by tomorrow. If you need anything, let me know.' As if Storm, who communicated only directly or, occasionally, by letter, was the kind of man to drop a quick text asking for a pint of milk.

Jude opened the gate for her and followed her along the lane towards Long Meg. 'How's your mum doing?'

'Don't tell me you're here to enquire about her welfare.' Geri stopped at the edge of the field. The shadows of Long Meg's daughters reached out towards them. As the brightness went out of the sun, the place acquired a strangely desolate air. 'I've given her a phone so she can call me, but she'll never use it. What do you want now? What am I suspected of?'

'I live locally. I'm out for a walk.'

'Just passing again? Okay.'

Somehow someone like Geri, who seemed the type to call a spade a bloody shovel, was easier to deal with than someone who wriggled and hid and lied with subtlety. Jude sensed that if she was lying and he challenged her she'd come clean, just like Storm. 'Fair play. I don't come up here that often. I'm trying to get my thinking straight and that means clearing out all the stuff that isn't relevant.'

'I see. And now you know I was around on the occasion of two deaths in these woods.'

'You didn't tell me about the first one.'

'You didn't ask me about the first one.'

'When I first met you down on the river path you said you came *as soon as I got Mum's message*.'

'Goodness. What recall you must have. I think you'll find I said I came as soon as I got my dad's message, but as you never recorded our conversation, we'll never know whether you misheard me.' She leaned against the nearest stone, her back to the sun so he couldn't see the expression on her face. 'I see exactly where you're coming from, and the last thing I'd want to do is lead you down the wrong path. I understand you're doing everything you can to stop these copycat suicides and so I'll do everything I can to help you. I have skin in this game. I have a teenage son.'

He hadn't forgotten. 'Then do you mind if I ask you a few questions?'

'I'll be delighted to be eliminated from your inquiries,' she said, dryly. 'Ask away. But before that, I should tell you something you probably don't know. Yes, I was here for the last two suicides and I shouldn't have misled you. But I was also in the area for the one before that. The poor girl who jumped off the bridge.'

'Is that right?' Now that was a coincidence, possibly a coincidence too far.

'Yes. I don't imagine it's relevant, and I can prove to you I was in Oxford at the time of the other death.'

She must have thought it through, to have an alibi in place. Odd, when there was no suggestion in the media that it wasn't coincidental, no conviction within the police apart from anyone other than Jude himself that it might be murder. 'I don't need you to do that.' It was something Chris would be able to verify independently, if asked, with very little trouble. 'Tell me a bit about yourself. You have an interesting background.'

'Now you sound like my therapist,' she said, laughing.

'You have a therapist?'

'As you say. I have an interesting background and life wasn't always easy. At one point in my life a therapist was a luxury I could afford and I tried a few sessions. Well, let me tell you. That was a waste of time and a bigger waste of money. It's a joke of a profession. Charlatans, the lot of them. In the end, time sorted me out.' She tossed her head, the first sign of unease, and the sun caught her blonde hair. Behind her, seagulls dipped and swooped over a field on the other side of the river. 'However. I'll tell you about myself and I hope you'll find it interesting but irrelevant.'

'I'm all ears.'

'Okay. My parents, as you know, dropped out of the modern life very early on. My dad did ten years in recruitment and was very good at it but it nearly sent him mad. My mother was always a hippy child and didn't get on with her family. Dad's grandparents are from up Carlisle way and he likes this place, so they've always drifted around from here to there, staying a few years in one place, a few years in another.'

Jude nodded. Cumbria attracted its fair share of those seeking an alternative lifestyle and he could see why. 'You weren't drawn to that life, then?'

'It was forced on me.' Geri's frown deepened. A brief scowl crossed her face. 'When I went to school the other kids had stuff and new clothes and watched telly. They were right up on all the latest gossip and the celebrity chat, such as it was in those days. They had nice things and they went away to exciting places on holiday. They had rules and I was allowed to do pretty much what I wanted, within our own little world. It was a bore. I did chores. It was positively medieval. I helped to cook and to clean and I sat round the campfire and was expected to enjoy it. Of course, I learned to love the place and I don't regret spending time close to nature.' She laughed. 'That's the one thing the shrink said that was true — that kids need boundaries and that I couldn't forgive my parents for not giving them to me. But when she told me that deep down I regarded it as borderline abuse, I was done with them all.'

'You've moved on, though.'

'Yes.' She stopped and looked down the slope towards

the Sentinel Tree. 'Maybe I still am a bit of a tree hugger at heart. I've tried to bring Josh up with proper sensitivity for the environment. Of course I went through a materialistic phase, and in fairness my parents taught me to work hard. Just not at the things other people thought were important. So I had a work ethic and I made the most of it. And as soon I was old enough I left home and changed my name.'

There was something about her rueful smile and self-deprecating glance that Jude found irresistible. He laughed. 'You must have been a Spice Girls fan.'

'When I was that age they were the peak of sophistication. Geri was my heroine for years after I outgrew the music, and I don't regret the name. For the first time people looked at me with a little bit of respect. It's a bit dated now, but I'd rather have a name I chose for myself than an airy-fairy name picked to reflect someone else's philosophy. One thing I did learn is that you have to be true to yourself.'

Jude watched as a sheep ambled its way through the stone circle. 'What then?'

'I went to university. Of course, I did things my way. When I was nineteen I had Josh, but that was okay. I'd seen a load of people managing everything with a baby on their hip. That worked out fine.'

'You never married?'

'That's a sly question, Chief Inspector. No. There was another thing I picked up from my upbringing and that was that sex is just an appetite, like eating or sleeping. I don't know who Josh's father is. Now you look shocked.'

He wasn't so much shocked — more taken aback by her complete frankness. 'Not at all. Just interested.'

'Then I'll expand. Love is something you have for lots of people. It isn't exclusive, or it shouldn't be. If you make it exclusive you introduce jealousy and possessiveness and those are ugly and unnatural characteristics. Very few animals are monogamous.'

Wings beating, two swans took off from the river at the bottom of the slope. 'There are some.'

'Yes. but humans aren't naturally so. I take sex as I find it, and so I'm completely free of guilt or responsibility. It brought me my son and I'm very happy with that.'

'And now?'

'I'm happy enough. My relationship with my parents isn't all it should be, but that's because I blame them for holding me back as a child and they dislike what they see as my materialism.'

'Did your therapist come up with that?'

Geri snorted. 'That's far too sensible a line of reasoning. I worked it out for myself. The therapist was hung up on my romantic relationships, but that's all a reaction, too. Neither of my parents has ever looked at anyone else since they met.'

'And yet you're back when your mother needs you.'

'Yes, but family. Family comes with obligations you can't shrug off.'

Or did it? Jude couldn't shake off the responsibility for Mikey but his father had succeeded without much trouble. It reminded him. It was time for yet another in his regular and futile attempts to bring the two of them back together again. Maybe the fevered sense of fear in the Eden Valley would be enough to prompt some kind of rapprochement. 'I can't argue with that.'

'I bought a house here because I could see this happening. I've tried to persuade my parents to move into it for the sake of Mum's health, but of course they won't. I've tried to persuade her to get treatment. I've probably tried too hard, pushed her too far. She won't budge. Now I'm here I'll stay for as long as it takes. I can get to Oxford easily enough on the train if I need to.'

'And your son?'

'He's off to Exeter uni at the end of the month to study computing, so he'll spend some time with me and his grandparents. If I can get him away from his computer to spend any meaningful time with them, of course.'

Another car drew up, another dog walker got out, acknowledging them before heading off down towards the riverside path. 'I've grown fond of your mother.'

'She mentioned you a couple of times. I think she likes you. You amuse her. But of course, you're a very handsome man, and she's as susceptible to good looks as I am.'

'I'll take that as a compliment.' He'd been standing a good three feet away from her, but he shuffled a little further away.

'Are you married?'

'No, but I have a partner. And I don't think it's a good idea for you to flirt with a detective when he's pursuing his duty.' But his lips twitched into a smile.

'Pursuing your duty? I thought you were just out for a walk.'

'I'm always on duty.' Becca had hated that about him.

'It shouldn't matter. We should all get back to nature and mate when it suits us. You should come around for dinner and we could discuss sexual morality over a glass or two of wine.'

'That would be entirely inappropriate.'

She laughed. 'If you change your mind, do call. And if you need any more information, you know how to get hold of me.'

'One more thing,' said Jude, as casually as he dared.

'Oh?'

'Yes. Just totally off topic, but I wondered if you'd come across someone called Adam Fleetwood?'

'Adam? Oh, yes. He's with a charity I do some work for. A bit of a charmer, I think, but as I say, I'm a fool for a good-looking man. Is he a friend of yours?'

'Yes, from way back.' Jude headed for the Mercedes and made good his escape.

FOURTEEN

Eden's End nursing home was less than four miles from Cave Wood, linked to it by the sinuous rope of the River Eden. When Becca passed through the lounge on the way back from dealing with her patient, she wasn't surprised to find it still buzzing over the latest tragedy. She thought the tone had shifted from the shock of the first few deaths; there was a definite sense of black humour peppering the staff's chat.

'Better take care if you're going out in the woods,' Ellie called to her as she passed. 'Want me to walk you to the car to make sure you're safe?'

'We're all too old to die like that,' someone chirped up from the back. 'Doomed to live a long life. Death's a privilege for the young folk, not for us old fossils.'

Becca thought this disrespectful, but it didn't do to look too po-faced. *Whom the gods love die young*, she remembered, from some distant corner of a past English lesson. She shook off the laughter that followed these remarks and made her escape. At least when she'd spoken to Mikey the previous evening he'd seemed cheerful enough.

It was a brave, blue-skied September afternoon in the Eden Valley, a day with one foot bracing for autumn and the other keeping a toehold in summer. On the front lawn of Eden's End, Leslie Chester was sitting deep in the shade of a chestnut tree. A cow stood by the fence, looking on with interest and swishing its tail against the flies but Leslie, who was normally alert to everything around him and never let Becca get past without a word, stared at her without seeming to see. He had a brown square in his hand.

The envelope, again. Becca took a swift look around to see if anyone was there to pay him some attention but the staff member who was out in the garden was picking up the knitting that one of the other residents had dropped, brushing dead leaves off it and laughing. Becca stepped off the gravel and onto the soft green grass.

'Are you all right, Mr Chester?' Yes, it was a brown envelope, but larger than the one he'd had before. She understood. 'Is it Nicholas?'

He nodded but said nothing, taking a photograph from the envelope and thrusting it towards her. She'd expected the same picture, Nicholas and his sister in the garden, but this was a class photograph that must be forty years old. The colour had faded in the same way it had in the snapshot he'd shown her previously; the clothes and hairstyles were as ludicrously dated, the smiles and scowls the same as those of any class of teenagers, fooling about instead of taking this matter of record as seriously as it deserved.

She scanned the photograph. There would certainly be people there she knew, even if she didn't immediately recognise them, links to the present in this picture from the past. It was why these deaths touched so many people in the Eden Valley and it was why Nicholas Chester deserved to be remembered. He must be in that picture. Her parents would know which one he was; they'd been at the same school, at around the same time. She took a wild guess, pointing to the figure at the end of the row. Sandy hair, glasses. He looked nothing like Leslie but there was a lack of shine on the picture, as if his father's finger had touched him, over and over again, in an attempt to reach into the past and bring him back. 'Is this him?'

'Yes.' Leslie's voice shook a little. 'He's dead. They're starting to die now, do you know that? I don't know why I have to live on. Maybe I have to survive until they're all gone.'

Becca disliked the idea that her parents' generation was starting to shuffle off, one by one. Dropping off the perch, her mother used to say about her grandparents' friends, and now the same was happening to their generation. In time it would come to her. 'He looks a lovely young man. You must have been very proud of him.'

'Aye. I was. He wanted to be a musician. He played the violin, so well. He was such a talent. He wrote it all in his diary.'

'Dad!'

Becca hadn't noticed the car draw up and the woman get out, but she was glad to see a woman she recognised from the local paper as Vanessa Wood, striding across the lawn as if there was some urgency. 'It must have been such a comfort for you,' she said, preparing to cede the conversation to the newcomer, 'having that to read.'

'I kept the diary,' Leslie said, wiping a tear from his eye. 'I have it still. I read it every day. I look at his picture every day. I think of those poor young people in the papers and I know what their parents are going through. It'll never leave them. They'll suffer, like I'm suffering, to the end of their lives. It's a curse, to outlive your children.'

'Dad.' Vanessa had reached them. 'Put the picture

away, now. It won't do you any good looking at it. And I'm sure—' she snatched a glance at Becca's name badge, 'Becky's got plenty of other things to do. She doesn't have time to talk to you.'

Becca was about to protest, but there was a grain of truth in what Vanessa said. She was a nurse not a psychologist and surely there could be no-one better for Leslie to have as a visitor than Vanessa. Becca hadn't known they were father and daughter but when you saw them together the relationship was clear. Thanking her stars at the timely intervention, she made a graceful exit. 'I'm never too busy to talk, Mr Chester, if it helps.'

'I'm sure he really appreciates the offer. Thank you so much for taking the time.' Vanessa was smiling at him but as she did so she tweaked the picture from his fingers and looked down at it. 'Put that away just now, Dad. I'll see if someone can get us a cup of tea and we can talk about Nicky if you want. Or we can talk about something different. Whatever makes you feel better.' Then she twitched the envelope away and the three rows of semi-familiar faces disappeared from Becca's view and into the flap.

She walked to her car and slid into the driver's seat. These days Eden's End, the scene of a murder inquiry the year before, always reminded her of Jude and she paused for a moment to think of him when they were together, folding himself into the passenger seat of her Fiat 500, his head almost touching the roof. Maybe it was time to catch up with him, have a chat about Mikey. Talk to him about the photograph.

She dialled his number. In the shadow of the tree, Vanessa was sitting next to her father, holding one of his hands while the other one pointed to the photograph. The two of them were smiling together. Forty years dead, Nicholas could still make his father laugh or cry as a living child might do. It was a gift, to tap into those precious memories. Lucky man, to have Vanessa. 'Jude. Hi. Are you busy?'

'As always.' He never used to be a man to answer personal calls at work unless they were from Mikey, to whom he was always available, but over the past year or so he'd loosened up. These days, on the rare occasions she felt the need to call him at work, there was a fighting chance that he'd answer, even if all he did was put her off until later. 'Anything I can help you with?'

'I don't know. It's this suicide thing. I've no idea what's going on.'

'Neither have I.' She sensed tension.

'It's not Mikey,' she said, hastening to reassure him. 'But I've been thinking. And anything might help, right?' It wasn't as if she had children, let alone teenage ones, or even any prospect of them at thirty-three and with no man on the horizon, but she was a soft touch for other people's grief.

'We always encourage people to come forward with any information, even if they think it's irrelevant.'

She tried to imagine him saying it, knew he was mocking himself and that he'd be smiling. 'I'm pretty damn sure what I'm going to say is irrelevant.'

'I can't talk now. Can I come and see you this evening?'

'I don't want to put you out at all.'

'You aren't. It'll give me an excuse to pop along and see Mikey. I don't want him thinking I'm obsessing about him.'

'Are you?'

A pause. 'Yes, probably. I'll see you later. I don't know when I'll get away.'

'Becca, eh?' said Ashleigh, as she and Jude parted in the car park at Carleton Hall. 'Interesting.'

'Not Becca at all. At least, yes. I'm going to see Becca. It's because she has something to tell me.'

'Something she couldn't tell you over the phone?'

That irritated him. Ashleigh was the one who took calls from the ex-husband she swore she no longer had anything to do with and, he was sure, occasionally met up with without his knowledge. Now she was questioning him about his relationship with Becca when it had long ago evolved into friendship and any meaning it had ever had was long dead. He still loved Becca, after a fashion, but he accepted it meant nothing and Ashleigh knew it. Jealousy became nobody. 'I'm sure she could have told me over the phone. I suggested meeting up so I can call in on my mum at the same time. It's a good excuse.'

'You need an excuse to go and see your mum?'

'You know what I mean. It's about Mikey.'

'It always is.'

He got into the Mercedes and watched her heading off to her own car, with a shuffle that was almost a flounce, but he let her go without calling her back to explain. There would be plenty of time later to kiss and make up, and he was already running later than he intended.

He drew out of the car park and headed the six miles or so southwards, through Askham and down onto the Haweswater road. To his left the brow of Lowther Fell shone with bracken in the evening sun and the curling, swirling snake of the river sparkled below it. Sometimes it was a wicked world, but it remained full of promise. Why had so many young people, with so much to look forward to, chosen to leave it behind them, so many in such a short time? What was it in that area, at that time, that drove them on? And who else would fall victim to it?

Becca was looking out for him. He got out of the car, as casually as he could in case anyone got the wrong idea, and turned to the gate, but she came down the path as she had done before and met him half way. From a shrinking pool of sunlight on the far side of the garden, Holmes watched them with disdain. 'Jude. Good of you to pop by. But as I say, it's probably nothing.'

'Yes, probably, but it costs you nothing to tell me and it costs me nothing to listen.'

'True. Okay. Did you know Vanessa Wood's father is a resident at Eden's End?'

'I didn't, no.'

'His name is Leslie Chester. I was talking to him earlier. He must be eighty if he's a day. I know these suicides have got people on edge locally, but it's so awful for him. His son died young. Forty years ago or so, and it's brought it all back.'

'Suicide?'

Almost irritably, Becca poked a strand of hair out of her eye. 'No. It was an accident. He was playing about on the viaduct at Eden Lacy and a train came along, and he fell. My heart breaks for him.'

He nodded. That would explain Vanessa's mission. He'd seen something in her eye, a cold determination to pursue a quest to the very end. Perhaps her father's misery had mapped out her career path for her. *No parent should have to mourn a child*, she'd said. In his job Jude saw many people pursue vengeance with just such steel, but others, like him, preferred to pursue justice or restitution. It was better to put the world right than add to its wrongs. 'Poor bloke. God help him.'

'He has Vanessa, I suppose, so he's in good hands. But it breaks your heart. He was showing me the boy's picture.

A class photo. He was at the grammar school, and he'd have been there with a lot of people we know.'

'Forty years,' Jude said, thinking about it.

'I was thinking. Maybe these things come back to haunt a place. Not literally. I'm not that superstitious. But maybe there's a pattern. And there was another thing about it.'

'What's that?'

'Did anyone tell you how much you look like your dad?' She dimpled a smile at him.

Mikey never stopped going on about that, especially when he was annoyed. *You look like Dad, you sound like Dad*. Then he'd storm off. 'Sometimes.'

'It's you in the class photo, to the life. Your dad was in Nicholas Chester's class at school. That was what made me think of mentioning it to you.'

Jude's father, David Satterthwaite, might have known Nicholas or Vanessa, though what they might learn from an old story was open to debate. 'Thanks. I might follow that up. I'm going to the football with Dad on Saturday. I'll see if he's got a copy of it.'

'It's almost certainly nothing.' Becca turned up the path and flipped her fingers at Holmes, who ignored her. 'I'll see you later.'

'See you. He turned his attention to other matters, rapping on the door of his mother's cottage, which was unlocked, and pushing it open.

'Oh, it's you.' Mikey was coming down the hall, his dark hair spiky with damp. 'Timing perfect as ever. I've just been to the gym and I've got pizza. Want some?'

'If there's any spare.'

'I've got no-alcohol beer, too, if you're in the mood to live a little. Though I'm having the real stuff.'

Jude followed Mikey through to the kitchen and out into the garden, lifting a can off the worktop on the way past. In the light he could see a bruise blooming on his brother's cheekbone. 'What were you doing at the gym? Boxing?'

'Not intentionally, no. But there was a bit of a bust-up.' Mikey shrugged.

'Oh?'

'Yeah. Some kid in there. I didn't know him but some of the others do. Apparently he comes in from time to time. One of the guys called him a dirty gippo. Me and a couple of others had to break it up.'

Jude sat down with his back to the house and watched the light on the fell, changing every minute as the sun dipped and the shadows lengthened. 'Too much testosterone, eh?'

'Something like that. He's not a bad kid. He belongs to the New Agers up at Long Meg, except he doesn't. A grandson, I think.'

'Josh Foster?'

'I don't know his name. He can look after himself, anyway.' And Mikey ripped the ring off a can with a satisfying pop.

FIFTEEN

'I know it feels like every conversation I have with you is about men, and I know this isn't how female friendship is supposed to work, but if you listen to me just this once, it'll be done. We can move on and discuss stuff like folklore and the cost of living and who's going to win the Costa Book Prize. And after that I don't want to hear you talk about him ever again.'

Lisa had taken up the confrontational stance that was her instant reaction whenever Scott's name popped up in the conversation. Used to it, Ashleigh was comfortable enough to be amused. 'All I said was that I wonder how he's getting on.'

'You don't care how he's getting on. Remember? Shall I quote it back to you? You said *just because he's only a few miles away doesn't mean I have to see him. I don't need to know what he's up to.*'

'There's no need to get touchy with me.'

'I'm not. I'm telling you. You've got someone who's good for you. You don't want to risk losing him because you can't get over Scott.'

If she lost Jude, it would be nothing to do with Scott. It would be to do with Becca. 'I'd be happy to talk about the Costa Book Prize, if only I had time to read any books.'

'Don't change the subject.'

'Okay. But I don't want to talk about Scott. I'm not interested in him. As I said before, and as you just quoted back to me.'

Lisa sat down with an exaggerated sigh. 'For God's sake. How is it possible that someone as sensible as you gets so stupid and irrational when it comes to Scott?'

The answer was obvious. It was because she loved him, or she had done once, and because there was no-one in life she would ever love the same way. It was no wonder she was so reluctant to let the good times go, even though they had come at the cost of his controlling toxicity. 'Let's just leave it. Anyway, I have work to do.'

'Ash. You know what you're like.'

'Yes. Busy.' She got to her feet and retrieved her iPad from her briefcase. Sensible and self-aware, that was what she was like. And pragmatic. No relationship lasted for ever and the one she had with Jude, which was based upon physical chemistry and friendship and yet perversely had never combined these two ingredients into love no matter what they whispered to one another in the darkness, had already endured longer than she'd expected it to. At some point, one of them would have their doubts.

Lisa followed her into the hall. 'You work too bloody hard. Leave the work and come to the pictures. There's a kickass action film on at the Alhambra.'

Above the irritation, Ashleigh was laughing as she headed upstairs. It was impossible to be angry with Lisa, whose good intentions always shone through. It was hard enough to be angry with Jude, who'd never tried to pretend that their relationship meant as much to him as the one he'd had with Becca and so had doomed it with his honesty. She'd always known there was no permanence to it, and for the first time she began to wonder how it would end and which of them would end it.

She laid the iPad down on the bed, sat at her dressing table and opened the drawer. She couldn't concentrate on her work with that kind of thought rumbling about in her head, so it would be sensible to take a few moments to calm herself down and rationalise her way out of the irritation Jude had brought on her. First he'd disappeared off to see Mikey; now it was Becca. He'd made it clear she wasn't his priority.

Guilt troubled her, nevertheless. He'd told her about it. She'd kept quiet about the occasional coffees she shared with Scott.

That was because coffee with Scott meant nothing to either of them, and so wasn't worth mentioning. Nevertheless it niggled at her, so she had to lay it to rest. From the drawer she took out a deck of tarot cards, wrapped in purple silk. If she had a guilty secret it was the cards, not Scott. Jude knew about them, and so did Lisa, but no-one else. The two of them gave her enough good-natured abuse over it and she could barely think about the amusement she'd generate if anyone at work found out. It wouldn't just be amusement. There would be a degree of scepticism and an inevitable loss of credibility to go along with it, and that was something she couldn't risk.

'Shall we talk about Scott?' she asked the cards, keeping her voice low so Lisa didn't hear and come racing in to tear another strip off her and strain the bounds of friendship. She dealt them out, five in a horseshoe, and this time she didn't follow her usual routine and turn them over, one by one, asking each a question, having each one address a specific issue before she knew what would come next.

'This time,' she said (to the cards? To herself?) 'I need to get a feeling for the overall.' Some things were too important to trust entirely to the Tarot and all she wanted them to do was to offer her some breathing space. She didn't even need to know what she had to think about. It was all there in her head — Scott and Jude and the patient, irresistible threat that was Becca Reid; love or sex or happiness — and all she had to do was find a solution.

It was for her to do it, not them. For the first time she doubted their guidance. It had been reflecting on a random draw of a card that led her to cut Scott off so completely in the first place, and now she knew how foolish that would sound if she ever confessed it.

She surveyed the cards. The Four of Pentacles, indicating that she was holding on too tightly — but to what? The Emperor, inhabiting his world of self-discipline, always sticking to the right road. She stopped and frowned at him, the card she always associated with Jude yet which had never come up in any reading since she'd met him. Usually the card that came up was the Three of Swords, the one that reminded her of Scott and his incurable infidelity. Auspicious? Inauspicious? Then the next one, the Empress, domestic and content, thoughtful, emotional and loving. Definitely not me, Ashleigh said to herself.

The last card, not remotely to her surprise, was the Hanged Man. Sometimes she thought that whatever she was thinking influenced the cards she drew rather than the other way round. She might have subconsciously identified this card of the dead as she'd cut the deck, shuffling it to the top and keeping it there, just the way the series of suicides in the Eden Valley kept shuffling to the forefront of her mind.

She looked at the card, deep in thought. There he was, the Hanged Man, suspended by his feet yet with the ghost of a smile on his face. It wasn't a card of death, but a card of sacrifice. There was a lot of food for thought in that.

When it came to her heart, she had nothing to fear; she knew that. Nothing to fear from anyone but herself.

When the doorbell rang, late on in the evening, Jude was standing in his stockinged feet in the kitchen with his fist clenched around a can of decaffeinated diet Coke, a joyless end to a thought-provoking evening. Late alerts like this weren't unusual and were rarely welcome. He made his way to the front door with care, and opened it to find Ashleigh on the doorstep.

'Well, this is an unexpected pleasure. Come on in.' He leaned in to kiss her. She smelled of cider and Chanel. So, after he'd cancelled their evening out in fruitless search of reassurance about Mikey, she'd gone out anyway. He could hardly hold that against her. 'What brings you over here at the time of night? Had an epiphany?'

'Yes.' She stepped inside but she kept her jacket on and made no move to follow him through to the living room. 'But probably not the sort you want to hear. I won't stop.'

'Right.' Consciously defensive, he stuck both hands in his pockets and looked at her as she stood on the mat just inside the open door. Adam Fleetwood, strolling past, peered in at them and laughed. 'Close the door, then. Whatever you have to say I don't imagine you want the whole street hearing it.'

'No.' She closed the door behind her. 'I've just been for a drink with Scott.'

'For old times' sake, as usual.'

'Yes.' For once she didn't look at him but instead peered beyond him to the heavy mirror fixed on the wall. Jude wasn't a man for mirrors and this one had been there when he moved in, so firmly screwed to the wall that it was too much of an effort to move it. Now it was perished round the edges where the silvered paint had begun to tarnish, so that when he saw Ashleigh's timeless yet expressive face in it he was briefly reminded of the faded photograph Becca had described to him of Nick Chester, fixed forever at the age of sixteen.

Something, some sense of foreboding that had crept into the house with the mention of Scott, warned him that this might be the last time Ashleigh looked at herself in that mirror, that she'd never tweak her hair straight or apply her lipstick in it again in the morning after a night with him.

'I hope he didn't drive home,' he said, to break the silence, waiting for her to say that he'd gone back to her house, or was waiting outside, or whatever else she had to say that would bring official notification of the inevitable.

'He got a taxi.' There was nothing wrong with her makeup but she fidgeted with it all the same, smearing a finger beneath her eye as if to pick up a stray flake of mascara.

'It's good to see you're getting on so well with him.' He wasn't a mean-spirited man, but he didn't see why he should make this easy for her.

'I always have done. That's the thing, Jude. Don't you see? I always will get on well with him. I like him.'

To Jude, it was evident Scott Kirby was controlling, self-absorbed and manipulative. That Ashleigh, who had always understood that, should claim still to like him was telling. 'As I'll always get on well with Becca. It's always good to be civilised with your ex-partner.'

'It's more than just civilised, though. You know it. It's because deep down I still love him.'

In the mirror he saw her close her eyes for a second as if she couldn't bear to hear herself speak the truth. 'Right.'

'You knew this was going to happen, Jude. Don't deny it. We both always knew this wasn't long term. We knew it wasn't love.'

He couldn't argue with that. It had lasted longer than he'd ever expected, especially once he'd met Scott and seen for himself both how keen she was to get away from a man who was persistent and churlish but never violent and how difficult it was for her to let him go. He'd once heard Lisa spell it out in a way he never would; Ashleigh was drawn towards Scott, the one man she'd loved, like the moth to the flame, knowing she'd be burned.

He didn't know Scott well but he guessed it would happen again. A brief smile crossed his face as he thought of Geri Foster and her philosophy of life, love and sex. It was a simple enough solution if you could stick to it, but Ashleigh's continued flirtation with the ghost of her marriage showed how hard it was to love inclusively. If you loved, you wanted to be the only person. That was why his resentment towards Ashleigh as she returned to Scott was so much less than it had been towards Becca when she'd taken up with the allegedly-reformed returning hero, Adam Fleetwood.

That was over now. Becca was single. 'I hope you're happy,' he said, to fill the gap.

She turned away from the mirror. 'I don't expect I will be. I've already tried to change him and failed. But I got to the stage when I have to try, just one more time. You have to make sacrifices.'

A strange choice of word. He might have understood it better if she'd said *take risks*. 'And I'm the sacrifice? I see.'

'I don't know if you are. Maybe it's me. I'm sorry Jude, and I don't want to hurt you, but you know what? I don't think you will hurt.'

His pride would, perhaps, but that was all. His heart wasn't hers to damage. 'I don't imagine I will.'

'And do you know something else? There's a silver lining to every cloud. Don't pretend you haven't already thought of it. Because now you're free and single, and so is Becca.' The deed done, face to face, she turned her back on him and placed a hand on the door.

Not that long before, at Mikey's twenty first birthday party, Becca had kissed him and avoided him for weeks afterwards, turning scarlet when they finally did meet. Later, in a moment of stress she'd thrown her arms around him for comfort and there had been hell to pay from Adam Fleetwood, her boyfriend at the time. But now? 'That ship sailed long ago.'

'Of course it didn't. Do you know what? Before I came out I read the cards.'

'You and your bloody cards,' he said, unable to resist the temptation to tease her even in these most serious of circumstances. 'Did they tell you I was the wrong man for you?'

'You know that isn't how it works. But I turned over two cards, the Emperor and the Empress, together. That's unusual.'

There were seventy two cards in a tarot deck. He did the maths as he had done for the roll of the die, for the suicides. The odds of any one coming up were one in seventy two. The odds of those two coming up one after the other would be very much more — less than one in five thousand by his rusty mental maths. 'How many cards in a spread?'

'Five in the one I did.'

That changed the odds again. 'What were the others?'

'I can't remember.'

He didn't press her, moving to open the door for her. 'I know you're right. It was always going to happen. But I admit I wasn't expecting it tonight.'

'Lisa will tear me limb from limb,' she said, dipping her head as if in apology, 'when I get home and break it to her. She could never stand him. But I have to try again. I have to give him just one more chance.'

'I see,' he said, though he didn't.

'We'll still be friends, won't we?'

'We'll always be friends.' When she stepped over the doorstep he followed her and gave a huge hug in the street, but he was acutely conscious that for all the closeness, all the intimacy, the touch of her cheek against his and the trailing golden hair she left on his shirt, there was no kiss at the end of it.

'I'm so fond of you, Jude. You know that.'

'Shall I walk you home?'

'It's okay. I'll be fine.'

He watched her down the street and there was no sign that Scott was lurking in the corner to take her back to his digs in Pooley Bridge or to take on the challenge of Lisa at the house in Norfolk Road. Over the road and a few doors down he could see, as so often, Adam sitting in his living room in his habitual pose — beer in one hand, tv remote in the other.

He closed the door and went into the living room. In a drawer of the sideboard he kept the deck of tarot cards Ashleigh had brought him back from a holiday in Sri Lanka. Jude was a tarot sceptic and the gift had been a joke, but he got them out nevertheless and sorted through them for the Emperor and the Empress. The deck was cheap and gaudy, made of thin card with the ink already fading on it, and she'd bought it because each card had a different representation of a tiny grey cat, yawning, hunting or sleeping. In the two cards in his hand the cat adopted an almost identical, pose, curled on the lap of the Empress, fast asleep, but on the lap of the Emperor one eye was open in an exaggerated, meaningful wink.

He stared at the cards for a while, thinking of the serenity of Becca and the knowingness of Holmes, before he tucked them away back in the pack, wiped the smears of cheap ink off his fingers and then, turning out the lights one by one, headed upstairs to bed.

SIXTEEN

'Did we find out anything more about Geri Foster?' Jude had strolled into the open office where Ashleigh and Chris had their desks and stood between the two of them, his question addressed to both. Ashleigh, who wasn't as good as he was at keeping her personal and professional lives separate, looked away from him, but not before he'd seen that her face was a flustered shade of pink.

'Nothing more than she's told us.' Chris looked vaguely regretful, as if he'd let them all down. 'Sorry. I got called on for something else. Is it important?'

'I've no idea.' Jude thought of Geri, resistant to some of his questions but choosing to answer others in enormous and irrelevant detail. If he hadn't deduced it from what he knew of her background, he'd have guessed she liked to keep control of the situation and that control, in her case as in so many others, meant keeping secrets for their own sake. Some, like the timing of her arrival in Cumbria, would be harmless. Others might not be. 'She wasn't straight with us. That's all. That always makes me wonder what else people are capable of.'

'I always think that about her folks.'

For all his innate scepticism, Jude remained convinced of Storm and Raven's general innocence. 'Do we know anything about her son? Mikey said he fell out with some of the kids down at the gym in town the other day.'

'A lot of the young lads hang out down there.' Chris was a fitness fanatic, outdoors in the daylight, indoors in the dark. 'They're always trying to outmuscle one another. Too much testosterone. That's the problem.'

It often was, but testosterone didn't usually manifest itself in anything other than a brief surge of violence, in Jude's experience. Young Josh Foster might not be a cold and calculating killer or an assistant in suicide, but according to Mikey he'd put a lot of people's backs up. That was always worth exploring. 'I don't imagine it's anything, but I think I'd like to take a closer look at the Fosters. Both of them.'

'Shall I go down there and talk to her?' Chris offered. 'I don't mind popping down after work.'

'I'll go.' Ashleigh looked up from her laptop and her expression, at last, mirrored him in neutrality. 'From what I've heard about her, she'd eat you alive. Raven's terrified of her.'

'And you think she won't eat you?'

'Not in quite the same way. Don't worry. I'll go along this evening. I'm not doing anything else.'

So, she wasn't out with Scott, then, he thought, but pulled himself up. They'd all become engaged with the suicides. Jude had briefed Faye on developments earlier that day and she clearly regarded it as less of a problem now Vanessa Wood had become more involved, looking over the press releases and issuing soothing statements.

Vanessa's open sessions in the evenings had, Faye informed him, been mobbed with the curious and the concerned, and her school sessions were also full. Everything that could be done was in hand and there was no need to spend precious resources on it.

In the meantime, Jude drove past the New Agers' camp to Long Meg and back most evenings, in the forlorn hope of finding someone suspicious or intervening at the right time to save a life. He saw nothing, and took comfort from the fact that no other deaths were reported. It was possible — just possible — that Vanessa's extra hours and expertise, along with the community's vigilance and every parent's concerns, were drawing the incident to a close.

'One other thing.' Chris sat back. 'I did a little digging last night, off my own bat. I thought I'd see if I could track down the owner of Eden Whispers.'

'Any joy?' There had been a new blog post up that morning, wondering about who might be next, asking its readers if they ticked all the boxes. *Could it be you?* the blog had asked, a snake inside the head of the vulnerable.

'Nope. I got so far but whoever it was has made sure they aren't easily tracked down.' Chris's look was almost pleading. 'We should get the professionals involved. It's way beyond me, and it's not just a blog. Eden Whispers has a Twitter feed. There are some niggling messages on there, and the engagement has gone up hugely in the last couple of weeks. A lot of the followers are young people, by the look of it, some of them local. It's the same sort of stuff.'

'Do they tag anyone? Target anyone by name? Specifically suggest people should take their own lives?' If that was the case he'd have a chance at persuading Faye there was a case to make, a crime committed.

'No, they're far too smart for that. I'd lay my pension

on the fact that there are a few direct messages that bear scrutiny, though. I'd love to see them.'

Maybe Jude could try again to persuade Faye. Even if they couldn't easily peel away the layers of cyber-secrecy protecting the blogger, they might find enough to identify potential victims. 'I can't ask you to spend any more time on that. But if you have any ideas, come back to me.'

Geri Foster's house was barely more than a cottage — a single-storey sandstone building with tiny windows, crammed onto a narrow terrace above the river between the hamlets of Great Salkeld and Eden Lacy. A skylight built into the attic suggested someone had squeezed an extra bedroom into it at some point. The exterior paintwork was peeling but the rest of the house was in good condition — new pointing, a few shiny grey tiles suggesting recent repair and a neat garden that pointed to the later stages of a renovation.

Ashleigh parked in front of the house and got out. It was a pleasant evening and Geri was in the garden that sprawled around the side of the house, sitting in an ancient wrought iron chair with a tall glass of golden liquid beside her. When she heard the car she turned, got up and strolled over to the front garden. 'Sergeant O'Halloran, isn't it? To what do we owe the pleasure?'

'I was passing.' Ashleigh had changed before she came along, to make herself more obviously off duty. 'I thought I'd pop in. Given how things are.'

'You people seem to spend all your leisure time in this small area. Your boss always seems to be passing Long Meg. But since you're here, come and have a drink,' Geri suggested.

'I wouldn't mind a diet Coke if you have one.'

'I think we can manage that. Josh!' she called in through the open kitchen window. 'Get yourself a drink and bring out a diet Coke, and come and make yourself sociable with a wandering detective.' She led the way along the path down the side of the cottage and waved Ashleigh to a second chair. 'He's a nice enough kid, and I shouldn't really complain because he does get out and about a lot. But he spends way too much time on the computer, and God knows what he's doing on it.'

'Most of them play a lot of games these days, don't they?'

Geri snorted. 'Maybe my parents were right after all. I'd be a whole lot more competent with computers if I'd learned to use one a lot earlier instead of being the only one at school who couldn't switch the thing on, that's for sure. But yes, you're right. You can play too many games.'

'But I'm going to study computing.' Josh Foster, broad-shouldered and with his hair cut short enough to intimidate, emerged from the house, blinking into the evening sun, and handed Ashleigh a glass of Coke without meeting her eye. There was a bruise under his left eye and another on his forearm. He sat down on a step that led to the lower part of the garden, where it fell away towards the river. It had, Ashleigh noticed, handy views across the river towards Cave Wood and the sandstone warren of Lacy's Caves, just about visible below the overhanging trees. Long Meg was on the back slope of the hill, out of sight, and a couple of hundred yards away the railway passed over the bridge from which Nicholas Chester had fallen to his death. It was a landscape of ancient and modern mystery, of sinister, sudden death.

'So you are.' Geri's attitude to her son was brisk and offhand, but she kept a mother's eye on him as he sat and stared across to Cave Wood, just as Ashleigh herself had done. 'Okay, Sergeant. Let's have the pastoral care spiel and get it over with.'

'I was wanting to check your mum's okay. And Josh, of course.'

'Yeah. I'm fine.' He put his glass down and rested his hands on his knees. His young man's muscles blossomed under his tee shirt, biceps rippling in the sun as if he were posing, consciously or unconsciously, in the expectation of admiration. 'Why wouldn't I be?'

'It must be upsetting, knowing that those young people —' Ashleigh ground to a halt as it occurred to her that while she knew exactly what not to say, the right form of words eluded her. 'Looking out over this.'

'Lacy's Caves are haunted, they say. By a madman, naturally. Obvious nonsense.' Geri picked up a pair of designer sunglasses from the table and put them on, another level of security to hide behind.

'Nah. I don't care,' said Josh, in answer to Ashleigh's previous question. 'I don't live here. What's it to me?'

'I thought you said you knew the lad. Charlie, was it?' said Geri, sinking a fair amount of Pimms.

'I met him in town, in the pub. He won't be missed. Introverted, selfish sod. Like the others round here.'

They all stared out at the river. On the path on the far side a dog galloped along, distantly followed by a hurrying, overweight man. A woman supervised two small children at the water's edge, where a dry spell had lowered the water level until it barely trickled over the weir.

'Did you ever see them about?' asked Ashleigh. 'Maybe the night that—'

'Nah. Only the weird Goth girl from Lazonby, but she's always hanging around. Never speaks to me, though. She thinks she's too good for the likes of us.'

Josh, Ashleigh concluded with interest, was a young man with a chip on his shoulder. 'I expect people are talking about it in town.'

'People talk a lot of crap in town. I don't have nothing to say to them.'

'What is this?' Geri turned to Ashleigh and took off her sunglasses. Her voice was calm but her eyes were narrow. 'I'm not sure I like where this conversation is going.'

'It was a genuine inquiry. We're still trying to find out what caused these young people to take their own lives and hopefully prevent any others doing the same.'

'I sincerely hope you aren't suggesting Josh had anything to do with those suicides. Just because those kids treated him like an outsider and wouldn't accept him as one of them.'

As far as Ashleigh understood things Josh surely was an outsider, someone who drifted up in the summer and drifted away again when the school holidays — or, in future, the university holidays — were over. 'I—'

'I thought the police knew everything.' Geri laughed, although she didn't sound friendly.

'I wish we did.'

'I'll tell you something for nothing and you can take that away and put this in your files. Josh was here with me at the time of the three suicides that happened when we were here.'

'I don't doubt it.' Ashleigh flicked a look past her to Josh, who was staring away from the confrontation as if it was nothing to do with him, watching a heron as it rode the air above the river with long, lazy flaps of its wings.

'It should be obvious to you he can't have had anything to do with it. If you're seriously suggesting a teenager has gaslighted four young adults he doesn't even know to their deaths, you shouldn't be in the force.'

In some astonishment, Ashleigh stared at her. 'I didn't suggest anything of the sort.' Geri was like everyone else in the area — on edge. 'What makes you think I did? Has anyone else suggested that?'

'No, of course not.' Geri looked down at her glass. 'That's my second Pimm's of the evening. I'm sorry. Alcohol tends to make me speak my mind even more than I usually do. Obviously I worry about Josh. But let's move the conversation on to something else.'

'It was the strangest thing.' It had taken Ashleigh a while to bring herself to call Jude. On any other day, even before they'd been in a relationship, she'd have done so instinctively but for the first time it felt difficult.

But it was business, not pleasure. She'd left the Fosters and driven into Lazonby. In search of inspiration, she'd headed up to Fiddler's Lane, parked on the verge and walked up to the bridge, remembering how they'd come there the day after Charlie Curran's death, how Jude had measured up the scene. It was possible this death was more than suicide, but there was no evidence the three hangings and Clara Beaton's overdose could have been anything else. 'She went after me for no reason. I asked after Josh, asked if he knew any of the kids who died and she came after me and accused me of accusing him of being involved.'

'Is it possible?' She imagined him sitting in the living room, half his attention on her and half on his work emails, or on the telly.

A train whistle blew in the distance and she turned towards it. It was the time of the evening when Tania had fallen to her death in front of the Langwathby train, the last on the line. She withdrew from the bridge, away from the driver's line of sight in case she spooked him into a panic, a fear that what had struck a colleague might happen to him or, in the worst case scenario, the same driver had returned to work, would see a figure and fear the worst. 'I suppose at one level it is. He's fit and strong. Guns of steel, even for an eighteen year old. He'd be fully capable of hanging someone.' Capable of pushing a woman off the bridge, too, whether or not she resisted. 'He didn't get on with a lot of people locally. He wasn't one of them and he resented it.'

'Did I tell you Mikey came across him in the gym? I don't think he took to him, either.'

'You said. He stood up for him, at least. The other thing about Josh is that he's a computer geek. I'd imagine he'd be perfectly capable of setting up something like Eden Whispers and hiding it behind layer upon layer of secrecy.'

The train whistle blew again and the three carriages rattled under the bridge and onwards. She watched it disappear.

'So,' pursued Jude, unaware of the backdrop, 'that's the case for the prosecution. But of course there's a case for the defence, too.'

'Yes. There's no evidence at all for any third party involvement. He wasn't in the area when Clara and Connor died and his mother will give him an alibi for the other three deaths.'

'I'm sure she would. Rightly or wrongly. But I think we have to remember. You don't have to be on the spot to gaslight someone.'

Eden Whispers had published a photo of the very bridge on which Ashleigh stood. They'd called it the *bridge to peace*. 'Are you sure you can't persuade Faye to pick up on that?'

'I can mention it again. But even if she agrees, she won't prioritise it. Getting anything back could take weeks.'

They shared a silence while a car came down Fiddler's Lane. She was conscious of the occupants watching her, taking note of anything unusual. She reassured them with a smile and a wave. 'Nothing we can do, then.'

'Nothing we can do until something else comes up. Let's just hope it isn't another body.'

'Let's hope so.' She waited for a second. 'I'll see you tomorrow.'

'Yes.'

Another day he'd have said *You could drop in on your way past* and she'd have hesitated, because Becca still got in her way, and Scott almost certainly got in his. As far as Becca was concerned, Jude could do what he wanted now. She'd arranged to meet up with Scott the next time they were both free, for a quick bite to eat for old times' sake.

For old times' sake. That should be her epitaph. 'I'll head home, then.'

'I'll see you tomorrow,' he said, and rang off.

SEVENTEEN

For the first time in what felt like months, Jude had managed to honour an arrangement to meet up with his father.

Their relationship was rocky at best, but they clung to its wreckage. David Satterthwaite pleaded love and fondness towards both his sons, along with a touching innocence in the matter of his broken marriage, but he lacked the will to make good on his words. The consensus was that he was wrong on at least one of those counts and had treated his wife badly when he'd sacrificed her to his mid-life crisis, but David never quite managed either to take up his responsibilities or offer an apology for failing to do so.

Jude, who had been old enough to bear the burden of his mother's near-fatal illness and Mikey's roller-coaster teenage years, was the only one of the family who still spoke to him and had to make a constant effort to keep communication open. Saturday afternoons at the football were the least painful way of doing so; father and son had season tickets for adjacent seats at Carlisle United, and the only time they were truly at ease together was in the tribal comfort of the stand, where every neighbour was a friend for a couple of hours on a Saturday afternoon.

Keen to pick his father's brains over the school photograph Leslie Chester had shown Becca, Jude made a special effort, and so far it was going well. They'd taken the train up from Penrith to allow themselves a pre-match pint, and negotiated ninety minutes of football without discussing anything contentious. David hadn't mentioned Mikey, though — hadn't even asked after his general welfare, let alone expressed any specific concern. If he didn't feel some primitive fear for his son, he must be the only parent in Eden not to do so.

'Pint?' David said, inevitably, as they walked back to the station. 'It's not often you manage to spare me a whole afternoon, so we should make the most of it. And it's in your own interests. I've got something for you.'

'You managed to find that school photo?'

'I did, and let me tell you, it got me off on a real nostalgia kick. We'd better look at it before I have my pint or I'll have a tear or two in my eye.'

That was more than likely. David had a weakness for a drink and a soft spot for amateur dramatics, a combination which sometimes ended badly. Jude, whose nature was immensely more practical and whose drinking was more restrained, invariably ended up as an interested onlooker or, if his father became mawkishly over-emotional, trying to control his irritation. 'That would be good.' And later, when David was getting sentimental, he might try once more to broker a peace deal between him and Mikey. The series of suicides had only reinforced his perennial worry that one day one of them would go out as normal and never come back.

It was irrational, he knew, and if he applied the same mathematical logic to the probability that he did to the

Eden Valley suicides, he wouldn't be concerned, but he'd seen it too often. Few people who got the call from the police to say their loved one had been the victim of accident or murder had expected it would happen to them. Most expressed bitter regret at things unsaid, sins unforgiven. If Jude could do anything to heal the rift between father and son, he would do it, because one day it might be too late.

David led the way into a city centre pub where he was all-too-clearly well known and spent ten minutes getting the orders, joking at the bar with the regulars while Jude checked his work email and was disproportionately relieved to find there was nothing immediate and no-one else had died. When his father returned with two pints, he thrust the phone back into his pocket and turned his attention to the matter in hand. 'Let's have a look at this picture, then.'

'What's the story with it?' David felt in his backpack and brought out an envelope with a cardboard backing, a larger version of the snapshot that Becca had described. 'Is one of my old schoolmates wanted for an international drug smuggling ring? I wouldn't be surprised to find some of them weren't keen on making an honest living.'

'It's interest, really. Becca said she saw someone looking at an old photo in one of the places she was working and thought she recognised you in it.'

'Becca, eh?' said David, exactly as Ashleigh had done. 'That's back on now, then, is it?'

'No.' Jude lifted his pint. No matter how much he might regret that Becca was no longer so integral a part of his life, he wasn't so foolish as to think he could change it, even after Ashleigh had so elegantly ended their relationship. When you lost trust in someone, as he'd done in Becca, you didn't get it back easily. He might still love her — he was honest enough, at least, to admit that — but love wasn't enough. Ashleigh knew that, too. Theirs had been a relationship between second-bests, fraught with difficulties as result, and in the end it lasted for longer than he'd thought. But it, too, was done.

For once David got the message, let that single word end the thread of the conversation. He placed the picture down on the sticky table top. 'Here we go. That's my old marras from way back when. That's me. As if you didn't know. You'll find that like looking in a mirror.'

Jude looked at it. He was dark, like his mother, where David's hair had once had a sandy tint before it faded to grey. That apart, they could have been the same person. In the picture David was standing next to Linda, the childhood sweetheart who'd become his wife. His arm was around her and she was smiling up at him where everybody else was looking towards the camera, but neither Jude nor David mentioned that. 'A bit. Yes.' The apple never fell far from the tree; there was more than a touch of Mikey in the image of his father, too. It had never occurred to him before how tough it must have been for Linda, confronted on a daily basis by the living images of the man who'd treated her so badly.

'Forty years ago, that was. More than. Makes me feel old.' Lifting his pint with one hand, David jabbed a finger at the picture with the other.

'I bet a few of them have dropped off the perch by now.'

'God, you're a morbid one today. Fifty-eight isn't old.' The finger hovered over it. 'Though now you mention it, there's a few have fallen by the wayside for one reason or another.'

They'd almost included Linda. With practised ease, Jude subdued the anger with his father that Mikey had yet to learn to control. 'You'd expect to lose one or two, maybe.'

'Natural wastage.' David laughed. 'Here's Nick Chester. That was a sad one. He was killed in an accident, just a few weeks after this picture was taken.'

'Oh?'

'It was a hell of a shock. I liked him. He was a good kid, a bit geeky and a bit bookish. Not into sport or our kind of music, not adventurous at all. He liked art and history and classical music. God knows what he was doing on the track.'

'A dare, maybe?'

'Aye, maybe. He was a good sort.'

In the photograph Nick Chester had had a grin on him as wide as the Mersey tunnel. 'Poor kid.'

'Yes. And there's this guy here.' The finger moved along to the other side of Linda, a youth with an insouciant expression, hands stuck in his pockets. 'What was his name again? Richard something? Richard Stoker, maybe, or Stokes? He came to a bad end.'

'Is that right?'

'Murdered,' said David, with relish. 'You're a policeman. You ought to know about these things.'

Jude looked at the later-to-be-murdered teenager with interest. 'I can't be expected to know the details of every homicide in the area over forty years. If it was local. Was it?'

'Yes. Or not local, exactly. After he left school he moved away down to Appleby. They found him dead in his garden over the Horse Fair weekend, a few years on. House broken into, cash and alcohol missing.'

'Did they catch anyone?'

'No. Must have been one of those…' David caught

himself up, sober enough to remember he must be politically correct. 'Travelling folk. That's what the talk was, at the time. The police never caught anyone, of course. Case unsolved.'

Jude allowed himself a wry grin. There was every chance whoever had been on the case had a clear idea who it might have been but couldn't find the evidence. The annual Appleby Horse Fair was a regular headache and he knew plenty of locals who took the opportunity to commit some petty crime or other under the umbrella of chaos, and hope the blame was conveniently shifted to someone passing through. 'Interesting.' If he found himself with a spare minute he'd look that up and see if it led anywhere. 'So that's two out of twenty dead.'

'Two out of twenty dead unnaturally,' his father corrected. 'Here's Clare. I dated her once.' Clare was standing behind Linda, grinning. 'She went to work out in Africa and picked up some nasty disease or other. Some fly bite, I heard. She died, what… about four years ago? And here's Mac. Finn McDougall. I never liked him. I lost touch with him after we left school, but I heard someone say he died. I don't know how.'

The class of teenagers would all be in their mid-to-late fifties by now, but surely in an area such as this the loss of four of them was way above the average? Imagining himself explaining this to Faye, Jude could see the scepticism in her face. But where was it coming from? Where did it lead?

'This guy.' David jabbed the forefinger down on the figure at the back of the picture. 'He was a hell of a lad. Trouble through and through. I don't remember his name, but I do remember that. He wasn't here long, just a year or so. His folk were tinkers. I mean travellers. If he isn't in prison by now, he should be.'

'Oh?'

'He killed a man. Lost his temper in a bar in Hexham or somewhere, and then did a runner. I remember thinking that wasn't like him to be so obvious. He was a sly bugger. I was always careful not to get on the wrong side of him. I never knew what he'd do if I upset him and I didn't want to find myself driving over Hartside one day with my brake cables cut.'

Jude looked at the picture and saw the boy had what his mother would have called a look of the devil about him. He was handsome, in a buccaneering kid of way, and stood at the end of the back row, sneering at the camera. One arm was visible, hanging by his side, and the fist was clenched. A murderer and a murdered man, in the same photograph. 'Do you think there's any connection with—?'

'With Richard? I wouldn't be surprised. They hated each other's guts.' David sat back from the picture, as though his memories were exhausted. Maybe the good ones were. 'Take the photo and throw it to your cold case team to keep them interested. It would be good if you could finger the bastard after all these years. Richard was okay. He didn't deserve his head cracked in like it was.' He moved to put the picture away. 'Steven Lawson. That was his name. He had a hell of a temper on him but a way with the girls.'

'That's not always a good combination.'

'I'll bloody well say it wasn't. You didn't want to get on the wrong side of Steve.'

Jude held up a hand to stop David putting the picture away, and it wasn't just because there was something curious about seeing his parents so obviously in love when many of his memories and surely all of Mikey's had evolved from a toxic atmosphere, constant rows, constant disappointment. David and Linda Satterthwaite, the epitome of the way that people grew apart, were a warning to everybody. 'Do me a favour, would you?'

'Aye, if I can.'

'Can you write me down all the names you remember? On the back of the picture.'

'Why?'

'I can find out another way, I suppose.' Linda would know, though he was reluctant to share this bittersweet memory with her. 'It might help us track down witnesses.'

'Aye, okay then. Why not?' David rooted around in his bag again for a pen and accepted the one that Jude produced from his pocket. 'And that's me almost done with my pint. I wouldn't mind another one while I'm writing.'

When Jude looked back from the bar he saw his father frowning over the images, then turning the picture over and beginning to write on the back.

Steven Lawson, the man who came and went, who blew through the Eden Valley and ended up killing a man further over the Pennines, was familiar enough to trouble him. It would be ironic if, instead of solving the mystery of the Eden Valley suicides, they ended up solving a cold case murder, forty years old.

EIGHTEEN

On the Monday, after the remnants of his weekend off had been spent trying (unsuccessfully) to persuade Mikey to take a step towards repairing his relationship with David, Jude had come in to work early. The first thing he did was hand the class photograph over to Chris with a request to follow up on it when he had a spare moment.

He sat down and opened his desk, scrolling through the emails. There had been no new developments on the Eden Valley suicides, thank God, other than a new post on the blog. Rather to his surprise, this asked the question: *Is this the Last of the Eden Valley Suicides?* There was no surprise to read through it and discover that it wasn't, at least in the view of the author. *Many more young people will yet find the escape route they crave from this toxic world*, the writer concluded.

He closed down the blog as a text came through. Faye, wanting an update and wanting it straight away. Vanessa Wood was coming in to give her perspective on the investigation, and she thought he should be there. *Now*.

When Faye texted rather than phoned it was always a

warning of her irritation. There had been increasing signs of it over the past couple of weeks and he could sense she felt meeting Vanessa was a waste of her precious time and of his. Faye was touchy about rank and deference, and he suspected she wasn't just a little in awe of Vanessa, but saw her as the only person who had any degree of control over the situation. As such, she must feel obliged to tolerate this intervention.

Picking up his pad, he made his way towards Faye's office. It was scarcely surprising she felt out of her comfort zone. He did, too. No matter how he tried, he couldn't get inside the head of someone who took pleasure out of leading — or driving — young people to their deaths.

'Chief Inspector.' Vanessa, who had been perched on the edge of a chair looking at the thick cup of black coffee Faye had made her as though it was poison, put the cup down and stood up when he came in. He thought she might be trying to exert some kind of psychological dominance over him, but it was a mismatch. She was tall, but he was well over six feet. In the background Faye, who was nominally in charge of the meeting, was clearly fuming. 'Thank you for finding the time to join us. I'm on my way up to the Community College just now for one of my open sessions, but I thought I might take the chance to update you on where I am.'

He murmured a polite greeting and took the seat Faye indicated. She was in one of her more brisk moods, he could tell, clearly keen to get this meeting over and done with within as short a time as possible. She, he knew, was the one who was picking up the flak from the local community over what they perceived as slack handling of the matter.

'I'll be brief.' Either Vanessa had picked up Faye's subliminal messages or she, too, was in a hurry. 'The response I've had from the young people of our community and their parents has been tremendous and overwhelmingly positive. I've been able to offer them strategies to handle their own feelings and also to deal with the matter if they suspect that someone else, friend or stranger, may be vulnerable to the kind of autosuggestion Eden Whispers is putting about. I'm quite confident that we're controlling this series of incidents.'

'The press are very much on board,' Faye said, 'and thank God for that. I always worry some journalist will fall into the trap and sell out for a clickbait headline.'

'Naturally they're on our side. Plenty of them will have young friends and relatives of their own. It would take a very hard-headed newshound to run a story that risks lives without a good deal of thought.'

'I understand that. But they're asking questions I can't answer. I don't imagine you can answer them either, but I'm going to ask anyway. Do you think this is over and if not, when will it be? And how many more young people will we lose?' Faye sat forward at her desk, resting her chin on her hand.

Vanessa allowed herself a moment's reflection. 'I can't say. I'm afraid I have to go with my more pessimistic instincts and say it probably isn't over. There's damage already done which we may not be able to undo. And I'm not a miracle worker. I can only help those who put themselves forward for help.'

'Have you spoken to a young woman named Izzy Ecclestone?' Jude asked. 'I appreciate there may be patient confidentiality involved here, but she's someone we do know has a fascination with death and particularly with Cave Wood. I'm no expert, and I know in most cases we only see what people want to show us. But she seems to me to be extremely vulnerable.'

'I do know Izzy, and I've reached out to her. I've spoken to both her and her parents. Yes, you're right. Izzy is a concern. But we can't keep her under lock and key and I'm not convinced she's a danger to herself.'

Jude thought of Izzy, ghosting through the trees, and of both Raven's and Mikey's instinctive concern for her. 'Really?'

'Yes. She's had plenty of opportunity to harm herself and hasn't done so.'

The irresistible thought of Mikey reared again in Jude's brain. Did Vanessa think those who were apparently stable were, in fact, at greater risk? But Vanessa passed on. 'If there's no more progress on this investigation, Superintendent Scanlon, then I should head off to the Community College.'

'There is no more. I don't think you understand our role.' Faye fought her irritation, too obviously. 'We deal with the law. There's no evidence the law has been broken.'

'No,' said Vanessa with a sigh, 'indeed not. But I believe there's a perpetrator — that's the word you use, isn't it? — and finding that person is certainly your responsibility.' She stood up.

Faye was about to say something, possibly inflammatory, and Jude found himself cast in the unusual role of peacemaker. 'Am I right in thinking you lost a brother, Dr Wood?'

Vanessa put her mug down. 'That's correct, Chief Inspector. Have you been checking up on me?' She smiled. 'I'd expect that, of course.'

'Not checking up. My father mentioned it. He was at school with Nicholas.'

'I see. Then he'd have been at school at the same time as me, though I was a few years younger. What's your father's name? There were a few Satterthwaites, as I remember.'

'David.'

'David Satterthwaite. No, the name doesn't ring a bell, I'm afraid.' She turned back to Faye. 'So, to conclude. There's no progress on identifying this mystery blogger?'

'Not as yet.' Faye met Vanessa's gaze straight out, to Jude's considerable admiration. He could see she wasn't about to admit they couldn't justify it. 'Whoever it is has been adept at covering their tracks.'

'Inevitable, I suppose.' Vanessa shrugged. 'I think we're in the dying stages of this scenario. If you want my view, we need to target all our resources on preventing any more deaths — which, in my view, we'll be lucky to do and, frankly I'm surprised there haven't been more — and after that the blog will die a quiet death of its own. You can flush out vulnerable people, but you can't create vulnerability. If we can identify the vulnerable, we can build resilience. The odds are stacked in our favour from here on, I'm glad to say. Goodbye.'

Faye saw her to the door and pointed her towards reception, then came back and closed the door behind her with an exasperated snap. 'What a waste of time. Nothing said that couldn't be said on the phone. That woman is on a power trip, if you ask me. She expects us to jump when she shouts.' She picked up the mug Vanessa had placed on her desk and frowned at the ring it had left behind.

'Perhaps we could look in a little more detail at the blog—'

'Don't try and gang up on me. Copycat suicides are unpleasant but they aren't criminal. And yes, I've looked at the blog and yes, it's distasteful but in my view there isn't enough there to consider it *encouraging suicide*. Which, as you know, is the letter of the law.'

Jude disagreed, but he understood the subtext. Pressing on with a criminal investigation into encouraging or assisting suicide meant a lot of work, much of it devolving to Faye. 'I read it as clear encouragement.'

'It's impossible to justify the resources that would require, and you know it. Besides, she said herself. We're on top of it. Pull up a chair. I've a whole load of other things I want to go through with you, and they're urgent in their own way.'

But Vanessa hadn't said that. He was about to argue with her, though there was no point, but he kept thinking about Vanessa's words even as Faye was rattling through budgets and resources.

He was losing concentration when there was a knock on the door. Ashleigh, anxious and businesslike, answered Faye's snapped acknowledgement by opening it and stepping inside.

'I've got some really bad news,' she said, without preamble.

And Jude knew, without being told, that Vanessa had been right. The series of suicides might be coming to its end, but it wasn't over.

'So who is he?' asked Jude, as he and Ashleigh headed down to Cave Wood once again.

Ashleigh checked her phone for the umpteenth time. Information was coming in by the minute and she fired it off as it appeared. 'He's Ben Curran, younger brother of Charlie. He's twenty-one. There was a little more than a year between them. Ben wrote an emotional tribute to his brother on social media that would break your heart, Chris says.'

It must have been bad if it could get behind the terminally unsentimental Chris Marshall's defences. Perhaps this death wasn't so surprising, if the tensions running so high in the community had collided with, and amplified, Ben's devastation at the loss of his brother. Jude spared a thought for the parents, already wrecked by grief, perhaps so much so that they'd lost track of their welfare of their son. 'Any other family?'

'There's a third brother, a few years older. He lives in Manchester.'

Jude turned down through Little Salkeld, lifting a hand to acknowledge the uniformed constable who'd closed the road. Would the parents be quietly relieved that their surviving child was away from the fevered atmosphere of the Eden Valley, or tortured by the thought of what he might do without their help and support? 'Who found him?'

'Not Raven, thank God. The farmer.' Ashleigh kept flicking through her phone as Jude manoeuvred the car past a parked-up police car and squeezed it into a gateway. 'He takes a turn around the woods last thing at night and first thing every morning these days, just to make sure.'

'I don't blame him. I do the same myself, if I've nothing else on. We'll stop here. I think it's as close as we'll get.'

Ashleigh unclipped her seatbelt as he stopped the Mercedes. 'He came down last night, he said, along this path. Either he was there too soon and missed him, or Ben heard him and hid.'

'He was in Lacy's Caves, is that right?'

'Yes, but he looked in there.'

Ben hadn't hanged. There had been a bottle of vodka and some pills. 'Do we know what he took?'

'Not yet.'

Jude's concern gave way to frustration. That was three deaths in Cave Wood, four if you included Clara Beaton, as he was inclined to do and Faye was not. 'This is ridiculous. We can't police these woods. It's impossible.' And if they did there were endless others locally where someone could choose to go and never be found.

They got out of the car and headed down the well-worn path, though quite what there was for them to see was open to debate. 'Isn't Geri Foster's house over there?' Geri, Ashleigh had told him as she'd briefed him on the way to the scene, had been on the scene again. 'It's a pity she didn't see anything.'

'I don't know if anyone's asked her about last night. There hasn't really been time. I know the bare bones. She says she took the dog for a walk and went up to see her parents, but by the time she'd made it to Long Meg the police were on their way.' She raised her hand to stop his intervention. 'I know it looks odd, but it didn't really surprise me. It's her routine. They're all early risers.'

Whoever had closed off the scene had extended it further than usual. Jude and Ashleigh paused for a moment on the path outside the blue and white tape and from somewhere in the trees the chattering of a red squirrel floated down to them.

'Do you think we should we look more closely into Geri?' asked Ashleigh, stepping off the path to allow the CSI team, clad in their white forensic suits, to pass by. Even the usually gregarious Tammy had nothing to say today, passing by with nothing more than an acknowledging shrug, head down as she approached the grim task.

'Probably.' Jude looked along the path. Lacy's Caves, a network of man-made caverns burrowed into the sandstone cliff, were just round a bend, invisible among a tangle of birch and holly trees. He was relieved about it, and at the same time a little ashamed at feeling that way, but he wasn't in the mood to look on the body of another young man, snatched away too soon. 'That's Eden Lacy. Which is her house?'

'That sandstone one, there. Standing out on its own a little.'

'A clear view of Cave Wood isn't evidence of a murder, I know,' he said, with a sigh, 'but she sure as hell is in a good place to see what's going on.'

'As is her son.'

'Yes. I don't have a good feeling about this.'

A ladybird descended on whirring wings and settled on Ashleigh's sleeve. She put a finger down and the creature crawled onto her polished nail. 'You were in with Dr Wood this morning, weren't you? What did she say? Not about this. About the whole thing.'

'She still says this is a normal sequence of events. The damage has been done and we can do very little to undo it. She said she thought there'd be more, but not many.'

'I hope to God this is the last.'

Jude thought of the parents again, and inevitably his thoughts went to Mikey, to how his father would respond if anything happened to him while the rage between them still simmered. Of the two, Mikey was the one whose pain he understood; David was the sinner who'd forced his sons to choose between their parents. It had cost Jude enough to keep up a civil relationship and he never mentioned it to his mother. Some people might kill themselves to spite those they left behind. It was just possible Mikey detested his father enough to do that. 'Yes. Hopefully.'

Tammy popped her head back around the corner. 'I just thought you'd want to know. An empty vodka bottle by his side, half a dozen blister packs of paracetamol, all empty. Place stinks of alcohol. I can't say when he died, but it's been a few hours.'

So Ben Curran had perished, presumably alone, in the small hours of darkness. 'Tammy, I know you always go over everything with a fine-toothed comb.' He was always careful not to insult her professionalism but this time he had to be sure. 'But under the circumstances—'

'Yeah, I know. I'll be extra careful.' She disappeared around the bend again.

'I never came here when I was younger,' Jude said to Ashleigh, looking along the green curve of the path. 'I was over the other side of town. But back in the day this was one of the places kids would come for an illicit drink. I don't imagine that's changed too much. But this is different.'

'Let's go back up and see what's going on up the road.'

Back where they'd left the Mercedes, Doddsy was busy with his clipboard, dispensing instructions and receiving information. Geri was standing in her characteristic pose with her hands in her pockets giving her account of events to a uniformed PCSO and — rather to Jude's surprise — Vanessa Wood was deep in conversation with Josh Foster.

Josh. In running gear, his face still pink with exertion. Leaving Ashleigh dealing with Geri, Jude strolled over. 'Is everything okay?'

'Yep.' The young man was noncommittal, but his hands were balled into fists and the look he gave Vanessa was less than friendly. He'd been out running, shoes crusted with mud and plastered with grass, tee shirt still damp with sweat. 'I was just getting a dose of advice I don't need about how to look after myself. But hell, I'm used to that.'

Vanessa stepped away, lifting her hands in apology. 'I've said I'm sorry.'

'You should never force advice on people,' Geri called over, from where she must just have finished with the PCSO. 'It's counterproductive. I thought you'd have known that. Being a professional. But I'm pretty damned sure you guys make this up as you go along. I'm only surprised the fake advice some so-called counsellors dish out doesn't drive more people to kill themselves. Still, whatever brings in the cash, eh?'

Vanessa shot her a look that was concentrated poison, but discretion triumphed. 'I'm sure you can always confide in your mother,' she said evenly, to Josh, 'but if you need to talk to anyone, you know where I am.'

Jude could quite see why these two women wouldn't get on; both very determined, each convinced she was right. Geri hadn't bothered to hide her dislike of therapists.

'Come on,' Geri said to her son, impatiently. 'We're done here. They know where to find us if they need to.'

'I wasn't expecting to see you here,' he said to Vanessa, when the two were out of earshot.

'I probably shouldn't have come along,' she said in a low voice. 'I'll give the woman that. But the farmer called me to let me know what had happened and said there was a young man around and he thought he might need help. I thought I'd better come down at once and talk to him. I'd only just got here. However, not every therapist is the right person for every patient.'

'I'm sure he'll understand that.'

She hesitated. 'You asked me about my brother, earlier. That's what made me come down.'

'I can see it might be difficult.' It was comforting to think he wasn't the only one whose professionalism was affected by the events.

'It is indeed. I can handle it myself, you understand. But when I visit my father he's distraught. The memories have come flooding back, of how he was when it had happened. Sometimes he conflates the past and the present, thinks the girl who fell from the bridge was Nicky. I made a grave professional error by rushing in just now, and I know DI Dodd would have called me in his own good time, but these deaths hit very close to home.' She looked across at Josh. 'I'll move on, and I imagine he will, too. He seems a reasonably secure young man in himself, as far as I can judge.'

Jude thought the opposite. Even without the benefit of Mikey's opinion, Josh's attitude spoke for itself and told of a huge chip on his shoulder, about life and the way everyone treated him. Maybe Vanessa's use of terminology was different and *secure in himself* just meant she didn't think he'd kill himself. 'I'm glad to hear it.'

'I don't think there's much benefit in my being here,' she said, after a moment. 'I came down on a whim.' She looked as if she was irritated with herself at some lapse in professionalism. 'It was a misjudgement, but a genuine one. I thought I might be needed. On reflection I see my time will be better spent elsewhere.'

Jude's own time would be better spent elsewhere, too. He waited for Ashleigh to come across to join him. She stood a good six inches further away from him than usual and he could see from Doddsy's raised eyebrow that his friend had noticed it. 'I'm no psychologist but I always think it's better to act than not.'

'Such a policeman's reply.' Vanessa's eyes lingered on young Josh Foster, disappearing along the path. 'Do you know the worst thing about Eden Whispers? It's that a lot of what it says is so very seductive for people who have problems, even confident individuals who don't think they do. Me. You. It offers us that temptation. It whispers in our ears that it's in our power to make everything all right by leaving this world behind. In that one moment when everything seems so overwhelming — a moment that comes to us all — it's so very easy to take that message on board. To stand on the edge of a cliff or stare into a bottle of spirits and hear that voice saying to you *just do it and everything will be all right*.' She turned. 'Goodbye. I'll obviously keep you briefed.'

They watched her go. 'Let's get back to the office.' Jude strode back in Vanessa's wake, nodded at the police officer on guard and flicked the key fob to unlock the Mercedes. 'I need to process this.'

'I know what you're thinking,' Ashleigh said to him, as he started the engine and drove down the lanes. 'You're thinking it's Josh, aren't you?'

'It could be.'

'I was wondering about it last night.'

Another time — even a few days earlier — she wouldn't have hesitated to call him, even late at night. 'Go on.'

'I was looking over the notes you made from your first meeting with Vanessa. All the deleted comments on the local Facebook group. And I looked back over the stuff on Eden Whispers. And I realised something. Do you remember the name of the poster whose comments started Vanessa off on the idea that it was deliberate?'

'Not offhand, no. Only that it was a pseudonym.'

'Okay. It was Four Hats Jose. I thought it was some kid having a laugh about something. But it's an anagram. Of Joshua Foster.'

Jude said nothing, negotiating the car around a bend in the road. Maybe now was the time he could persuade Faye that there was a real and present threat, and that it was time to find out who was behind Eden Whispers.

NINETEEN

'Right.' Jude closed the door of the incident room behind him and took a seat beneath the whiteboard. He was glad to have his back to its gallery of fresh faces, alive only in the memories of their families and friends, their potential doomed to be unfulfilled. 'What do we think? Because I'll tell you what I think. There's a hell of a lot more to this than meets the eye.'

He looked across at Aditi Desai, the one additional detective Faye had been able to spare for him. It had been enough of a struggle to get Aditi on the team and if the case was as complex and sinister as he suspected, they would still be woefully under-resourced. 'Have you been able to find out anything about Ben?'

'There wasn't that much to find out.' She placed his picture on the table, with care. Ben Curran had been a young man, and the photo showed him in football kit, wreathed in smiles. Families often chose a picture of their lost ones in their happy moments, the way they liked to remember them. 'He and his brother were close and he was devastated by his loss, but there's no evidence of any previous depression of mental health issues. He worked on a farm. He was popular. He'd had a couple of girlfriends but nothing serious or long term, and he wasn't in a relationship when he died. He played a lot of sport and was very much one of the lads.'

'Did he leave a note?'

'No note. He'd told one of his friends he didn't know how he was going to manage without Charlie but the friend didn't read anything suicidal into it. The opposite. I haven't finished speaking to all of his friends, but nothing's obvious so far. His phone's in the hands of the digital forensic guys just now, so we can see who he'd been in contact with. But that'll take a while.'

'Okay.' Jude had expected nothing less. He moved on to Chris. 'Let's talk about Eden Whispers. Is there anything new?'

'Not much. Just a news flash kind of post saying that some else had died — *found peace* it says here, which is just about as much in breach of the code as you can get.' He shook his head in disgust. 'There's a reference to Ben *drinking with his brother in heaven*, which implies they've picked up some gossip along the way.'

'We haven't issued any statement about it yet,' Ashleigh said, 'but news travels so fast around here.'

'I have my ear to the ground down in the town.' Chris sighed. 'But Ash is right. I've never known a bush telegraph like there is in this area. There were plenty of people who knew.'

Mentally, Jude ticked a few of them off. He could safely rule out the police or the CSI team, because none of them would have risked a disciplinary offence by speaking off the record, and Vanessa's professional reputation wouldn't stand a breach of trust. Beyond that, there were many whose silence couldn't be so easily guaranteed. There was the farmer who'd found the body and who had been indiscreet enough to call Vanessa before the police did so, his wife, the farm hands who'd been there when he'd come back up with the story. There were Geri and Josh, once again on the scene. There were Storm and Raven, and the assorted dog walkers who'd arrived at the riverside path and been turned away again, without any information but with eye-witness accounts to season the gossip. It was all too easy to see how the name and the likely cause of death had found their way into the public domain. 'There's nothing we can do to contain it. But I want you to keep your eye on that blog and see if there's anything that comes up that gives us a clue as to who it might have been. Beyond that, I don't know what we can do.'

'Yeah. There are ways of finding out who's behind it, but they're beyond my skillset. You'd need to get your mates on the tech team onto that, as well.'

Jude rolled his eyes. Even with Faye's authorisation and support he wouldn't expect any urgency from the digital forensics team.

Ashleigh's phone pinged with a message and she looked down at it. 'That's Tammy. Jude, this is interesting. There were two empty vodka bottles in Lacy's Caves. She's sent them off to the lab but she thought you'd like to know that she'd put her house on the fact that one of them contained vodka and the other contained water.'

There was silence around the table. 'Water?' said Aditi, puzzled. 'Why?'

Several possibilities flicked through Jude's mind. The bottles could have been there a while. Ben could have brought water with him. Tammy's initial appraisal might be wrong. Or it could be something altogether more sinister. 'Let's go straight to the worst case, shall we? If it's water. If it wasn't Ben who brought it. Then I think—'

'Someone sat with him, pretending to drink while he drank himself to death. Or positively encouraged him to do so.' Ashleigh's face was serious. She avoided his eye. 'I know there are other explanations for it, but it's so… elegant. You can see it, can't you? You can see exactly how it might have happened.'

He nodded. 'It'll be interesting to see what we get from the bottle.' Not everyone realised how closely they investigated a suicide scene. The alternative — that someone did know and had taken steps to prevent identification — would be equally telling. 'If there's DNA we'll have a lead and if not…well, that'll be interesting in itself.'

'That's progress,' said Doddsy, nodding. 'This is the first of these deaths that we can look at as being probably more than a suicide.'

'Exactly.' Jude couldn't suppress an unbecoming sense of vindication. Faye would struggle, now, to resist escalating the matter. 'Let's move on. Chris, did you find anything else?'

'Yep,' said Chris, noncommittally. 'I had a rare bit of fun with your photograph.'

Chris had had the class photograph blown up and had annotated it. He handed copies out round the table. Jude lifted an eyebrow but stayed silent, taking the opportunity to look at it again, in a more detached manner than he had done in the pub. 'Talk us through it. Was it worth the effort?'

'You can be the judge. If nothing else, I think you've set a cold case running.'

'Oh?'

'Yes.' Chris moved his finger along the lines of schoolchildren. 'Nicholas Chester. Dead. Fell from the Eden Lacy viaduct. Jude, your mum, your dad, obviously. Another couple of random people, both alive and well. One of them runs a self-catering business at the back of Skiddaw. One lives in Leeds. This is Richard Stoker.' He tapped a finger on the picture. 'Your dad was right about him. He was killed following a break-in at his home in Appleby during the Horse Fair, six years after this picture was taken. There was no sign of a struggle so it looks as if he was taken by surprise. The house was ransacked. There are fingerprints on the system but they couldn't match them at the time. I had them checked again. Still nothing.'

Six years after the photo would have been too early for DNA results. 'And the conclusion?'

'The case is still open. There were no suspects, no-one saw anything, nothing that was stolen was ever traced. It looks like an opportunist crime by someone who's never attracted the attention of the law, before or since.'

There were plenty of those. Jude thought, once more, of the New Agers. They were an easy target for those seeking a criminal, but their life was more or less static, confined to a small area of Cumbria. They were passive, too, and generally open, lacking the mobility of the majority of the thousands of travellers who came every summer for the Appleby Horse Fair and the cunning of the few who broke the law. Ironically enough it was the likes of Raven and Storm who were regularly accused and investigated, who co-operated and were cleared. The clever criminals got away with it. 'Go on.'

'This is a lady called Clare Mahoney. She went off to become a doctor in Africa. She never came back to Cumbria and died of a fever caused by a reaction to an insect bite, four years ago.'

'At least we can reasonably assume that's nothing to do with this,' said Ashleigh, with unwarranted cheerfulness.

'I think so.' Chris ran through half a dozen others, each of them still alive and some of them prospering, some still local, others not. 'And now this. Finn McDougall. He moved on from Penrith and ended up working in Lincolnshire.' He looked up, with a sly smile. There was very little theatre in procedural policing, but somehow he found it. 'He's dead. Do you want to guess how?'

'Not suicide?' Ashleigh leaned forward and looked at the picture. Jude sat back, watching her. He'd spent a long time studying the photograph, didn't need to see Finn McDougall's face.

'No. That would have been too much of a coincidence. Although it's interesting enough. He was killed. In a break-in at his home a year after Richard Stoker died.' Chris smiled at them again, not because any murder, even an old one, was a matter for amusement but because another piece of the puzzle had appeared to them. 'He lived in Lincolnshire at the time. Again, nothing was stolen but cash. There were fingerprints at the scene, and as with Richard they don't match any named individual on the database. But there's one key difference.'

'It was the same person?' Jude sat forward, intrigued.

'Yes. The crimes are linked. The person who broke into Richard Stoker's home and killed him also did the same to Finn McDougall. In both cases the assumption on the files is the same — that it was a member of the travelling community and the motive was robbery.'

The more recent of the two cases had been cold for well over thirty years. It was surely inconceivable that the perpetrator could be caught now, without either a very good reason for reviving the two cases or a more substantial new lead. 'Interesting.' Jude turned back to the photo. 'What about the rest of the class? Tell me one of them was murdered and Faye will have a meltdown.'

'Nothing so obvious. As I pointed out. Most of them are alive and well. But see here. Paul Curran.' Chris tapped a finger on one of them. 'This is where it gets interesting. He's the father of the two Curran boys who died in Lacy's Caves.'

'Okay.' Chris might find it interesting but Jude was unsurprised. There were only two secondary schools in the area; it was hardly surprising that lives overlapped. 'Anything more?'

'Here. Sharon Ford. She lives in Carlisle now. She married a man called Turnbull. He's not in the picture.'

'Turnbull?' It was Ashleigh who cottoned on first. 'Don't tell me. They had a son called Connor.'

'No. She was a teen mum. They had a son called Robert. Connor Turnbull is her grandson. Next to her we have Jimmy Kennedy. Daughter, by his second marriage — Juliet.'

'Stop right there.' Jude had been so sure of foul play and now the web of connections was tighter, and wider, than he'd imagined. Faye would have to throw resources at it. 'You're telling me that out of this class of twenty four, two were murdered, almost certainly by the same person, and we have links to four of our six suicides.'

'Yep.' Chris was struggling to control his excitement. 'There's more. Tania Baker's mother, Lucy, didn't go to the same school but she lived next door to Sharon Ford, and they were thick as thieves. So that's five out of six.'

'And the sixth? Clara?'

'I drew a blank with that one. Her family are incomers. But another friend of Sharon and Lucy was a girl called Liz Battersby. She went on to marry a man called Ecclestone, and their daughter is—'

'Izzy.' Again Ashleigh got there first, that fraction of a second before anyone else.

DEATH IN THE WOODS

'Right.' Jude frowned. 'If we exclude Clara, we can trace all of these suicides and two connected murders back to one class in one school forty years ago. Have I got that right?'

'That's what it looks like.'

They were all looking at Jude, and he in his turn was looking at the photograph. This wasn't about numbers; it wasn't about a rolling, rising probability or a distrust of coincidence. None of them could be unaware that if death was picking off the smiling faces of this class, tapping on the shoulders of their children or grandchildren, it brought the matter closer than was comfortable to Jude himself — and to Mikey.

'Okay,' he said, more briskly than he intended. 'I'm satisfied we've demonstrated enough of a connection to escalate it, and to bring these two cold cases back into play. First up, we need to warn the Ecclestones. Ashleigh, I'd like you to do that. Aditi, I need you to speak to all the suicide victims' families again, about what happened when they were at school. Now let's move on. Is there anyone else in this picture who we can connect to this case?'

'There's this guy. Steven Lawson.'

Jude looked at him again and the niggle that had kept in the back of his brain rose up again. 'Yes, tell us about him. He's wanted for murder, isn't he?'

'He is. And now no doubt we're all thinking the same, about his two classmates if nothing else. He had a reputation as a troublemaker. He had links to the travelling community. He blew through the place, never settled at school, never made friends. Clever, but not a man for his books.'

'Do we know where he is?'

'No. He's rather slipped through the net. Changed his name, perhaps, and most likely rubs along in the grey economy. That's if he hasn't left the area altogether. Or the country. He wouldn't be the first to do that.'

Jude stared at the picture again, for a long moment, focussing on it, and then it came to him. He sat back. 'I know what it is. Ash, have you noticed? He looks like Josh Foster.'

TWENTY

'So,' said Jude. 'This is my problem. I'm happy in my own mind that there's some connection between Josh Foster and the suicides. It all points to him, except that he wasn't born when Richard Stoker and Finn McDougall were murdered. But I think there's a connection. I think there has to be. I just don't know what it is.'

Ashleigh was sitting in her car in Lazonby, waiting to nerve herself to speak to the Ecclestones and warn them to keep a closer watch than ever over their daughter. Jude's phone call had given her a moment to prepare herself. 'Do you want me to go down and talk to Josh again? I don't think he'd thank me for it.'

She pulled down the driver's mirror, not to look at herself but to keep tabs on the woman who'd just walked past and given her a long, hard stare on the way. Sure enough, the woman had her phone out and the rumour mill would be in full swing. *That detective was up at the Ecclestones. That's not good news, mark my words.*

'No. We already know Geri's hostile to us, though God knows why. But we need to do something.'

There was no question. A connection between a class of school kids forty years ago, two cold case murders, six youth suicides and a young man with a chip on his shoulder? 'What does Faye say?'

'I've been trying to talk to her all day. She's busy. I'd better get on.' He rang off.

When the interested bystander was out of sight, Ashleigh got out of the car and walked up the path to the Ecclestones' neat semi. Izzy, dressed in black, was visible fluttering past an upstairs window and as Liz Ecclestone opened the door, the house shook with the vibrations of heavy, modern rock music.

'Come in,' said Liz, when Ashleigh had flashed her warrant card and introduced herself. 'Come on through to the kitchen. It's quieter there. I'm not going to tell our Izzy to turn that racket down. I don't take a lot of comfort from any of the goings-on around here, but at least I know when she's playing that music, she's alive and well.'

It was was enough to kill yourself in your own home, while your family went about their business blissfully unaware of your torment, and in Ashleigh's view the fact that none of the Eden Valley suicides had chosen that route further strengthened the connection between them. Someone standing beside Tania, encouraging her to jump from the bridge; with Charlie or Connor or Juliet, helping them choose a branch from which they'd hang; sitting beside Ben in the cave, looking out at the river and pretending to drink themselves into oblivion beside him.

Could that person be Josh Foster? And if so, what connected the Eden Valley suicides to the deaths of Richard Stoker and Finn McDougall, all those years before?

'I don't want to worry you unduly.' Ashleigh had rehearsed this, over and over again, but her script went out of the window as soon as she crossed the threshold. Liz Ecclestone was a hard-faced woman who, she immediately sensed, wouldn't take kindly to soft-speaking. So much the better. She could tell it to her straight. 'Nothing to worry about. I wanted to talk to you a little bit about your schooldays.'

'My schooldays? What the hell does that have to do with what's happening to kids these days?' Liz had been baking. There was a large mixing bowl on the kitchen table and a dusting of flour on the floor. A lump of grey dough, roughly flattened to half an inch thick, sat on the kitchen unit. 'I'll carry on with this, if you don't mind. You sit down and tell me what you want to know.'

Ashleigh sat. 'We're trying to establish some link between these unfortunate deaths, and one of the things that's come up is the parents.'

'Aye, well. That's no surprise. This is a small enough place. I'm one of those that has time for offcomers, but there's plenty as sticks with the friends they've had all their lives. I'm more broad-minded than some I could mention.' Liz turned the dough over, slapping it hard down on the surface, sending a cloud of flour rolling across the formica and over the edge like an avalanche. The music throbbed in the thin walls of the house. 'But yeah. We brought up our kids together in this village. They know each other, even if they're not friends. Izzy knew Tania and Juliet, god rest their poor souls, and I know their mams and dads.'

Thump, thump went the dough as Liz hammered it on the worktop. 'All this has made me think. I wasn't that nice a girl when I was at school,' she said, and her voice wavered a little. 'Teenaged kids never are. Girls are the worst, for my money, but the boys can be right harmful buggers too. I don't think I was good to people when I was our Izzy's age. I see them doing it to her. Making fun of folk because they're different and never understanding why it hurts. I always want to turn it to good, now. I tell Izzy that. Don't you go doing harm to man nor beast, I always say to her, and I'm being paid back in spades for anything I might have done, because she turns all her misery inwards. Serves me right.' She kept on working, her forearms dusty with flour as she hammered the dough. 'I suppose when I look back we were all a bit weird. But you get a group of people who are weird in the same way and they pick on someone who's different. To them. That's what we did back then.'

'Who did you pick on?' The music skipped forward, as if Izzy was bored of it. Ashleigh recognised the next track: Billie Eilish, this time, the music of the disillusioned teen.

'Some gypsy kid,' said Liz, raising her voice. 'He was a mardy beggar. Chip on his shoulder the size of Helvellyn, and determined to make life difficult for everyone, so we did the same for him. He was only here for a couple of years. The lads were all afraid of him, though they'd never admit it. The girls were all sweet on him to start with, but we soon realised he was only after one thing. When he got it that was enough. When he left, he didn't have any friends to his name. But that's no excuse for the way we all behaved to him.'

The music stopped, as if Izzy was in an unsettled mood. Liz turned to switch the oven on.

'And have you seen him since?'

'No, I never seen hide nor hair of him for forty years.' She rolled the dough into a ball, tipped it into the mixing bowl and placed a cloth over it. 'I can't even remember his name.' She carried the bowl over to the oven, turned it on low and slid it inside. 'It was years ago. He's long gone.'

'I think you should keep a very close eye on Izzy,' said Ashleigh. And the music started up again.

DEATH IN THE WOODS

When she'd taken Liz Ecclestone through the byways of her schooldays and learned nothing more than she already knew, Ashleigh drove slowly back to Penrith the long way round, through Great Salkeld and diverting down the dead-end track that led to the Fosters' house. There was no sign of life there, and Geri's Range Rover wasn't anywhere in view. It was half past five so, rather than go to the office, she headed back home to write up her notes there and think the matter through.

On another day she'd have called in on Jude to share a bite to eat and chew over the day's events and maybe, if the mood took the two of them, stay over. That wasn't going to happen now she'd taken the initiative and shifted the relationship back to what it was before, that of colleagues. She frowned as she thought of him, comparing him with Scott. Lisa was right about how much better a bet he was for a partner than her ex-husband, but for all her common sense, Lisa had never understood love.

Leaving Jude had been the right thing to do. She'd had to end the relationship before she could fall into the trap of getting serious, before the whispers of *I love you* that they shared for form's sake could take on any kind of sincerity. If she hadn't gone, she'd have risked giving up her heart to him and finding he couldn't give his in return.

But the alternative was Scott, and he was a risk. He loved her but he couldn't help himself. And she couldn't help herself, either.

Made for each other, she said to herself, and headed home.

TWENTY-ONE

Everyone had left the office but with nothing to do that evening, no real reason to go home, Jude stayed late, tying up the last bits of admin on his to-do list, the things he needed to tackle on the half a dozen other cases he was working on. Faye was out of the office on a training course, but he dashed off an email to her anyway, yet another plea for her to apply to the relevant authorities and bring all possible resources to bear to find out who was behind Eden Whispers. Even if she agreed, there would be a long wait for an answer. It wouldn't be a priority when there were cases of stalking and other potentially violent and unarguable crimes to be investigated. But it was all he could do.

When his enthusiasm for work finally ran out, he allowed himself a few moments longer to mull over the case. If, as he suspected, Josh Foster was Steven Lawson's son, what were the ramifications? Geri had said she didn't know who his father was but Geri, he was quite convinced, was capable of delivering a seamless lie, just as she was capable of selecting which truths she wanted him to hear. This innate ability to pick and choose her moral obligations might be something she'd learned from her upbringing, or it might be something she'd picked up along the way as a means of self-defence.

It didn't matter. If Josh was the technical genius behind Eden Whispers, then what? Could he have done more? Was it credible to suggest he'd played at being mates with the vulnerable, that an arm around Tania Baker's sad shoulders had tipped her to her doom in front of the 9.48 from Carlisle to Langwathby? Was it conceivable he'd sat in Lacy's Caves with Ben Curran, commiserating with him over the loss of his brother, talking up his grief and handing him the bottle in which his sorrows had ultimately drowned? And had he accompanied others to the woods, handed them the rope, helped to haul them up, or even pushed them from the branches?

It was possible, but why? A young man with an inevitable chip on his shoulder, he might have a grievance if he knew his father had been bullied for being different. He couldn't have killed Finn McDougall and Richard Stoker — but his father could have done that. Steven Lawson had a reputation for violence, was wanted for murder and was a member of the travelling community. He would have had every opportunity to roam the country, track down his victims even when they'd moved away, and carry out an opportunist murder. Both had been in their homes when they died. Neither had resisted their killer.

Maybe both had welcomed an old foe who appeared bearing an apparent olive branch, and if so both had paid the price.

If it were Josh, with or without his probable father's connivance, who'd pursued this feud into the next generation, there was every chance the series of suicides was not, as Vanessa had contended, almost over. Cold fear washed over him as he thought of how Mikey had intervened in the fight after someone had called Josh a *dirty gippo*. The generation before had called his father much worse and now, perhaps, he was making them pay for it.

Mikey. Jesus. If revenge was indiscriminate, if Mikey's innate good nature wasn't enough to save him, if the sins of the parents were to be visited upon their children and if, as was all too possible, David Satterthwaite was one of those against whom Steven Lawson held his grudge, then not only was Mikey at risk but the shadow extended to Jude himself.

He checked his watch, shut down his laptop and headed for the car park. Next day he'd sit down with Faye and somehow persuade her to authorise a full investigation into Eden Whispers. He'd put out an alert to find Steven Lawson. Before then, he'd make time to call by and speak once more to Mikey.

There was a risk. As Ashleigh had reminded him as she manoeuvred him carefully out of her bed with a promise of friendship and her former husband back into bed with the promise of God-knew-what, there was a risk to everything. He evaluated it as he drove down through Askham, slowing to check the crowd sitting outside the pub to see if Mikey was among them. The most likely problem was that Mikey would finally have enough of being told what to do and go off and do the exact opposite, but surely even he wasn't stupid enough to do that. But what he might do, being good-hearted, was to take a chance if he bumped into Josh, feel sorry for him, try to make up for the behaviour of his mates.

As he arrived in Wasby, he pulled the car up outside the cottage just as his mother was leaving. She was turning the key in the front door and the burglar alarm was bleeping as she walked down the path. So Mikey wasn't there. He rolled the window down. 'You're just off out, I see.'

'I'm doing the taxi run. Mikey's been over to Newcastle and I said I'd pick him up at the station and run him round to some mate's birthday do.'

'I'll do it for you, if you like.'

'Thank you, but I'm going for a swim afterwards.'

A pity. If he'd known he could have had Mikey as a captive audience and not had to take his chance on meeting Becca, who was at the window of her cottage, no doubt waiting to come out so she could get the latest update. 'Tell him not to stay out with the wrong sort.'

'Are you worried about him?' Linda stopped in the act of opening her car door.

'No, not at all. It was a joke.'

'Hmm.' The look she gave him was a searching one. 'Sorry you've had a wasted journey.'

'No, it's fine. I wanted a quick word with you anyway.'

'I'm already running late.'

'Mikey can wait another two minutes.' Jude got out of the car and strolled over to his mother, as casually as he could. 'You're doing him the favour. I wondered if you remember anything about someone called Steven Lawson. You were at school with him.'

'Goodness. Well, that's a long time ago.' She crinkled her face and looked towards the distant fells. 'No, not much. The girls were all a bit keen on him and the boys all hated him, but Steven could look after himself as I recall. If I'm honest I don't really remember too much about that time of my life.'

'You weren't one of the girls running after him, then?' he joked.

She made a face. 'Most of the time I was mooning after your father and him after me. A fat lot of good that did me, in the long run. Yourself and Mikey excepted, of course.' She got into the car, but wound the window down so they could continue the conversation as she turned it in the lane. 'When I think of it, I do remember that Steven always seemed very angry. You couldn't get through to him. He didn't know how to return a smile for a smile.'

That made sense. 'Do you know what happened to him after he left school?'

'I heard he'd killed a man in a fight.' She twisted her head to see as she reversed. On the other side of the road Holmes appeared, fixed Jude with his yellow eyes and, fighting shy of the car, slunk under Becca's gate and out of sight.

'Do you keep up with any of your old schoolmates?'

'No, not really. I thought we were a very unlucky class, in a way. There was poor Nick, of course. He was a lonely soul. And then Clare, who was a saint in human form, dedicated her whole life to charity and then died. And those two boys who were killed. And of course, there was nearly me.'

Jude leaned across and kissed her quickly on the cheek through the car window. 'Let's not talk about that. We all have narrow escapes.'

'I know. And now there are these suicides. There's so much sorrow in this world. I'm so proud of everything you do to stop it.' And she stuck her foot on the accelerator and drove off before he could respond to the compliment.

He stood watching her for a moment, hands in pockets, and took a moment to reflect as the sun dipped below the western line of Rough Hill. He couldn't bear to think what his mother would do if she lost Mikey because Jude and his team couldn't solve the puzzle of the Eden Valley suicides. It would be unimaginable failure.

As he stood there he sensed, rather than saw or heard, the front door of Becca's cottage open. The grey swirl of feline smoke that was Holmes whisked up the path towards the door and stopped halfway.

Jude turned, the scene replaying itself as it had done a few days earlier. Becca, dressed in jogging bottoms and a baggy tee shirt as if she'd come to the end of her tether and given up for the day, stood on the doorstep, watching him. He waited. In an unusual quandary, Holmes dithered between them, unable to decide who to favour and who to slight, then gave up on the decision and stalked off, tail vertical, nose in the air.

'Holmes,' Becca said, a trace of irritation in her voice. 'What time do you call this? I thought you were inside.'

She caught Jude's eye and her irritation turned to amusement. 'Don't mind me. I'm just talking to the cat.'

'Maybe you need someone different to talk to.' He hadn't meant to say that. It just came out, a thought finding expression in a way he'd trained himself never to do.

'Maybe.' She advanced a few steps down the path, and he sensed her uncertainty. 'I know I shouldn't ask, but are there any updates? On the suicides.'

'No.' He was reluctant to talk work, even though he'd half intended to ask her, yet again, to keep an eye out for Mikey. There was no need; she was already on the case. So there must have been some other impulse that made him stop and wait for her when he'd had plenty of opportunity to drive off. 'At least, nothing I can tell you that isn't in the public domain.'

She came a bit closer. He knew her habits, knew she liked to get in from work and sink into a hot bath, and that must be what she'd done. Her hair was still damp, her face pink and pearled with moisture, and the fresh smell of Body Shop foam bath overrode the rising tide of night-scented stock from the border next to the wall. 'I'm keeping an eye on Mikey, as much as I can. I think he'll be all right.'

'Thanks.' He mustered a smile to cover his uncertainty. A ridiculous, unarticulated thought was crystallising in his brain, even as he looked at her and listened to his heart. She didn't look directly at him. Maybe she was thinking the same.

But she'd never say anything. She thought he was still dating Ashleigh. 'I'll keep watching over him, though.'

'Like an angel,' he said, in words that sounded so unlike anything he'd ever said to her before that she looked at him in surprise.

'My goodness,' she said, twisting the hem of her tee shirt in what looked like anxiety, 'What's come over you tonight? That's very fancy talk, for you.'

Adam Fleetwood, who'd always been handsome, popular and charismatic, had a stock of chat-up lines like that, and had over-employed them until he became a standing joke. With age Adam had also acquired cunning, and from what Jude had heard around the town he'd learned to be more subtle. But the lines he'd used had worked with Becca. He knew she was thinking that. Her face wouldn't have gone so shamefully scarlet otherwise.

'I wondered,' he said, and took a few more steps up the path until he was standing close to her. At the edge of his vision Holmes seemed to realise there was something going on in which he might have a passing interest, and scuttled down the length of the flowerbed before cutting out and pretending to be casual as he strolled across to play gooseberry.

Holmes, Jude always thought, was on his side. To keep him that way, he dipped a hand down to touch the cat's soft grey head. 'I hoped we could let bygones be bygones.'

'We have. Haven't we? I mean, we wouldn't be having this conversation if you weren't…' She took a deep breath. 'So forgiving. Because I know you think I behaved badly and you're probably right, but I do want us to be friends.'

It was his turn for the deep breath, as if there wasn't enough air for both of them. 'We could be more than friends. Couldn't we? I might as well be honest. I still feel about you the way I did…before.'

'Before I let you go?' Becca claimed Holmes, scooping him up in her arms and holding him against her until he turned a reproachful head away and looked at Jude with the ultimate feline expression of contempt, though whether it was for Becca's weakness or Jude's it was impossible to tell.

'Yes. I thought I'd get over it, but I might as well be honest. Maybe it doesn't hurt like it used to but it still hurts. It always will. I'll always miss you.'

'Really?' She clutched Holmes more tightly and her voice chilled him. 'And does Ashleigh know you think this way?'

'I imagine she does. Does that matter?'

'She's your girlfriend. I'd have thought it matters a lot.'

'She isn't my girlfriend any more.'

'Right.' She lowered her head, rested her cheek against the top of Holmes's soft grey head. 'As of when?'

'As of Wednesday.'

'I see. And did she end it, or did you?'

'It was always going to end.' Though it had lasted longer than he'd thought it would. He tried to read Becca's expression but she kept her head down, avoiding him.

'She did, then.'

'Yes.'

'Okay.' Becca lowered Holmes towards the ground and he jumped free at the last minute, wriggling away and off again as if to avoid the ending he sensed coming. 'So. Your girlfriend dumps you and you come round here and try and hit on me again. Great.'

'I'm not trying to hit on you. I miss you. I love you. If it had been up to me we'd never have split.'

'We split because you were never around. Because there was always something else that came up. Because other people's needs were always more important than mine. Because your work was more important than your friends. That's why.'

'I think I've learned my lesson now.'

'Really? Give me one example.'

'I turned up at Mikey's twenty-first—'

'Late, because something happened at work.'

'But I turned up,' he pleaded, taking a step towards her. The something had been a murder and an arrest. She didn't understand.

'There's another thing, Jude. You always promised you'd change and you never did. I appreciate your honesty and I'll be honest in return. Of course I still care for you. I always will. I think I probably still love you, in a way, and I really want you to be happy. But you'll never change. I don't want to be married to your sense of duty. I've had enough of that. I want someone who'll put me first.'

'I'll do that. I swear I'll—'

'But you promised before. I want to believe you'll change, but I know you won't. So I'm sorry, Jude. No.'

She waited for a second to allow him time to answer but he couldn't find the words either for acceptance or argument and so she turned away and headed back up the path.

He shrugged it off, for her benefit at least, and turned his back, but there was a hollow where his heart ought to have been and a numbness where a few moments before the blood had been hammering through his veins. It had been folly to try and win her back in the first place and if he'd had the slightest chance of success, he'd sacrificed it in the heat of the moment, snatching at it as if it was the one opportunity he'd have.

That was Ashleigh's fault. She hadn't put the idea in his head but she'd fanned the flame and tripped him into declaring himself too soon. He knew she hadn't done it deliberately but the effect on him had been the same as that of Eden Whispers, intentionally or otherwise illwishing the vulnerable and prompting them to believe that the answer was simple and immediate.

'I expect I'll see you then,' he said over his shoulder, not caring if she heard. From here onwards he'd have to avoid her for the sake of his self-respect. Becca would confide in her sister, because she always did, and Kirsty would tell her husband, who was close friends with Adam Fleetwood, and from there the news of his humiliation would spread among his peers.

'I'll see you.' And then: 'Oh, Jude!'

He turned back more quickly than he should have done, the devil that was hope rearing up only to die when he saw she'd only paused on the doorstep and still she wasn't looking at him. *Go on*, he willed her, *say it was a mistake*. 'What is it?'

'It's what I was coming out to say to you before this nonsense.'

So it was nonsense. Now he knew what a fool he'd been. 'And?'

'Leslie Chester. I meant to say to you before and I forgot. He told me he has Nicholas's diary. I don't imagine it's important but I thought you might be interested.'

'Thanks. I'll ask him about it,' he said, and waited until she'd gone inside and closed the door, until he was sure she wasn't coming out again, before he turned to head home.

TWENTY-TWO

'I wondered,' Jude Satterthwaite said, standing in Vanessa's cramped excuse for a consulting room and regarding thoughtfully, as if he was trying to read her mind, 'if it would be okay for me to call in and visit your father at Eden's End.'

The man was doing his best, Vanessa knew, but he and his colleagues were almost endearingly ineffective. Anyone with half a brain would have tracked down the source of Eden Whispers straight away, and the nonsense about resources and priorities and time that Faye Scanlon had spouted at her was all too obviously a smokescreen for the fact that they either weren't in a hurry or didn't have the capability.

Or didn't have a clue. She'd never been a great fan of the police but she had more time for Superintendent Scanlon than she had for DCI Satterthwaite. The man annoyed her. 'I don't think you can hold my father responsible for shepherding these young people to their deaths, Chief Inspector, no matter how desperate you are to find yourself a villain. He's a little too old for that. In any case, he has a rock solid alibi. He hasn't been out of Eden's End since I took him out for lunch at Easter.'

Easter Sunday that year had chanced to fall on Nicky's birthday, which had made it a difficult occasion. Everyone around them in the restaurant had been enjoying themselves on a fine spring morning, and she'd struggled to jolly the conversation along. Her father had wept, silently but copiously, throughout the meal and Vanessa had been impatient with him. She still hadn't forgiven herself for it. These days Leslie's emotional wellbeing was all that mattered.

'I don't think we've ever suggested anyone's shepherded them to their deaths,' he observed, after a moment's thought.

'Then perhaps you think he has the technical knowhow to run Eden Whispers? On the office computer, perhaps? Not to mention the psychological grip of the nuances. Which, by the way, are many and complex.'

She thought he tried not to sigh. In her experience the man was usually fairly equable but he didn't seem in the best of moods that day. 'I don't think that, either. It's much simpler than that. Someone told me your father has a diary that your brother kept, and I wondered if it might give us a lead. That's all.'

'I don't quite understand what poor Nicky's accident has to do with this matter, if I'm honest with you.' Having kept him standing purely because she could, she finally waved him to a seat. When he'd popped his head around the door claiming he was just passing, she'd assumed he'd come to update her on the progress of the investigation. It appeared not.

'I can't stay long.' He remained standing, one hand on the door as if he was indeed in too much of a hurry to talk to her, but he met her gaze when she challenged him to and didn't look away. 'I might as well be honest with you. I don't imagine there will be anything in the diary but if, as I believe, your father was talking about it in the context of the local suicides, there's just a chance there might be something in it that will help.'

Someone at Eden's End must have been talking. It was understandable. Everyone felt the deaths so keenly they were desperate to help, seizing on something they'd heard or thought or feared, until it was hard to see what was real. If Jude Satterthwaite was following every one of those leads, as he was surely obliged to do, the case would drown in irrelevance long before he could reach any kind of conclusion. The suicides would end and only one person would be content with the way things had gone — the perpetrator.

'My father is nearly ninety,' she said with a sigh, 'and he'll have nothing to tell you. He's very frail and although he's mostly lucid he can become confused.' The memory of Leslie's tears struck at her. At least five families would suffer as he had done. 'Old people often conflate the past and the present. I'm astonished you don't know that.'

'My late grandmother used to talk about the old queen,' he remarked, conceding the point, 'and we were never quite sure whether she was talking about the Queen Mother or Queen Mary.'

'Precisely. My father has seen this on the news. He's heard the carers in the home talking about it.' She'd warned them not to, knowing how it would play out in his mind and his soul, and now it was all happening exactly as she feared. She'd have to go into Eden's End and read them the Riot Act. Again. 'Dad will be keen to help, I'm sure, but it'll be a waste of your time. Even after all this time he's only thinking of Nicky.'

'You feel your brother's death very keenly,' said

Satterthwaite. 'That's right, isn't it? Is that what motivates you?'

God help her; he fancied himself as a bit of a psychologist. There was nothing more dangerous. At that moment, she hated him. 'Nicky's death destroyed my mother and broke my father's heart. I saw at first hand how the death of a child affects the parents. Regardless of the circumstances, when a parent — or anyone *in loco parentis* — loses a child, they blame themselves. The only relevance my brother's death has to this is that it's made me determined to make sure such a thing never happens again.'

'And so say all of us,' he remarked, with a touch of levity. 'You don't know anything about a diary, then?'

'I know Nicky kept a diary. Many teenagers do.' Two of the district's lost teenagers had done so, and their grieving parents had shared their children's innermost thoughts with her in an attempt to understand where they'd gone wrong. All had found things in there for which they could reproach themselves, and it had added to their burden. Vanessa allowed herself an ironic smile at the way of the world.

'But you don't know where it is?'

'To be honest I haven't given it a thought in years. If I'd known at the time what I know now, I'd have advised my parents to destroy it without reading it. If I thought about it all, that's what I'd have assumed they did.'

'Perhaps your father didn't.'

'Maybe he didn't. I certainly wasn't aware of him having kept it and he never mentioned it to me.' She paused, wondering whether she'd be rebuffed if she offered to be helpful. 'I'm going down to see him this evening. Would you like me to ask? It would be less disruptive coming from me, I think.'

'I'd like to talk to him about it myself.'

'Leave it until tomorrow.' Irritation rippled through Vanessa. 'He's old, he's very distressed. He really doesn't need anyone else reminding him about Nicky, least of all the police. But if you must do it, give me a chance to warn him and explain why you want to talk to him. He's far more likely to cooperate if he knows it's coming. And I'd like to be there when you see him.'

He thought about it for a moment. 'I don't see why not.'

Outside in the square an ambulance siren squealed. In the reception area behind Jude, Vanessa's secretary, Maisie, answered the phone. 'Yes, Dr Wood will be around tomorrow. Drop in any time after eleven.'

Vanessa inclined her head towards the door. 'I'll see you at Eden's End at ten, then.'

'There's one other thing,' he said, and paused.

Vanessa took a guess at what he was about to say. 'Your brother will be fine, Chief Inspector.'

A flicker of surprise crossed his face and for a moment she thought that wasn't what he'd been going to ask. But the surprise was followed by almost immediate relief, so her guess had been right after all, and she'd hit on what that was worrying him. 'You think so?'

'It's natural for you to worry. You're a clever man, I know, but you're a sensible one, and I'm sure he is, too. Stop worrying about him.' Mikey Satterthwaite had turned up at her drop-in session and loitered in the waiting room while Vanessa been listening to Izzy Ecclestone expound on her fascination with death and the mystery of what lay beyond it, but he hadn't come in. Having escorted her there, he'd escorted her safely away again and politely refused Vanessa's invitation for a chat. You couldn't reach people who didn't want to be reached, but she fancied

Mikey had a level head on his shoulders. She'd have loved to have talked to him; whatever reassurance she'd just offered his brother, the younger Satterthwaite was bound to have major emotional issues.

'I'm a bit happier for hearing that.' He wouldn't be, of course, though he managed a rueful smile. Reassurance was impossible. He'd lie awake at night like half of the local population, waiting for bad news.

'Good. We all have things that trouble us, Chief Inspector. No-one is too old or too strong or too clever to have problems, and it's normal and natural to look for the easy way out. I shouldn't really say this because I wouldn't want people to think death might be the answer, and I'd never do so in a professional capacity.' Sometimes she lied to her clients. All therapists, she thought, did so. 'But sometimes it is. Izzy Ecclestone, for example. The attraction she feels for that tree. It's unhealthy. They should cut it down. It has an appeal for a certain type of person. It only ends one way.'

His eyes narrowed slightly, as if he didn't like what he'd heard. 'I'll see you at Eden's End at ten tomorrow, then,' he said, and left.

TWENTY-THREE

'I'm buying,' Jude said, as Doddsy preceded him in to the Golden Cage at Lazonby. 'But for God's sake don't let me drink myself into a stupor tonight. I've got a lot of work to get through tomorrow.'

Doddsy, who was handily teetotal and therefore an ideal drinking partner when restraint was called for, lifted an eyebrow as they shouldered their way through the busy pub. It was a sunny evening and the locals seemed keen to make the most of it. 'One of those days, eh?'

'You can say that again.' Jude was too intense, too aware of his position and his responsibilities to be a heavy drinker. In a bizarre way it occurred to him that this was just the kind of thing that Becca, though no serious drinker herself, would regard as symptomatic of his obsessive nature. That evening, after a frustratingly unproductive day which had ended with Vanessa Wood neatly fingering his deepest fears, was one in which he wanted to drink enough to stop himself lying awake at night and drown the niggling voice in the back of his head that whispered about Mikey.

'Then I'll buy. Because I'm that mean I won't get you the kind of measure you'd get for yourself and tomorrow will be a whole lot easier on everybody.'

Doddsy's calm always rubbed off on those around him, and he'd assessed the situation accurately in a conversation of just a few words, which meant Jude wouldn't need to justify his mood. Thank God his friend could be trusted to keep the situation neutral and deliver Jude back to his house in Wordsworth Street in reasonably undamaged condition. Already the temptation to drink himself into a stupor was passing. 'Make mine a pint of Eden Gold, then. I'll go and get a seat outside where we don't have to listen to the folk at the next table talking about how we should be doing our job.'

Doddsy threaded his way through the table to the bar. Both the bar and the beer garden were unusually crowded, as if the sun had tempted everyone out to make the most of it. It was a lively yet lazy evening, where the sun and the beer drove the customers to ever more intense discussion with increasingly little consequence. Jude loitered in the doorway, taking his habitual look around, before heading out into the beer garden and occupying a table by the low, riverside wall. From there he had a view along the curve of the Eden and the thick green tangle that marked the edge of Cave Wood and concealed Lacy's Caves. In a moment of weakness he texted Mikey just to check where he was and the reply, a barrage of outraged emojis, almost made him smile. Quite why Vanessa had been so sure of Mikey's safety was beyond him, but she knew her job.

There were reasons other than Vanessa's superciliousness and Mikey's bad temper to further sour his mood. Adam Fleetwood was standing in the middle of the beer garden talking to someone, and as Jude watched Geri Foster appeared, strode towards him and greeted him with a kiss on each cheek. Jude turned his back. He could imagine the laugh that would come to Adam's lips when he heard how Becca had rejected him. And that wasn't the worst; the worst was that there was no more he could do, no more questions he could ask. He knew the answer. Becca loved him, but not enough. He'd done his best, and his best wasn't good enough.

'Here.' Doddsy negotiated the obstacle course of the beer garden, slid the pint down on the table in front of Jude and settled down in the seat opposite him with a tall glass of orange juice and lemonade. He, too, had taken a long look around. 'Look on the bright side. If you're looking for a woman, you won't go short, and if you aren't we'd better leave now. I saw your Spice Girl friend in the bar.'

Jude had told Doddsy about Geri's blunt approach to life and love, and it raised a smile. It was hardly a surprise that she was there; the Golden Cage was local. 'Yeah, I saw her. I think I can protect myself against a predatory female. But I won't need to. She's with Adam Fleetwood.'

'Nope.' Doddsy double-checked. 'She's on her own.'

Jude didn't look for himself. He trusted Doddsy's eyes and ears, and it made sense. Geri and Adam knew one another but it didn't follow that they'd socialise, nor mean anything if they did. The Golden Cage, with its huge outside space and its geographical connections to the local suicides, was the pub of the moment. It had been his idea to come, for that very reason, but it had been a mistake. They should have chosen somewhere else. 'Waiting for someone, you reckon?'

'Could be.'

Jude looked towards the bar in time to see Josh Foster come out and scan the garden, swinging a car key on his finger in a jaunty manner, before he strode over. Jude's curiosity got the better of him. He half turned. Neither Josh nor Geri, seated two tables away, had a drink in front of them. Waiting for friends, then. He drew on his pint, pulled his chair round so he could look in their direction without being obvious. Josh also swivelled, but away from him, looking down the river towards the sandstone cliff in which were concealed Lacy's Caves. Was that significant?

'Interesting stuff, eh?' Doddsy said, under his breath. 'She's a good looking woman, mind you. I like a bit of character.'

'You're spoken for.' Jude drank again. It didn't take much more than sunshine, a pint and some good company to help him start on the road to recovery. Ashleigh ending their relationship hadn't come as a surprise, and Becca's rejection was just the reprise of an old song. Even Adam's vindictiveness seemed, at that moment, like a vanquished ghost. He'd survive. 'What will Tyrone say?'

Doddsy laughed. 'I don't think he needs to worry.' He lowered his voice. 'Seriously, now. What do we reckon about Josh? Do you think it was him?'

'I certainly think it could have been.'

Josh said something to his mother, who turned to him and laid a careful hand on his arm. If he was guilty, did Geri know? Jude thought not, given the way she was looking at her son, the concern on her face.

He sipped again. He was drinking too quickly, he knew, reliant on Doddsy to keep him under control, but he didn't slow down. Something about Josh and Geri compelled him to keep watching. The two of them were laughing, now, but Geri stopped laughing first.

'I think so, too,' Doddsy said, still in the low tones although there was no-one within earshot and the hubbub from around them would have drowned them all out. 'But supposing he is behind Eden Whispers, eh? We've all read the blogs. Subtle as you like. Nothing overt, all suggestion. Are we sure that's enough to constitute an offence?'

'That's one for the CPS to worry about, but I think so. If it was him, I can't believe Eden Whispers was all he did. He can't have got that lucky. Maybe that's what happened to begin with. But after that, maybe not. After that he might have moved on to give a helping hand.' Or, in the case of Tania Baker, a push. 'Maybe the phone records will show something, when we get them.'

The Fosters turned again, this time to a man who was making his way across the beer garden towards them, hands clutching an assortment of glasses and with a couple of packets of crisps clenched by their corners in his teeth. He took the seat next to Josh, pushed a glass with a can of Coke inside it across to him, dropped the crisps on the table.

Forgetting discretion, Jude stared at him. The man had thick grey hair that skimmed his shoulders and a beard that was darker than his hair. A gold earring flashed in his left ear. He had, Jude was quite sure, never seen him before in his life, yet he was startlingly familiar.

'See him?' said Doddsy, in a near-whisper. 'Look.'

Jude put down his pint. When the man smiled the flash of his teeth and the crinkle in the eye were an exact reflection of the look on the face of the young man next to him. 'Yeah.'

'That's Steven Lawson, isn't it?'

It was there in front of them. He was an older version of Josh who, in his turn, was a template drawn from that old school photograph. 'It sure as hell is.'

'Right. Then we need to get him picked up now.'

'Agreed,' said Jude under his breath, regretting the half a pint he'd drunk too quickly. Steven Lawson wasn't just wanted for murder; he was possibly complicit in two other killings and had questions to answer over the Eden Valley suicides. 'We don't want him giving us the slip.' Just as he'd done forty years before, when he'd ghosted his way out of a crowded pub and vanished, leaving a man dying behind him.

As casually as he could, Doddsy reached for his phone. 'You keep watching. I'd better call for backup, I think, as I'm the one who's stone cold sober.'

As Doddsy dialled, got through to the control room, Jude watched the next table but one. When they got Steven Lawson into custody, they'd know for certain the extent of his crimes. He wasn't a betting man but he'd lay money on the fact that Lawson's fingerprints would match those found at the murders of Finn McDougall and Richard Stoker. 'He must have been behind it, then. He put the kid up to it. Eden Whispers. And maybe he did the others himself.'

'Slow down,' Doddsy said, closing down the call. 'Let's make sure it's him first. Let's see if his dabs match up.'

'His dabs don't need to match up for him to be hauled in for the Hexham murder.'

'I don't know how these guys live with their consciences.' Doddsy sighed and took a deliberate look elsewhere. 'Imagine. You know you did it. Everyone else knows you did it. You're wanted. Don't you expect the knock on the door, every day of your life?'

'Not if you're arrogant enough to think you've got away with it.' Jude, too, dipped his head to look less obvious. There was no way Steven Lawson could know who they were, but Josh and Geri did. And if they told him, even if he didn't realise how closely he was tied into the web of death that someone had spun across the area, if he realised the police were taking an interest he'd melt away like the summer snow.

On the other side of the beer garden, Josh looked up and turned sharply towards the man who must be his unacknowledged father. The man pushed his drink to one side and stood up.

Jude sighed in frustration. 'He knows who we are.'

'There's a patrol car on its way,' Doddsy said, 'but we don't want to lose him, do we?'

'He might not go anywhere if we don't chase him.' Jude turned his head away, pretending to be casually disengaged, and Doddsy did the same, but they both kept half an eye on the drama going on a short distance away.

Yards away, Steven Lawson looked across at them, measured up his chances just as they were doing. He was, Jude knew, fifty-eight, the same age as David Satterthwaite. He looked lean and mean and fit but he didn't look like a man who could outrun either of them, over a short or a longer distance.

Lawson said something to Josh, who stood up and reached for the car key he'd placed on the table, but Geri was swifter. She closed her hand over the key and snatched it away. 'Joshua Foster.' Her raised voice reached them over the now-empty table between them. 'Don't you even think about it!'

Lawson lost his caution. 'What the hell are you doing? Give the kid his key. I need a lift and I need it now.'

'It's my key, it's my car, and I say who drives it. I'm not having him getting mixed up with anything dodgy.'

'It's not dodgy, you stupid cow. But I need to get out of here.' He'd lowered his voice but Jude could still hear him. 'If those are the police, like he says—'

'They are the police. But they're drinking in a pub, not turning up in uniform. They don't know who you are. It's us they're looking at. Doing a runner and drawing attention to yourself is really going to help, isn't it?'

He snatched at the key, caught her wrist and broke her grip, twisting it free. Geri's cry of pain crashed through the sound of a summer evening and the father of her child snatched the key and broke for it across the crowded beer garden, overturning chairs as he went.

Jude and Doddsy took off after him, hampered by the falling furniture, through the chaos of the bar, out into the street.

'Stop!' shouted Doddsy, but Jude was concentrating on the man in front of him. They dodged through the darkened bar. His hand clutched at thin air as Lawson swerved to the doorway and burst out into the street. Fending off the door as it swung back in at him, Jude followed.

He was under no illusions. Lawson would be heading for the Land Rover and if he got to it, it would become a weapon. He put on a spurt. 'Stop! Police!' The Land Rover was parked on the pavement, illegally, but Lawson must have realised he hadn't time to reach it and make an escape. He ran past it, fruitlessly. Jude was a confident runner and tackled steep hills with ease; he made it to within arm's length, reached out to grasp Lawson's shoulder and the two of them crashed into the gutter.

'Get off him!'

Jude hadn't realised that Josh had come after them and he, youngest and fittest of them all, had easily overhauled them. Lawson fought like a rat, though he must know he had no realistic chance of escape, and Josh's young man's fury was behind him.

'That's enough, lad,' Doddsy was panting from somewhere above as Josh rained blows down on Jude. The tussle went on, futile and brutal, until just a few moments later a police patrol car screeched to halt beside them and two constables got out to join the fray. And that was it. Within a minute, Steven Lawson and his son were in handcuffs and a second car was drawing up.

Jude, off duty and with half a pint of Eden Gold inside him, got to his feet, shook himself off and stepped back. Tonight it was a problem for someone else and he wouldn't have to worry about it until the next day. He stepped back and ran a cautious hand over his shoulder. Bruising, nothing more, and that was lucky. Young Josh was handy with his fists; an interesting detail. He looked back to where the customers were beginning to spill out of the pub onto the street to see what was going on. A third police car drew up and Tyrone Garner got out, looked up and down the street with a broad grin.

'Enjoying your evening off, boss?' Tyrone said to him, though it was Doddsy on whom he turned his dazzling smile. 'Looks like it's an interesting one.'

'You can't even get a pint in peace around here,' Jude grumbled, reaching into his pocket for a handkerchief and wiping blood from a grazed knuckle. 'Is anyone else coming along? Who's on call? This isn't just your average brawl. We'll need a detective. You'd better get statements.' Not least from himself and Doddsy.

'DS O'Halloran is on duty this evening. Now. Not just a brawl? Then these guys…?'

'One for murder,' Doddsy said, 'and one for obstructing the police in the execution of their duty.' He turned to the officers in the other two police cars. 'Get them taken down to custody, would you? We'll fill you in with what happened and then probably get out of your way and look after our bumps and bruises, eh?'

When Jude had given Tyrone his statement he stepped away, leaving Doddsy to give the uniformed officers what little direction they required, and turned to see what happened to Geri. She was standing on the pavement outside the pub, the fingers of her right hand clutched around the fingers of her left, and when she saw him she walked towards him. 'Oh, well done, Chief Inspector. An excellent night's work.'

He ignored the sarcasm. 'Are you hurt?'

She looked down at her hand. 'Bruises, that's all. It was an accident. Really not worth making all that fuss about.' She looked along at the police car, with Josh already in the back. 'You'd better not be going to lock my son up.'

He shook his head at her, feeling the beginnings of a bruise throbbing on his shoulder where Josh had struck him. 'What do you think we're going to do? He was trying to stop us making an arrest.' Josh would get bail, he was sure of that. Geri would know it, too, and must be trying to provoke him. 'You saw it.'

'All I saw was a young man trying to protect an older one. I'd have said that was admirable.'

'For God's sake.' Finally, she'd pushed him too far. 'Let's not pretend. In your words, the man did a runner. What do you expect me to do? Watch him go?'

'I don't know what I expected, but three police cars is overkill. What's he supposed to have done?'

He looked at her, read her cold simmering fury. 'Why did you tell me you didn't know who Josh's father is?'

'I don't know. For certain,' she qualified, when he lifted an eyebrow. 'Steve's an old mate. I see him from time to time, when he's in the area. And that doesn't answer my question. What's this all about?'

'He didn't tell you about his past then?'

'He doesn't tell me anything, and I don't ask. He's a free spirit. I like that, and I respect it. So no, I don't know anything about it, except that he has a healthy suspicion of you and your people, because he and his people get the blame for everything you get wrong.'

'He's been on the run for the best part of forty years.' That was no secret. Anyone who wanted could look up on the internet and find the hue and cry that had followed the Hexham murder and the warrant that was out for Steven Lawson's arrest.

'Forty years? Your people have very long memories,' she scoffed.

'We do if it's about murder.'

The blood drained from her face even though she somehow maintained her expression of scorn. 'Is that right? I can quite see why he didn't mention it to me. Or to Josh. Careless talk costs lives and all that.'

'More lives,' he corrected her.

She turned away with an impatient shrug. 'I'm done with this. I'll tell your man what I saw and then I'm going home for a triple vodka.'

'DS O'Halloran is on her way here just now, Madam,' said Tyrone, intercepting her smoothly, 'and she'll be very interested to speak to you.'

Two steps behind Geri, Adam was lurking like a shadow. 'Want a lift when you're done, Geri? I'm going your way and I don't mind waiting.' He looked at Jude and Doddsy and laughed.

'Thank you, but I haven't had anything to drink.'

'You need to keep your nose clean with these guys,' he said, with another sideways look. 'They'll fit you up if they can't get you any other way.'

'I can look after myself, thank you.'

'If you need someone who saw it the way it was, not the way they wanted it to be, you just ask me, okay?'

'Don't be bloody ridiculous,' said Geri, and pushed past him.

'Let's brief Tyrone and get out of here,' said Doddsy with a sigh.

No-one would listen to Adam's embroidered version of events; the personal grudge he bore Jude in particular and the police in general was too well-known. Nevertheless he was a constant thorn, rubbing away at Jude's peace of mind as Mikey did, and Becca, and now Ashleigh herself.

Ashleigh would have a job on her hands interviewing Geri, he thought to himself as he followed Doddsy back to his car and left Tyrone charming statements out of the witnesses. He'd find out soon enough how it went.

TWENTY-FOUR

Vanessa was already at Eden's End when Jude arrived, sitting with her father in the lounge. She stood up when she saw him, but she kept a hand resting on Leslie's shoulder as if she were his bodyguard. She gave Jude an amused look; she could hardly fail to notice the fresh bruise on his cheekbone that sat so ill with his sharp work suit that Chris had joked it made him look like a bouncer at a Mayfair nightclub.

'It's the police, Dad,' she said, bending down to him, her voice carefully neutral as if not to harm him. 'Remember what I told you. They aren't here to upset you. You aren't going to get into trouble. DCI Satterthwaite just wants to talk to you about Nicky.' Then she straightened up and addressed Jude, quietly. 'Can we keep this short? This whole thing has been very distressing and I don't want him upset again.'

Nodding his acceptance, Jude declined a seat, but held out his hand to Leslie Chester. 'Mr Chester. Thank you for sparing me a few minutes. I won't keep you long. I wondered if you have Nicholas's diary.'

Vanessa rolled her eyes as if he'd got it wrong already. A fat tear rose in Leslie's already-rheumy eyes, overflowed and trickled down his cheek. 'No.'

'You did have it,' Vanessa prompted him, her fingers tightening slightly on his shoulder, 'didn't you?'

Lesley looked to her instead of Jude. 'You know, Vee. I kept it for years, but I never really read it. After he died I opened it up but it hurt too much. I understood how we'd let him down.'

'Dad. I've told you over and over. You didn't let him down.'

'I know he said we didn't, but we must have done. Otherwise he wouldn't have died.'

'But if it was an accident—' prompted Jude, fascinated.

'Yes. It was an accident.' She sat down and took Leslie's hand. 'We'll talk about it later, Dad. But the Chief Inspector needs to know if you still have the diary.'

'Tea? Coffee?' Ellie Jack, the head nurse, rumbled the tea trolley past them. 'Come on Leslie, sweetheart. Let's find you a cup of tea.'

Doling out coffee wasn't part of Ellie's job but even she had to pitch in when they were shorthanded. 'Dr Wood? Chief Inspector?'

'We aren't staying,' Vanessa said, speaking for both of them, and Ellie, who was intolerant of other people's intolerance, for once found herself in common cause with Jude and gave him an exasperated look. She dispensed Leslie's tea and biscuits with characteristic swiftness and moved on.

'Okay, Dad. Thanks.' Vanessa patted his frail hand. 'So now you know, Chief Inspector. Dad doesn't have the diary. As I told you.'

'What did you do with it, Mr Chester?'

'Threw it out,' Leslie said, indistinctly. He held the cup

and saucer on his lap and the teaspoon trembled, ringing against the china. 'Before I came here.'

Vanessa's shrug was aimed at Jude. 'Thanks, Dad. That's all. I know that was difficult. We'll leave you alone, now.'

Her protectiveness was dutiful but misplaced. Jude rarely left an interview with a question unanswered. 'I wondered if you remembered anything else from the diary.'

A second tear followed the first, then another, and another. Vanessa produced a tissue, then stood up and addressed herself to Jude. 'I understand you had to ask, of course, and I do realise you can't pick and choose your moments. But if you won't leave, I'll have to get the manager.' She steered him away towards the door. 'If I'd known the diary was important I'd have looked for it, but when Dad had his clear-out before he came here I didn't look through the bags. God knows what else went.'

'Can't be helped,' Jude said. 'Thanks for being so understanding.' Though she hadn't been.

She dipped her head. 'All right. I realise I was a little short with you, but Dad's been very distressed over this whole business, and that upsets me. That's no excuse, of course, but I'm sorry nevertheless.'

Thanking her, he excused himself and left. As he paused to sign out, Ellie appeared from one of the corridors, white plastic pinny tied around her waist and a tea towel flung over her shoulder. 'Chief Inspector. My, you've been in the wars, haven't you? I heard there was a bust-up at Lazonby last night. Was that you?'

Ellie could be just as cantankerous as Vanessa, but the obvious dislike which framed the psychiatrist's dealings with him was absent. He smiled. 'I was just having a quiet pint in my free time.'

'Trouble always finds you, doesn't it? Do you have a minute?'

'Of course.' Jude knew Ellie of old. She was waspish, astute and made her own self-interest her priority. If she had something to say, it was likely to be worth his while to listen.

'Shall we step outside?' She swiped her key fob to let them out of the building and followed him across the gravelled frontage to stand by his car. It was parked to the side, invisible from the windows of the lounge. 'I couldn't help overhearing what you were saying to Leslie.'

Jude suppressed his amusement. Couldn't help hearing? Ellie Jack was an avid gatherer of information, someone who missed nothing. 'Sorry if I upset him. I imagine there's been a lot of talk about the suicides.'

'Probably too much, if I'm honest.' Ellie, who was normally brazen in challenging everyone about everything, fidgeted with the plastic pinny, rolling its edges between slender fingers. Above them, the breeze rustled in the yellowing leaves of the big chestnut tree that dominated the lawn. 'In this place anything local is exciting, and everyone knows someone who's caught up in it. I'm sorry for poor old Leslie, but he wasn't being entirely straight with you.'

'Is that right?'

'Yes. You mentioned a diary. I heard him say he doesn't have it, but that's not true. I've seen it.'

'Really?' Jude had had a sense that Leslie was holding something back, but with Vanessa there he couldn't press the issue. 'When?'

'As recently as last week. He was reading it in his room when I went in to give him his warfarin. That must have been the Wednesday. There's no mistake. It was a notebook — A5 size with a brown paper style cover on it. Very tattered. Someone had written on the front. You know the way teenagers do. *Nicky's Diary. Top Secret*. I remember, because it made me smile and later I felt guilty about finding it so funny.'

Jude allowed himself a wry smile of his own. Ellie wasn't prone to guilt. 'You're sure?'

'I'd swear to it. He kept a couple of photos in it, in an envelope. He'd showed them to me once.'

As he had done to Becca. 'What were the photos?'

'I can't really remember. One was a boy he said was his son. The other was a group picture. I didn't really pay a lot of attention at the time. I was busy, and he can talk for hours if you let him.'

'Is that right?'

'If he doesn't have his watchdog with him. And I'll tell you something else. I took a bit of a liberty. You'd better not rat on me. But I ran down to his room and had a quick look in the drawer where I saw it, and it isn't there. I had a quick look in the other drawers. No sign.' She pivoted on one foot, turning her back on Jude and staring out towards the horizon as if to distance herself from what she'd just said, what she'd done. 'I thought you ought to know.'

'Thanks. I appreciate that.'

Unexpectedly, she turned back and smiled at him. 'You've given me a bollocking before for not telling you stuff I thought was trivial in case it was important. But you'd better not tell anyone what I've said. Because then I'll get a bollocking from that daughter of his, not to mention the boss. Can't do anything around here without getting on the wrong side of someone.'

Without a word of goodbye, she marched off, not the way she'd come but around to the side entrance of the building, no doubt so Vanessa wouldn't see her. Left alone, Jude leaned on the bonnet of the Mercedes in the sun, reflecting on what she'd said and checking his messages. It was obviously impossible that Leslie could have anything to do with the Eden Valley suicides. If he'd destroyed the diary it was most likely to be because he felt it cast some blame towards him for the loss of his son. A pity Vanessa hadn't read or interpreted it.

If she hadn't. It was extremely unlikely she didn't know what was in it, but plenty of people colluded to keep information from the police to protect their reputations or a family secret, rather than to hinder an investigation.

He flicked through his messages. Ashleigh. *Call me about last night.*

A few days before that message would have had an entirely different meaning. Now it just meant she'd got something to say about the fracas in the pub. He called her back, waiting while the phone rang a couple of times, wondering if she'd had to interrupt an evening with Scott to head down to Lazonby or whether she'd been sincere when she'd claimed she was playing it cool. He and Doddsy had left before she'd arrived. 'Any joy?'

'Not a lot of joy with anything. No.' Her sigh, at the other end of the phone, was fractious. For a moment Jude's sour temper weakened. In the months that they'd known one another they'd become friends. You might stop sleeping with someone overnight but you didn't shed the emotional intimacy as easily. Sometimes that hurt. At other times it was a comfort. After Becca had ended their relationship, the very thought of her had been wounding but he was happy enough to hear Ashleigh's voice. That was just as well. Many a workplace romance had hit the buffers less neatly. 'The opposite, in fact. My night's work didn't turn out anything like I was expecting.'

'Why not?' Surely he and Doddsy couldn't both be

wrong. 'It was Steven Lawson, wasn't it?' He opened the car door and slid into the driver's seat.

'Oh yes. That was all very straightforward. He admitted who he is, the warrant stands, the CPS are going ahead with a murder charge. He says he's going to plead not guilty and fight them all the way, but that hardly surprised me. But we have a real headache, Jude.'

'I'll say. And a lot of other aches, too.' He felt in the compartment between the front seats for a packet of paracetamol and a bottle of water.

'Wait until you hear this. We took his fingerprints and Chris got the guys to run them through the database to see if there was a match with the ones from the Stoker and McDougall murders. I've just got the results.'

'Is there a match?'

'No. It wasn't him.'

Jude took a moment to think about it, popped two tablets, washed them down with a swig of tepid water. He'd been so sure. 'There's nothing else to tie him to the killings?' His phone pinged with a message. He looked down at it. Mikey. *Can't get hold of Izzy*. God, that was all he needed. Panic rose within him and he fought it down.

'Nothing at all.'

'Okay.' Jude put Ashleigh on speaker and his common sense reasserted itself. He flipped off a quick couple of questions in reply to his brother. When had Mikey last heard of Izzy? Where was she last seen? 'What about Josh?'

'Charged with assault. Released on bail.'

Went for a bike ride. Didn't say where, came Mikey's succinct reply.

'Right.' *Leave it with me*, he messaged back, snatching a quick look across the valley. 'What does Geri have to say about it?'

'Insists on his innocence, of course. But honestly, Jude. You don't need me to tell you. Just because Steven Lawson can't be definitively linked to two murders almost forty years ago it doesn't mean Josh is nothing to do with the Eden suicides.'

'No.' But Jude was only half listening. Strictly speaking, he didn't have the time to go careering the four miles up to Cave Wood to see if he could find Izzy Ecclestone, but if he could somehow justify it as a trip to speak to Geri, it would do no harm and barely add three quarters of an hour to his day. And it might save a life. 'Are the two of them up at Eden Lacy?'

'I think Josh is there now. She came to pick him up this morning, and she said something about going to see her parents.'

Geri was brisk to the point of being offhand, but she was properly dutiful. Her mother was fading away before her eyes, barely a shadow, and she looked the type who'd stick it out to the end so she could leave with no regrets. She was no Leslie Chester, tortured by unnecessary guilt. 'I'm at Eden's End. I think I'll pop up there just now.'

'Do you want me to come along?'

He considered. Sometimes a second person made a difference and Ashleigh had a sense for things he missed. Raven liked her, and if there was anything to be learned about Izzy's state of mind, Raven would be the one person who knew. 'If you can spare the time.'

'I was up half the night. I think I'm probably almost on my lunch break, such as it is. Shall I see you up there?'

'Yep. See you.'

He pocketed the phone, drove out of the car park and swiftly covered the four miles or so to Long Meg and the New Agers' field. As he'd hoped, Geri's Land Rover was pulled up off the edge of the track that ran through the stone circle. He took a quick look down past the Sentinel Tree but no body hung from it, no bicycle lay abandoned against its trunk. He hadn't expected it; all the suicides had taken place at night, or when the despairing darkness had closed in on its victims and light must have seemed so distant as to be unreachable.

Ashleigh's car appeared in the lane a minute or so later, just as he was letting Mikey know there was no sign of Izzy. 'Okay?' he said, as she got out.

'Oh, fine.' He thought she sounded weary, as if the long night had taken a toll on her. 'What about you? I don't know if you've seen Doddsy this morning, but he's got a wonderful black eye.'

'I'm fine, too.' The paracetamol was already at work on the aches and pains. 'But bothered.'

'I know.' She frowned at the tree. 'If it wasn't Lawson who killed those other two, who was it? And how is it connected to the suicides, if it is? And I think it is.'

'You don't have any clues from the cards?' he asked her, daring to joke.

She frowned. 'I'll be honest with you. I suspect the last lot of advice they gave me did more harm than good. What are we here to talk to Geri about?'

'Nothing, really.' For once he was the one driven by gut instinct, but he couldn't see what they might learn from this visit, whether it was from Geri, from Raven or from the elusive Izzy herself. 'I wonder if it's even worth talking to her.'

'This isn't like you.' Her brows crinkled again, this time, he thought, with concern.

'Well, what are we going to ask her? If she knows anything about Josh, if he is implicated, she isn't going to tell us.'

'She wouldn't let him help Lawson get away. That's what Doddsy said.'

'No, but I don't get the impression Lawson is anything more than she says he is — an old friend who happens to be the father of her son. She'll think he can look after himself. Josh is different.' Geri was a woman who would kill for her child. 'Maybe we won't speak to her, after all. Sorry about the wild goose chase.'

'You sound so defeatist.'

He looked across the field, through the gap in the fence towards the New Agers' camp. Geri was standing with her hands on her hips, Storm behind her with the expression of a small boy making faces behind the teacher's back. In the background a line of washing sagged in the damp morning. Raven must be somewhere out of sight.

'I don't think this type of talking helps,' Geri was saying, her voice drifting across to them on the wind.

With Ashleigh in his wake, Jude edged closer.

'There's no point in pretending,' said Raven, her voice given some carry by an unusual note of exasperation. 'We're all going to die at some point. It's just that I'm going to die soon.'

'You'll live a whole lot longer if you let me look after you instead of being so bloody stubborn. If you come and stay with me then at least you can be comfortable and we can enjoy a bit of time together. And I don't need to tell you that this needn't have happened if you'd been sensible in the first place and seen a doctor.'

In the background, Storm confined himself to a helpless shrug. Once upon a time, Jude knew, he'd been a forceful character, at the top of his professional game. When he'd discovered inner calm and a resistance to aggression, his confrontational streak must have wasted away like an atrophying muscle. It lived on in Geri, standing no nonsense.

'But death comes to everyone when it's our time.' A clearer, younger voice piped up. Jude and Ashleigh exchanged glances. Izzy. 'Some people die young. It's natural. You shouldn't interfere with Nature.'

'I don't need your input. Especially not if you're going to be irresponsible. For God's sake, don't we all have a responsibility to live?'

'Perhaps you should go, Izzy,' Raven said. 'Come back and see us later, if you like. You know we're always here.'

'You can come and see Mum when she's comfortable in my house,' Geri directed. 'It'll be a whole lot more convenient for you. Really, it's no wonder everyone goes on about murder all the time, stuck in this sinister old wood.'

Jude and Ashleigh exchanged glances. No-one but the police was talking about murder. Even Vanessa seemed to see Eden Whispers as sinister and dangerous but not explicitly criminal.

'I'll see you.' After a few seconds' silence, Izzy appeared through the gate into the lane, wheeling her bike. Turning left towards them, she pushed the bike along the track into the stone circle.

'Morning, Izzy.' Jude smiled at her. His soul had been leaden for days, since Becca had turned him down, but here at least was a spark of cheerfulness.

'It's okay,' she said. 'I'm not going to do anything stupid. Mikey would kill me if I did.' A weak smile. 'Nothing's wrong?'

'No,' Jude said, 'nothing at all.'

'Were you looking at the tree? It's gorgeous, isn't it? Did you know that this is part of an ancient forest, and that trees used to be thought of as a ladder between this world and the next? The locals call it the Sentinel Tree and no-one knows why, but I think that's the reason. It's a gateway to the underworld. But only the dead can travel that way, so only the dead will ever find out.'

The tree, Jude judged, wasn't that old — a couple of hundred years, perhaps, but nothing like the age of the other two oaks that grew within the circle, still alive, their thick trunks gnarled yet still optimistically sprouting new growth. The Sentinel Tree was graceful in its death, its bare branches bleached white by the sun and the rain, stripped of twigs and bark. 'It's a fascinating legend.'

'I don't think it's a legend. I think it's true.' Perhaps deterred by their presence, Izzy turned her bike and, where the track became a road, got on and cycled off, without a backward glance.

In the field, Geri continued to castigate her mother, in the face of her father's helpless annoyance. Jude turned his attention once again to the Sentinel Tree. It was clear why Izzy was so attracted to it. It had a commanding silhouette, its branches reaching out like beckoning fingers, inviting the unwary — or the all-too wary — to partner it in a dance of death. It was easy to understand how Izzy was constantly drawn to something she must know wasn't the right course. People were. They were compelled to do wrong things, or things that would hurt them, or other people. Mikey, pursuing a vendetta of silence against his father when forgiveness would have helped everybody. Becca, rejecting him a second time when she must know she still loved him as much as he loved her. Ashleigh, trying again and again with Scott and always doomed to suffer for it. What was it Vanessa had said? *I can only help those who put themselves forward for help.*

'I hope that ruckus in Lazonby didn't ruin your evening,' he said, for something to do, still standing looking at the tree. A bird — a sparrow — dived into its embrace and settled on a branch.

'It did, a bit.' She looked in the same direction, almost certainly thinking the same. How could they save Izzy Ecclestone when they couldn't even save themselves? 'I was out with Scott. Just for a walk, just to see how things went.'

'I see.'

A pause. 'Aren't you going to go on at me about him?'

'No.' Another bird flew in to the tree, to the same branch. The first bird shuffled along an inch or two.

'Lisa would.'

'Lisa's your friend. I'm your ex-lover. If I say anything it'll sound jealous and possessive.'

'I like to think you're still my friend, too.'

For the first time, uncharacteristic resentment rose within him. 'For what it's worth.' He avoided her gaze but he knew she'd be looking at him as if she could work out what he was thinking. Maybe she could, and he didn't want her to see it.

'I meant to ask you. Did you go and see Becca?'

'Yes.' He did look at her, briefly, and then looked away again, back to the Sentinel Tree and its long, pale, beckoning fingers. *Come and die*. No wonder Vanessa thought is should be cut down. 'Not that I should have bothered. She wasn't interested in trying again. So that's that. I won't mention it again.'

'I'm so sorry.'

Ashleigh was very touchy-feely and any other time she'd have crossed over to him, laid a hand on his arm, but today she didn't. Today their friendship was very much secondary to her futile love for her worthless ex-husband and Jude himself had been cast aside by both of the women he cared for, like a branch washed up on a sandy spur of the river bank. Where did that leave him? With nothing but constant concern about Mikey and his father, about everyone but himself.

What was it Vanessa had said? *No-one is too old or too strong or too clever to have problems, and it's normal and natural to look for the easy way out.* And with that came the implication that the easy way out might be the attractive one. Even Vanessa, the woman putting her time and her effort, her emotion and her experience, into saving lives, had explicitly acknowledged that sometimes it was easier to let go.

'Jude!' said Ashleigh, with sudden vehemence. She moved towards him swiftly and her hand, belatedly, came down on his arm. 'Stop thinking like that!'

He snapped out of it, shocked at himself, at the ludicrously glib and easy way he'd fallen into such negative thinking. He wasn't like that. He was positive and forward-thinking, a problem-solver not a man who surrendered to circumstances. 'No. You're right. I don't know what came over me.' He turned his back on the tree and saw Ashleigh's face white with fear. 'How did you know?'

'Because I thought it, too. And I'm not like it either. But somehow it came into my head. That actually when things get complicated it might just be easier—'

Things didn't come into your head. Someone put them there. It was the website, Eden Whispers, sliding into the subconscious. And, more explicitly, it was Vanessa Wood, confiding. *I shouldn't really say this because I wouldn't want people to think death might be the answer…* 'Is it possible? That it was Vanessa, putting those ideas into those kids' heads?'

'I don't know.' She let go of his arm. 'Actually, of course I know. Yes, it's definitely possible. Definitely. It's a question of whether she did. And whether we can prove it.'

Jude's mind was whirring. 'We can try. My money says she was behind Eden Whispers, and all those posts she claimed to have seen on the Facebook group. We know she was counselling some of those kids, at least.'

For once, Ashleigh looked bewildered. 'But she was the one who drew our attention to that.'

'Yes, presumably because she reckoned we couldn't or wouldn't trace it. She'll be smart enough to hide her tracks — the name on them was an anagram of Josh Foster, remember. She'll have done it to put the blame on him. She must have known we'd find it eventually, so she pointed it out to us.'

'She double-bluffed us. Oh, God. She'd know exactly what to say to tempt people to their deaths, of course. And she had the perfect access to pick off the ones she wanted to hurt, encourage them to die when they came to see her, and then offer genuine help to the others.'

'Yes. We'll have to prove it, of course. But I don't think Faye will argue any more about getting authorisation to see who's behind it. We know what we're looking for, now.' The caller usage records from the victims' phones, when they got them, would be revealing and almost certainly damning. He stepped back, out of the shadow of the Sentinel Tree, and was surprised how easily it let him go.

'There are the two cold case murders,' said Ashleigh, following him into the sunlight. 'What about them?'

'It's possible she could have done them. We need proof—'

'We also need a motive.'

Jude stopped and thought of Vanessa's cold, intense, suppressed fury, of Geri's antagonism towards counselling, of Josh's resistance to questioning. 'I've an inkling. I think we'll find it in Nicky's diary.'

'Did Leslie have it, then? Did you get it?'

'No.' Jude thought of Leslie, of Ellie Jack's smart but inappropriate move to check it out as if she were the policeman. 'He definitely had it, but he doesn't now. Vanessa must have taken it. That's what it'll be. And if she didn't destroy it she'll still have it. So I reckon now we have enough evidence to ask a magistrate for a warrant to search her house — and to arrest her.'

TWENTY-FIVE

Jude hadn't realised how close to the scene of the Eden Valley suicides Vanessa lived — a bare mile and a half from Lazonby. As he got out of the car he saw Ashleigh looking towards the village, too obviously thinking the same as he was. You could walk there from here, across the fields, unseen or unremarked. You could meet someone on the railway bridge without passing a house.

Vanessa wasn't at home. 'I didn't think she'd be here,' he said to Ashleigh. 'At work, I imagine. We'll go along there afterwards, and see what we can find.' The warrant covered her office as well as her home. 'But I have a feeling if we find the diary, it'll be here.'

'I think today is one of her open session days at the school,' said Ashleigh.

Jude had sent Doddsy down to see if he could find and arrest Vanessa — something Jude would normally have taken on himself. In this case, he was more interested in uncovering Nicholas's diary. He turned to the uniformed officers who were just getting out of the the cars behind him. 'Looks like we'll have to force entry. You lads can get on with it.'

He left them tackling the door while he strolled around the side of the property and assessed its location in more detail. It was a nice enough spot. You couldn't see Long Meg and her daughters itself, but if you knew where to look you could see the spot on the horizon behind which it lay, and you could see the dark shadow of Cave Wood, too.

A crash and a shout from the front of the building brought him back to the job in hand. He strode around to the front, where the four uniformed policemen were waiting for instructions. 'Are we good to go, Boss?'

'Yep. You know what we're looking for. Any computer equipment, anything which might be a written record of any offence, or which might be any evidence of an offence. Specifically, a schoolboy's diary.'

They listened, then shouldered their way in to the silent property and began the search. Jude and Ashleigh followed.

'Vanessa always seemed so confident, didn't she?' Ashleigh said, with a sigh.

He nodded, reviewing his interactions with the psychiatrist. He'd seen dislike and challenge in her attitude, but now he understood. She'd been probing for his weakness; latterly she must have begun to wonder how much he knew, how much he suspected. Her number would be on all of those young people's phones; with time and intent, her messages would be accessible.

It was entirely possible Vanessa had hidden the diary, or destroyed it. On balance he thought the former, because if it was in any way incriminating she'd surely have got rid of it long before. There must be some sentimental value to it, for her father if not for herself, if Nicholas's death still gripped them both so tightly.

He left the uniformed officers to look in the living spaces and began his own search in the downstairs room Vanessa used as a study, pausing for a second to stare out of the window. The house was an old one, solid sandstone with walls a foot thick and views, like Geri's, across the Eden Valley. You couldn't see Cave Wood form this window, or even see the river itself, which wound its serene way beneath steep sandstone cliffs.

The desk yielded nothing. The bookshelves were stacked with psychological texts and included, he noticed, a few heavy volumes on medical psychology and suicide counselling. Among them was a bound copy of Vanessa's doctoral thesis, in the name of Vanessa Chester — a long and complicated title in scientific language he barely understood, but which dealt with adolescent suicides. He flicked through it, scanned the abstract. Vanessa had studied what to say to the potentially suicidal so it followed, therefore, that she must also know exactly what not to say. Interesting, and evidence. He placed the thesis in an evidence bag and also salvaged a back-up hard drive from the desk. God knew what secrets that would reveal. But there was no diary.

They moved on, opening every box file and every drawer, going through the shelf of cookbooks in the kitchen, learning about Vanessa from her possessions and yet not finding anything that gave her away. In the living room, the row of photographs on the mantelpiece revealed her family, including the image of Nicky that Becca had described to him, but most were of Vanessa and her parents. In the pictures of Vanessa as a child, she looked open and interested. Nicholas's death had had far-reaching implications, turning her into a bitter woman.

'No computer, though,' said Ashleigh. 'Do you thinks she's tried to destroy it?'

'I expect she keeps most of it at the office. Don't worry. We have the back up.' And when they'd searched the office they'd have the laptop, too.

'It looks like that's it,' he said, at last, to the constables, once they'd combed the entire property and failed to find the diary. 'You can get this hard drive back to the office so the tech lads can have a look at it. Someone needs to stay and get someone to make sure the property is secure.'

'She might have been right, then, about not having it.' Ashleigh sighed as he followed her out and closed the door.

'We didn't find it. That doesn't mean she didn't have it. She could have hidden it, or destroyed it.' There had been no ashes in the grate, no sign of a bonfire in the garden. The shredder in Vanessa's office had been full, but when he'd raked though it he'd seen nothing that resembled a forty-year old, brown paper covered diary. 'Remember those two lights Raven saw in the wood on the night Juliet died? It makes sense, now. One of them could have been Vanessa.'

'Making sure Juliet killed herself?'

'Or helping her.' Whispering to her, too, that whatever she was obliged to say professionally there was another truth, an easier way than fighting. 'She might have thrown the phone in the river in case there were any texts that might link them.'

'But she said they'd been in contact. She'd have had a legitimate reason for texting her, perhaps.'

'If it looked like a suicide she'd think no-one would bother checking the phone records.' Now Faye would harass the tech team, and they'd soon know.

He was still thinking of phones when his own rang. He looked down at it. 'It's Mikey. Give me a second. I need to speak to him.' In such fevered times any scruples he had about dealing with personal matters on work time went out of the window. No-one would hold that against him. 'Everything okay?'

'You tell me.' Mikey was in an unusually chirpy mood. 'I'm playing detective and tuning in to the local gossip network. Izzy says your guys are up at Dr Wood's place. Is that right?'

'Yes,' Jude said, rolling his eyes at Ashleigh to indicate that this was trivial, 'but I can hardly tell you why, can I? So don't look to me for the chat.'

'I'm in Penrith having lunch with Izzy,' Mikey said, regardless, 'and her mum was on the phone about it. Someone saw the cars up at the house. And I'm guessing you're looking for something, even if you can't tell me what.'

'What's this about? I don't have time for jokes, Mikey.' There were lives on the line, but he wouldn't say that, with Izzy Ecclestone, frail, vulnerable and over-interested in death, listening in.

'I'm not joking. I'm deadly serious. Izzy says, have you looked at the flagstone in front of the cooker?'

Jude thought about the kitchen, a traditional one with a woven rug on the floor in front of the built-in range. He'd seen one of the constables lift the rug, look and put it back. 'Yes.'

'Did you find anything?'

'No.'

Ashleigh had been listening in. Her eyebrows flicked upwards and she moved towards the patrol car. 'Hold on a moment. I don't think we're finished here.'

'Call yourself a policeman?' said Mikey. 'Look again. Izzy used to go and play with the girl who lived there before Dr Wood bought it. She says there's a flagstone you can lift and hide things. It's quite big. Izzy and the girl left a kind of time capsule in there.'

'Mikey,' Jude said, 'if this is helpful I'll buy you a pint.'

'If it's helpful? I'm telling you. I don't know what you're looking for, but whatever it is that's where it'll be.'

He hung up. Two of the policemen were heading back up the path as Jude turned again towards the house and opened up the door he'd just locked. In the kitchen he lifted the blue rug and rolled it back. It took a second look to see that one of the flags was less well set than those around it.

He helped himself to a knife from the kitchen drawer, dropped to his knees and inserted the blade between the flags. It came up easily; he slid four fingers under the slab and lifted it.

Inside the cavity beneath it, a foot square and a foot deep, was a plastic M&S carrier bag. When he lifted it out he saw a jam jar, crusted with dust underneath. Izzy's time-capsule. *Izzy and Lou*, the message on the outside said, painted in what looked like black nail varnish.

He stood up and removed the bag, laying it on the kitchen unit under the eyes of Ashleigh and the two uniformed officers. Inside was a large brown envelope. He opened that, too. There it was. Nicholas Chester's teenage diary, curled with age and, he thought, stained with Leslie's tears. It fell open at a page marked by the class photograph that Leslie had shown Becca, or a copy of it. A copy, he guessed, because this one had been marked, lines drawn across individual faces as though they were ticked off. His parents, thank God, still smiled out of the picture and some of the others he knew from the annotations his father had written out for him in the pub and the thumbnail bios that Chris had looked out. Those ticked off were either dead or grieving for their lost children.

He opened the diary and skimmed the schoolboy scrawl. Every now and then a name was marked in the modern fluorescence of a highlighter pen, as if someone had been through it in detail, ticking off things to be done. He skimmed a few pages, rapidly, caught his mother's name. *Linda…kind to me today…* Then he flicked to the end, because that was where the truth would be. Nicky's diary, he saw from a swift glance, would need some textual analysis, but the impression it gave him was clear.

'Now we know. It wasn't an accident. He killed himself.' The quiet, musical teenager had attracted the cruel displeasure of his classmates and they had made his life miserable. He had gone to Lacy's Caves and hidden there because they rode their bikes past his house and laughed, because they waited for him when he went out. And one day they'd found the place he went to preserve his sanity and had followed him there, too. 'Look. Here it is.' He read it aloud. '*I can't take it. They'll be sorry when I'm dead. I'm going to do it.*' That was where the diary ended, dated the day before the boy's death..

'But the train driver's statement—' said Ashleigh, bewildered. 'I went back to it. He said Nicholas was trying to get out of the way and fell.'

The witness statement had been clear, but so was the diary in front of him. 'He must have changed his mind at the last moment.'

'Oh God, I see. And fell, so it sort of was an accident but yet not. And that explains why Leslie is so determined that it was his fault and he failed his son.'

'It looks like this is all we need from here,' said Jude, to his audience. 'It may not be definitive evidence of any murder, but it certainly indicates Vanessa has had some kind of input into what's been going on.' He handed the carrier bag and its contents to one of the constables, who placed it in an evidence bag and labelled it. 'Let's get back to the office and sort this out.'

'You don't think she's done a runner?' Ashleigh asked, as he turned towards Penrith.

He shook his head. Vanessa and her father had been working towards an objective and that objective was achieved. The highlighted names had been those who were dead, or whose children were dead, and the only other name was that of Izzy's mother. Perhaps, ironically, it was Izzy's very vulnerability that had made it too much of a risk for Vanessa to attempt to gaslight her, with so many people watching out for her welfare. And his parents' names had been in the diary but not highlighted and not, he'd seen with relief, in any negative association. Thank God they hadn't been in the group who'd mocked and harassed their classmate, and the one mention he'd seen of his mother had been in reference to her kindness.

That must be why Vanessa had been so sure Mikey would come to no harm. His parents had committed no sins for which he must be sacrificed, for which they must atone. Her taunting of Jude himself had been no more than an attempt to express her power.

He got out his phone and called Doddsy. 'Interesting stuff from Vanessa's house. We found the diary. Did you have any luck hauling her in?'

'Nope,' said Doddsy, brief to the pint of terseness. 'No sign of her.'

'You tried the Community College?'

'Yep. She was expected but phoned to say something had come up. She's not at her office and her secretary doesn't know where she is. She missed an appointment there this morning.'

Jude paused. Where would Vanessa go, when she knew the game was up? 'You've got people looking out for the car? Blue Peugeot, I think.'

A twitch to his left. One of the constables — the one

he'd left on watch at the door — was looking suddenly alarmed. 'There was a blue Peugeot came past while you were searching. Slowed in the lane and then took off again. I thought it was just a rubbernecker.'

'Okay,' Jude sighed in frustration. 'Doddsy. Looks like she knows we're here. She may have made a run for it. You know what to do.' Another call, number unknown. 'I'm putting you on hold just now. Hello? Jude Satterthwaite speaking.'

'Hello again, Chief Inspector. Ellie Jack here, at Eden's End. Just a quick call, but I thought you'd like to know. Vanessa Wood's here, just arrived. Came roaring up the drive like she was in the Sweeney, she did, and stormed into the place with a face that would turn the milk.'

'To see her father?'

'She sure as hell isn't here to see me,' said Ellie, cheerfully. 'I expect I'll see you in a few minutes, then, shall I?'

TWENTY-SIX

Vanessa was looking out of the window of Leslie's room when the Mercedes with the two detectives in it came crawling up the drive at a respectful pace, rather than the wheel-spinning, rubber-burning speed she'd expected when they came to arrest her. Her heart sank when the liveried patrol car came along behind them. They'd better be on their game. She was pretty certain they couldn't get her for murder, but Jude Satterthwaite had struck her as the creative sort. He'd think of something, though a good lawyer must be able to argue that even Eden Whispers probably wasn't illegal, just a breach of an unenforceable voluntary code, and there was no record of the words she'd whispered in the ears of the dead. Even the texts and messages she'd sent had been carefully phrased and could be read entirely innocently.

She hoped.

She would be struck off, of course, but she was only a couple of years away from retirement and professional disgrace was a price well worth paying. 'Dad. I want to talk to you.'

'Of course, Vee.'

'Yes. It's very serious.'

The car stopped and the chief inspector and sergeant got out and strolled towards the front door, for all the world as if they were there on a casual visit. Somewhere in the reception area the bell rang, long and loud.

'I won't be coming to see you any more.'

There was a short silence. Most of the time Leslie was sharp as the proverbial tack, but he was showing increasing signs of short-term memory loss. From time to time she had to repeat herself. So much the better. It would save her the effort of making a full confession to the police. 'Why's that?'

'I might have to go to prison. Because of Nicky.' Even if she didn't, he would. Or maybe not. Surely he was too old and infirm to be locked up? But murder, after all, was murder.

He folded his hands tightly over one another. The door to his room was open and she heard soft footsteps in the carpeted corridor. She turned her back on the door. The footsteps stopped and no-one came in, but she felt their shadows and their silence. Jude Satterthwaite and Ashleigh O'Halloran had found the room and they would stand and listen to her confession before they took her away.

'Prison?' said Leslie, his voice quavering. 'Why?'

'Remember how you told me what you did to Richard and to Finn?'

On that prompt, he dug in the inside pocket of his jacket. Out came the class photo. Vanessa took it from him, reached into her bag and took out a pen. It didn't matter what happened to her. What mattered was that he had some kind of payback for what had happened to him, for all the years of misery and guilt that had followed Nicky's death. Now, of course, without her to remind him every visit of what she'd done, he'd forget the other parents who would suffer just the way he had for the mistakes they'd made, whose children had died because they'd driven Nicky to his death. In future he would remember only his own grief.

But she would know. Every time she'd visited, every time she'd talked him through her actions only for him to forget again, she saw the same satisfaction, the same understanding and the peace that came from knowing someone else would suffer what they'd made him suffer. Wielding the pen with vicious satisfaction, she slashed through two of the images. 'Richard and Finn, both dead. You killed them. Well done. I'm proud of you. And I did the others.'

'You killed them? They said they killed themselves.'

'Clara gave me the idea,' she said, for the detectives' benefit. She hadn't had to intervene on that occasion, and nor had she wanted to. Clara's parents hadn't known Nicky, but their grief had been first a reminder and then an inspiration. Vanessa had tried to save her and failed. 'I was seeing Connor, who was struggling with mental health issues. It was easy. He was deeply insecure.' Another figure defaced, another parent mourning a child. 'Sharon Ford. Remember, she had a daughter. Tania. She jumped off the bridge.'

'Did you push her?'

Vanessa hesitated. Why confess to murder when she didn't have to? 'I was with her when she jumped. Because I'd set up a website, you see.' Now they had her computer the police would find it, find everything she'd done to goad the youth of the Eden Valley to their deaths. In a strange way she was proud of herself. 'There were the Currans.' Their father's face, too, was disfigured by the malicious slash of red pen. 'I went with Charlie to the woods that night and watched him die, and I thought of you and of Nicky. Jimmy Kennedy's daughter, too. And I went with Ben to Lacy's Caves.'

'Nicky used to go there. It said it in the diary.'

'Yes. That was a happy coincidence. Ben said he used to go there and drink with his brother, so I suggested we meet there to see if it would help him move on.' She'd never intended that it should. 'I brought vodka, and water in a vodka bottle for me. And the pills.'

'Vee.' Leslie's hands were shaking, but she knew he understood. She took his old hands in hers and thought of Nicky, as she knew he would be doing. 'You were always so clever.'

She thought she'd been a little too clever, on balance. Nicky had liked Jude Satterthwaite's parents but she'd never believed they were entirely blameless. That, along with his assumed authority, was the reason she hadn't been able to resist taunting him with the ridiculous suggestion that he, too, was within her control. He never had been, and it had only been a matter of time before he recognised the dangerous nature of the things she was inspiring him to think. Pride was a besetting sin. If she hadn't fallen victim to it they'd still be looking at everything as inexplicable, powered by a malicious but anonymous online troll. 'I know. I have to go now, Dad. The police are here. They'll want to talk to you soon.'

'Goodbye, Vee. Thank you. And I'm sorry.'

She got up and bent to drop a quick kiss on the top of his head. 'It'll be difficult now. But I promise you. It was worth it.'

As she turned away from him, Jude stepped forward. 'Okay, Dr Wood.'

She dipped her head. 'Of course, you heard that.'

'We did. You might be interested to know we found the

diary. I'm placing you under arrest, on suspicion of encouraging and assisting with the suicides of Juliet Kennedy, Ben Curran, Charlie Curran, Connor Turnbull and Tania Baker. I'd like you to come with us and make a formal statement, now.'

The litany of names gave her a thrill; they were a roll of honour, a tribute to Nicky. 'Of course.' As she walked out behind him, Ashleigh O'Halloran fell into step in the rear, as though they were expecting her to run. 'What about Dad?'

'We'll be interviewing him later. I'd like to send someone down to take fingerprints first, if you don't mind.'

As if it made any difference whether she minded or not. 'Of course.'

She got into the back seat of the car and the sergeant got in beside her. Jude Satterthwaite started the engine but let it idle for a moment, watching her through the driver's mirror. He was a clever man; she understood, now, just how much so. There was value in keeping your cleverness hidden, rather than flaunting it.

'Why did you try and make it look as if it was Josh Foster?' he asked.

She fidgeted. Another example of being too clever. 'I didn't know where Steven Lawson had gone. He was the ringleader. Everybody hated him, but they were scared of him, too. They picked on him but he took them on and they all turned on Nicky instead.' Like a pack of wild animals. 'Read the diary. It's all in there.'

'You must have known he was Josh's father.'

'Not for certain.' If she had done, she'd have pressed further, tried harder to exert her influence over Josh and drag him down, too, though she knew she'd have struggled against his mother's common sense. 'At one point I heard a rumour he was back and that Geri Foster was dating him. I don't know her well, but she was always knocking around this place, because of her parents. Her mother was local, and whatever Geri says, people do have a strong sense of their roots. But no. I wasn't sure.'

He let the engine tick over for another moment. 'What about Izzy Ecclestone?'

'What about her?'

'Her mother's name is in the diary. You highlighted it.'

Vanessa thought of Izzy with what passed for sympathy. 'I never did anything to try and hurt Izzy. The opposite, in fact. I treat her as you'd expect me to treat a client. I did my best for her.'

'May I ask why?'

She leaned back against the headrest. She was suddenly very tired. 'In my professional opinion, Izzy isn't saveable. She has so many complexes, so great an obsession with death. Time, and her own frailty, will take care of her for me.'

'I see,' he said, in a voice that was rich with irritation, and he put the car into gear and headed off down the drive towards Penrith.

TWENTY-SEVEN

It was too late, but Ashleigh couldn't rid herself of the feeing — of the fear — that ending her relationship with Jude had been a mistake.

She got the cards out of their hiding place in her chest of drawers, sat down and began to shuffle, sliding them through her hands the way Raven did, with the ease of practice. It had been a while since she'd looked at them, as if, for the first time, she didn't trust them.

Scott had texted her as she was leaving work, and she hadn't replied. A sick feeling lurked in her heart, of impending self-destruction, surely too much like that which had troubled Tania and Connor, Charlie and Ben and Juliet and which must still linger in the darker corners of Izzy Ecclestone's soul.

Normally full of sound common sense, she didn't need anyone to tell her that what she was thinking was wrong. She wasn't about to take her own life but handing it over to Scott amounted to much the same thing. She looked at the message on her phone. *Enjoyed our walk, as far as it went. Let's try again.*

He'd moved up to Cumbria for the summer and surely that meant something. He'd done it to see more of her, or so he'd assured her, and she couldn't see any other reason why he'd have come. Scott was a man who liked crewing yachts in the Mediterranean rather than teaching hordes of kids to windsurf in the chill of Ullswater.

It was flattering, but she'd been flattered before. Ashleigh was no fool. If she went back to Scott there was every chance the vicious spiral of their marriage would repeat itself. They'd begin well; she'd be at work and he'd be bored; there would be temptation in his way; and, because he was Scott and couldn't resist a good-looking woman, he'd fall.

She turned the deck of cards face up. She'd taken what she interpreted as their advice and ended the relationship with Jude, on the delusion of sacrifice. With hindsight — always with hindsight — she understood how her subconscious mind worked. By letting Jude go, by giving him another chance to make it work with Becca, she'd thought she was freeing herself up for another chance with Scott. But Becca hadn't played ball and now she felt nothing but guilt.

If only she could turn the clock back.

She dealt the cards out, five of them face down, then picked up the five and shuffled them back in the pack. For the first time she felt they'd let her down and she didn't trust them not to do it again.

When she fanned them out in front of her, it occurred to her that there were too many cards in the deck she didn't want to see again. She could have done without Death, and the Three of Swords that always came up when she thought of Scott and which never offered her any comfort, but it was the Hanged Man that she selected. It wasn't just that it was the card that had prompted her to step away from a relationship that looked as if it was becoming serious and back into one that had almost destroyed her. It was that every time she saw the Hanged Man's serene face as he dangled by his feet from the trees she thought of the futility of that loss.

The deck wasn't complete that way, but it removed any chance that particular card would remind her of her folly. She smiled, shuffled again and began to deal.

TWENTY-EIGHT

When it was all done, when Vanessa had been questioned and released on bail, when Leslie's fingerprints had been taken and matched with those found at the scene of Richard Stoker and Finn McDougall's murders, Jude found himself at home on a bright summer evening. The charge sheet for Leslie's case was in Doddsy's hands and that for Vanessa, which promised to be more complicated, was one he was inclined to put aside. As Becca had kept telling him, you could work too hard.

Maybe now he'd learned the lesson, but it was too late. If things had gone differently he might have called her and suggested a walk or a drink, but he couldn't see how they could ever resume the comfort of their former relationship, or even their friendship.

Ruefully, he thought of Ashleigh. When they'd parted in the car park after work he'd asked her, without intent, what she was planning for the evening and she'd shrugged and not answered. What had she been thinking in the shade of the Sentinel Tree? What damaging ideas had Vanessa fertilised in her brain? They'd been together for the best part of a year and he knew her weaknesses well.

He sighed. It was none of his business. If she wanted his help or advice, she'd have to ask.

There were, he judged, two hours of good daylight left, and he decided to take advantage of them and go out for a run. In the mood to punish himself, he set off up the hill, along Beacon Edge, towards Great Salkeld. It was a dozen miles or so, something he was more than capable of, though he hadn't run that far in a while. He'd pay the price for it in the morning, on top of the aches he still carried after the tussle with Josh and his father.

There were a dozen other places he could have run, but he turned his face to the east, strangely drawn towards the River Eden, as though he had some unfinished business. But as he ran, with the wind behind him and the declining sun on his back, nothing came to him.

Why would it? There was nothing to finish. Vanessa had confessed and no-one else need die. His concern for Mikey, and for himself, was unfounded. A wave of relief washed over him and he laughed as he ran.

At the turning point in his route, just before the village of Great Salkeld, he saw a familiar figure. It wasn't the Geri Foster he might have expected, striding along the roadside holding the dog to heel. This Geri Foster was shuffling along with one hand up to her face, dabbing at her eyes, and the Labrador on its extending lead was gambolling as far away as it wanted.

He slowed as he approached, to make sure he had some breath left to speak to her. 'Are you okay?'

'Oh,' Geri said, stopping by the roadside and stuffing the tissue into her pocket. 'It's you. Tired of bringing the guilty to justice, are you?'

'I'm never tired of that.' He stopped. She'd been crying. 'Are you okay?' he repeated.

'Do I look okay?' She shortened the lead, pulling the dog back under her control, turned and headed down towards the lane towards her cottage. 'No. I'm not. I know you think I'm a callous bitch—'

'I've never said that.' Despite himself, despite the awareness that every step he took away from home was another step he'd have to take back and that the mile he'd have to go to be sure Geri was all right was a two mile addition and would end with him running in the dark, he followed her.

'No, you never have, but you must think it. You think I only care about myself. And Josh.'

'Where is he?'

'Gone to the pub.'

'Right.' At least he'd be spared the awkwardness of that encounter. Even if he weren't the subject of a criminal charge for assault, Josh would be understandably hostile.

They walked in silence for a while, at a brisk pace. Geri had her back to him again and was feeling in her pocket for the tissue. Her voice was gruff. 'Sorry. I've had gin and it always makes me teary. I thought I'd walk it off.' She yanked the lead and brought the dog, already tiring, to her side. 'I'm worried about my mum, that's all. I've given Dad a phone in case he needs me, and I charge it every time I visit, but he never calls me or answers when I call him. I know Mum's dying and I know she's quite happy to die, but I'm not happy to let her. How can I watch her fade away in that filthy field when she could be so comfortable with me? If she insists on refusing treatment, fine. That's her right. But at least she'd be warm and comfortable.'

Jude thought of Raven, content to see the stars at night and walk in the woods, saving Izzy Ecclestone's life through warmth and common sense, not psychiatry. 'She's living her life the way she wants to.'

'I know she is. And I feel frustrated that she is, and that she won't let me help. Normally I wouldn't give a toss what people think but I hate the idea people will look at me and think I'm the selfish cow who left her mother to die in a tent in the middle of a muddy field. And I think I'd even cope with that, if it wasn't for all these poor kids killing themselves. And with all these awful suicides I worry about Josh, because he's all I've got. This is all such a bloody mess.' The sniff turned to a sob.

The last thing Jude wanted was to get himself caught up with Geri and her worries. He looked to the west, where the light was fading and a stripe of purple cloud had settled like a weight on the hills. 'I can reassure you on that score, at least.'

'Oh, right.' Geri was recovering herself now. 'You've managed to find some miraculous solution have you?'

'I wouldn't say that. But I think we've found out what caused it and put a stop to it.'

They were in sight of Geri's cottage now. Jude half-turned, checking the distance, resenting it. He should have made his run shorter and turned earlier for home. Now he was lumbered with too many difficult questions on top of Geri's self-pity, but he kept walking. She intrigued him, and he had nothing else to do.

'Oh, you've fingered Vanessa, then, have you?'

That surprised him. 'What makes you say that?'

'You have, then. It came to me in a flash, earlier on today. That was one of the other reasons I hit the gin. I don't often do that, but I couldn't bear the thought that something might happen to Josh, especially when you so obviously suspected him of having something to do with it. And then I understood. Pointing the finger at him that way.

It must have been a grudge against me. I was going to call you tomorrow, when I'd sobered up.'

'Why would she have a grudge against you? If it was anybody, she had a grudge against Steven Lawson.'

'It comes to the same thing.' They'd reached the gate to her cottage now and she opened it, slipping the dog's lead. 'Come in and have a beer, and I'll tell you about it. Josh can drive you home when he gets back.'

'Not if he's been to the pub.'

'He doesn't drink.'

'I'd still rather not. I can't accept favours from someone who's charged with assault.'

'It's a lift, not a brown envelope full of cash. Why do you have to be so pure? Have a soft drink, at least. You look as if you need it, if you've run all the way from Penrith.'

A cold drink on that warm evening was undeniably welcome. He followed her into the house. 'So what's the story with Vanessa?'

'You obviously haven't checked on her background.' She turned to him with a malicious smile. 'Not doing your job, Chief Inspector.'

Vanessa's cunning had been to entrench herself among the good guys. They'd had no reason to check out anything more than her professional credentials. That would change. Her background and motivation would form a key part of the prosecution case, one of the main topics for him to delegate the next day. 'Not yet. Do you want to make it easy for me?'

'Well, why not?' She opened the freezer, dropped some ice into a glass. 'Apple juice? You know my views on sex, of course. Easy come, easy go. It works for me.'

'Glad to hear it.' It hadn't for him. He couldn't manage a relationship without emotion, without love, and now he knew he didn't want to. 'It doesn't for everyone.'

'I know that now. When I had an affair, if you want to call it that, with Steven, he was also seeing Vanessa. She's much closer to his age than I am. I knew about her and it didn't bother me. I never saw the relationship as a serious thing and neither did he. He's much more in tune with my thinking on that than you are.'

Jude, drinking the cold glass of apple juice, suppressed a wry smile.

'The trouble is, Vanessa isn't on the same wavelength. It was after her marriage broke down and she was looking for another relationship. She thought he was serious about her and she blamed me for breaking it up. Wrongly, of course. Steve's never committed to anything in his life and she was foolish to think he would, but love is blinding. She got jealous. They fell out. He left her. And she accused me over it and told me that one day I'd pay.'

'And you think that twenty years after—'

'She has a hell of a long memory.'

And she could bear a grudge. It would be interesting to know when Vanessa learned about her father's murder of two of Lawson's classmates. Was it possible Steven's casual approach to relationships had spared him from becoming close to Vanessa and, possibly, from becoming the third of her father's victims — or the first of her own? 'Did she know he's wanted for murder?'

'I doubt it. He went about under a different name. Not many people have memories that long and that sharp.' Geri sighed. 'She's a clever one, Vanessa. And cold. And she has power. It's the reason I hate therapists so much. It's why I thought she might have something to do with it. Because she has power and she knows how to use it.' She looked at him. 'I'm pretty damned sure you're the same, but you use your power for good. She uses it to feed her pride and her ego. I can't tell you how much that scares me.'

'You might have mentioned it to me.' Jude finished the apple juice and put the glass down.

Geri's phone, on the dark wooden dresser, rang and she snatched at it. 'Dad. You've remembered how to use the phone. Wonders never cease. Is Mum all right?'

Jude moved a step closer, but he didn't need to. Storm, who'd probably never used a mobile phone, was shouting. 'No, she's fine! But there's a car up at the stone circle!'

'It'll be a dog walker,' said Geri, soothingly. 'You must know that.'

'No! It's been abandoned! The driver's door is open!'

'There's no need to shout,' said Geri, with exasperation. 'I could probably hear you without this thing. Right. Anything else?'

'Yes,' said Storm, calming down. 'Someone's taken our washing line. And I don't know what to do.'

'Taken the washing line?' She looked across at Jude, in obvious alarm. 'Well, I—'

'The car,' Jude prompted her. 'What's it like? What's the number?'

'It's black. A little black car. It says Fiesta on the back.'

Jude had felt the first feelings of panic even before Storm reeled off the registration plate. His fingers were already flicking at his phone. 'That's my mum's car.'

'Your mum?' Geri looked at him again, this time in astonishment. 'Why would your mum—?'

'It's not her. She's away. It's Mikey.'

She looked blank.

'My brother.' The phone rang, but Mikey didn't answer. He waited until it flicked to voicemail. 'Mikey, ring me back. I need to talk to you.' Then he stuck it in his pocket. 'I've got to get over there.'

'Who's that with you, Indigo?' said Storm, plaintive and confused.

'It's Inspector Satterthwaite. Never mind why.'

Jude went to the window. Less than a quarter of a mile away as the crow flew, Mikey could be in Cave Wood, thinking — doing — the unthinkable. By road it was five miles at least. But the river was low. 'I'm on my way over.' He turned to Geri, who'd already picked up on what was going on and had opened the back door for him. 'Can I get down to the river from here?'

'Yes. There's a path of sorts, but it's steep and—'

'Great. Call 999, tell them what's happening, and to send someone over to Cave Wood.' He jogged down to the end of the garden, down the steep slope, pausing to call Mikey once more. 'Mikey. I'm on my way. But I need to know you're all right. For God's sake, call me!'

Nettles and brambles snagged at his bare calves as he careered down the slope to the edge of the river. After all, he'd misjudged Vanessa. Nicholas might have thought kindly of his mother but his father was a different matter, capable of thick-skinned insensitivity and a blithe lack of awareness of other people's feelings. It would be too cruel if Mikey were the final, innocent, sacrifice to her vengeance and her vanity.

The irony was that his father, who thought mainly of himself, would get over his loss very quickly.

Jude inched over the cobbles at the water's edge. It had been dry and the water was low, but the channel deepened in the centre and the water funnelled into a treacherous flow. On days like this the Eden was benign, but he knew it to be full of tricks. He stepped from stone to stone, until eventually he had to go deep. Water filled his shoes. Mid-calf, then knee deep. Behind and above him, Geri was shouting something into the phone, but he couldn't make out the words.

'Mikey!' he shouted, but there was no answer.

In the middle of the flow the cold water reached his waist. Jude waded on, as fast as he dared without losing his footing. If he fell he could get swept yards down the river before he regained his footing. Testing the next step, he slipped as the stone gave way under him. Struggling for balance, he struggled and managed to regain his footing, taking a huge stride out of the worst of the current and praying that his foot made stable ground. It did, but his phone slipped from his hand and into the water. He didn't stop to retrieve it but jumped for the bank.

On dry land, he shook himself like a dog while he tried to work out where Mikey might have headed. Lacy's Caves? But he'd taken the rope. So into the woods, then. Or the Sentinel Tree. Mikey had been spending time with Izzy. Hadn't she said something about it being the route to the underworld, accessible only to the dead? Crazy, of course, but now she had to be taken seriously.

'Mikey!' Somewhere up on the hill a dozen crows rose with an angry clatter from the dense trees. Had Mikey disturbed them? Above him, in that direction, the river bank was steep and he set to scrambling up it. On a normal day there would be plenty of walkers on it but this late in the evening it was a silent, desolate place. In the woods above him a magpie chattered its annoyance. He followed its cry. 'Mikey!'

'Jude?' Mikey answered him, bewildered but thank God, definitely Mikey. And close. 'What the hell are you—?'

He crashed towards the voice and broke through a

barrier of brambles. In a clearing, Mikey stood with a hand on a tree, shocked.

Jude got to him, grabbed him by the shoulders, needing to feel he was real and alive. 'No, what the hell are *you* doing? How could you put me through this? What will Mum say? What will she do?'

'What are you talking about?' Mikey shook himself free. 'It's Izzy.'

'What?'

'Izzy. I've lost her.'

'What do you mean?'

'We were supposed to be going to for a drink. I went to her house to pick her up and there was nobody there. Her parents are out. And her bike had gone. I knew she'd be here and I thought I saw her in the trees so I went after her, but I can't find her. We have to stop her, Jude. We have to. I don't know where she is.'

But Jude could guess. 'Up at the stone circle,' he said. 'She'll have gone back to the tree.'

Izzy sat with her back against a slender birch tree as the spliff in her fingers burned down. She felt pleasantly content, and the flurry of excitement in her belly was the promise of a new adventure. It would be a wonderful thing to die.

'Izzy! Where the hell are you?'

She liked Mikey Satterthwaite. It was strangely touching that he cared so much for her he didn't want her to die. In another world, an alternative one that she wanted to live in, she'd have been happy to open up a bit more to him, but there was so much in this world to be afraid of. If you loved someone — if you even cared for someone — all you did was add to the grief around you because, sooner or later, you were going to die.

Surely sooner was better.

She stood up, a little unsteadily, and crunched her way over the soft leaves underfoot towards the edge of the trees. She hadn't had to go far in once she'd realised Mikey was looking for her. That was the wonderful thing about the trees. They were her co-conspirators, sheltering and protecting her.

In the middle of the stone circle, the Sentinel Tree beckoned her towards it, its bleached limbs pink in the setting sun. She walked up to it and placed her hand against its smooth, dead trunk. Who knew what had killed it while the two on the other side of the stone circle clung on, thickened and distorted with age? Disease, maybe; or perhaps trees, like people, sometimes lost the will to live.

She untwisted the rope from around her waist. It was part of death's plan for her, waiting in the field behind Storm and Raven's tent and all she'd had to do was lift it down. Eden Whispers had told how those who wanted to make a success of suicide checked their knots and she'd done that before she'd smoked her joint, while she was in control of her senses and unlikely to make a mistake. With the rope gripped in her left hand, she began to scale the tree.

'Izzy? Where are you?'

The trunk was smooth, but there were enough places where she could get a grip. She'd always been good at climbing, so lithe and light — like a cat, her PE teachers had always said. Now she was beyond the first of the branches, now the second. How high should she go? She swung herself up to the third branch and edged along it, maybe ten feet above the ground. There, she wound enough of the rope round the branch to be sure she wouldn't hit the ground, looped the noose around her neck and sat to take her last look on the sad world.

'Izzy!'

She lingered. The sun was declining in the west. Mikey, crashing around in the woods, was getting nearer, but he wouldn't reach her in time.

'Izzy!'

She'd miss him. Bracing her hands one on either side of her on the slender branch, she eased herself forwards until she was barely balanced and then, with a flutter of excitement, leaned forward.

'Izzy Ecclestone. Get down from there right now!'

Storm. She hadn't seen him approach, but he was barely five yards away. The twist threw her off balance and, in an unwinding spiral of rope, Izzy fell.

Jude and Mikey broke out of Cave Wood just in time to see the black-clad figure balancing in the Sentinel Tree like an oversized crow. Jude was the closer, by a few feet. He turned up the hill, surging forwards, but the six mile run and the fording of the river had turned his legs to lead and Mikey powered past him. 'Izzy! Christ, no, don't!'

But she did. Even as Storm appeared, shouting, below the tree, Jude saw her slip forward, saw her drop and then, as he redoubled his efforts, there was a sharp crack. The branch snapped and branch, rope and Izzy crashed together to the thin, sheep-mown turf.

Storm had reached her first but Mikey brushed him aside and dropped to his knees beside her. 'For Christ's sake, Izzy, what are you doing? Can't you see how worried I was? Why did you do it? For God's sake, why did you have to scare us like that?'

Jude slowed to a walk. When he made the last few yards Izzy was sitting up, a bemused expression on her face, and Mikey was on his knees beside her, with his arm around her shoulders. He forced himself to be calm, because God knew what had gone through the girl's mind, or what she was thinking. Mikey's passion was understandable but not necessarily helpful.

'This wasn't meant to happen.' Izzy looked up at Mikey, in breathless, wide-eyed surprise. 'I was meant to die, but I caught my arm in the rope. You startled me.' She glared at Storm. 'It was like it was trying to hold me back. Look.'

She disentangled herself from the washing line and held out her arm. A red weal stood out on the pale skin where the rope had slowed her fall. There wasn't so much as a scratch on her neck.

A small silence encircled them. The wind rustled in the wood but the leafless branches of the Sentinel Tree were still.

'Are you okay, Izzy?' Jude asked.

'I think I've hurt my ankle.'

'Right,' Mikey said, 'we can sort that. We'll get you up to the hospital to get it fixed and we'll get you some help — some real help — and Jude will call your mum and let her know what's happening and everything will be all right. Because I'll make damned sure it is.'

'I thought I was going to die,' Izzy said, in tones of utter wonderment. 'I was so sure. The tree was calling to me.'

Mikey got to his feet, gave her his hand and held her up. 'You want to listen to me next time, not a dead tree.'

'We'll take you up to the hospital and get you checked out, Izzy. Then we'll get you home,' said Jude. 'Mikey, you can drive. And you can run me home afterwards, too.'

'I'll go and tell Raven everything's okay.' Storm backed away. A blue light flashed in the background and Jude moved to reassure them that everything was in hand.

Mikey got out his phone and checked his messages, putting them on speaker and playing Jude's panicked messages back. 'Ha ha, you were a bit worked up there, weren't you? Did you think I was that much of an idiot? Bit of a fuss about nothing, in the end.' He laughed and winked at Izzy, who winked back. 'Right. Let's get moving. It'll be fine now I'm in charge.'

'Wait a minute,' said Izzy. 'There's Raven.'

Raven was thinner than ever, frail in the gathering gloom. She hesitated a moment before she shuffled across to them. 'Izzy. My dear, dear girl.'

'It's like that first time we met, isn't it? Down here in the woods? It seems a long time ago.' Izzy dashed a tear from her eye. 'You were so kind to me. And do you know, you were right after all, weren't you? It isn't my time to die.'

It was after midnight by the time Jude struggled back home and managed to rustle up something to eat. The call came through on the landline and for a moment he stared at it in perplexity, because no-one but the few ambulance-chasers and scammers who'd got round his ex-directory shield ever called him on it. 'Hello.'

'Jude.' It was Becca, sounding wary. 'Sorry, I know it's late but I couldn't get you on your mobile.'

'It's in the river.'

'In the river?' A pause. 'Did I wake you up?'

'No. But I've had a difficult evening.'

'Oh, I'm sorry. It wasn't important—'

'It's okay.' He took the phone to the living room and sank into an armchair. 'I'm always glad to hear from you.'

He heard her sigh of relief. 'Well. You know I never presume, but I was a bit scared. I know your mum's away and Mikey went driving off like a bat out of hell and isn't back yet.'

Mikey was staying with Izzy until her parents, who had been out with friends, could get home. 'Yeah. It's been a bit of a nightmare.'

'Is everything all right? I know there's been a fuss at Eden's End, too. Ellie called me.'

'Yeah,' he said again, short of words. He could imagine her, picking at her hair, twisting it round her finger. It had been a lot more comfortable when Becca called him without anxiety and he could answer without fear of overstepping some invisible line he didn't know she'd drawn, but the sound of her voice still did something to his heart.

'If there's anything I can do to help—'

'Thanks.' He rallied. Vanessa had shown him his weakness and that meant he could turn it to his advantage. He loved Becca and always would; fighting it was as futile as hoping for something to come from it. Loving and losing wasn't the end of the world. If Vanessa had understood that, five young people would have lived. 'It's all good. A friend of Mikey's went off on her own and he was worried about her. But it turned out fine. She'd had a fall and hurt her ankle.'

'That's good news.' She laughed. 'Sorry. I'm wasting your time.'

'Never.'

'I tried to call you and so I got worried. It was a silly reaction. I'm as hysterical as everyone else these days. But I'm glad you're okay.'

He waited to see what came next, but nothing did. No

sudden profession of love, no plea for forgiveness. It didn't matter. You had to let these things go. He was a better person than Vanessa Wood. 'You can call me any time.'

'We are still friends, aren't we?' she said.

'Always,' said Jude with a sigh, and put down the phone.

ALSO BY JO ALLEN

Death by Dark Waters

DCI Jude Satterthwaite #1

It's high summer, and the Lakes are in the midst of an unrelenting heatwave. Uncontrollable fell fires are breaking out across the moors faster than they can be extinguished. When firefighters uncover the body of a dead child at the heart of the latest blaze, Detective Chief Inspector Jude Satterthwaite's arson investigation turns to one of murder. Jude was born and bred in the Lake District. He knows everyone… and everyone knows him. Except his intriguing new Detective Sergeant, Ashleigh O'Halloran, who is running from a dangerous past and has secrets of her own to hide… Temperatures – and tensions – are increasing, and with the body count rising Jude and his team race against the clock to catch the killer before it's too late…

The first in the gripping, Lake District-set, DCI Jude Satterthwaite series.

Death at Eden's End

DCI Jude Satterthwaite #2

When one-hundred-year-old Violet Ross is found dead at Eden's End, a luxury care home hidden in a secluded nook of Cumbria's Eden Valley, it's not unexpected. Except for the instantly recognisable look in her lifeless eyes…that of pure terror. DCI Jude Satterthwaite heads up the investigation, but as the deaths start to mount up it's clear that he and DS Ashleigh O'Halloran need to uncover a long-buried secret before the killer strikes again…

The second in the unmissable, Lake District-set, DCI Jude Satterthwaite series.

Death on Coffin Lane

DCI Jude Satterthwaite #3

DCI Jude Satterthwaite doesn't get off to a great start with resentful Cody Wilder, who's visiting Grasmere to present her latest research on Wordsworth. With some of the villagers unhappy about her visit, it's up to DCI Satterthwaite to protect her – especially when her assistant is found hanging in the kitchen of their shared cottage.

With a constant flock of tourists and the local hippies welcoming in all who cross their paths, Jude's home in the Lake District isn't short of strangers. But with the ability to make enemies wherever she goes, the violence that follows in Cody's wake leads DCI Satterthwaite's investigation down the hidden paths of those he knows, and those he never knew even existed.

A third mystery for DCI Jude Satterthwaite to solve, in this gripping novel by best-seller Jo Allen.

Death at Rainbow Cottage

DCI Jude Satterthwaite #4

At the end of the rainbow, a man lies dead.

The apparently motiveless murder of a man outside the home of controversial equalities activist Claud Blackwell and his neurotic wife, Natalie, is shocking enough for a peaceful local community. When it's followed by another apparently random killing immediately outside Claud's office, DCI Jude Satterthwaite has his work cut out. Is Claud the killer, or the intended victim?

To add to Jude's problems, the arrival of a hostile new boss causes complications at work, and when a threatening note arrives at the police headquarters, he has real cause to fear for the safety of his friends and colleagues…

A traditional British detective novel set in Cumbria.

Death on the Lake

DCI Jude Satterthwaite #5

Three youngsters, out for a good time. Vodka and the wrong sort of coke. What could possibly go wrong?

When a young woman, Summer Raine, is found drowned, apparently accidentally, after an afternoon spent drinking on a boat on Ullswater, DCI Jude Satterthwaite is deeply concerned — more so when his boss refuses to let him investigate the matter any further to avoid compromising a fraud case.

But a sinister shadow lingers over the dale and one accidental death is followed by another and then by a violent murder. Jude's life is complicated enough but the latest series of murders are personal to him as they involve his former partner, Becca Reid, who has family connections in the area. His determination to uncover the killer brings him into direct conflict with his boss — and ultimately places both him and his colleague and girlfriend, Ashleigh O'Halloran, in danger…

ACKNOWLEDGMENTS

There are too many people who have helped me with this book for me to name them individually: I hope those I don't mention will forgive me.

I have to thank my lovely beta readers – Amanda, Frances, Julie, Kate, Katey, Liz, Lorraine, Pauline, Sally and Sara – who offered support and suggestions throughout the process. I'd also like to thank Graham Bartlett, who kindly advised me on aspects of police procedure. Mary Jayne Baker delivered, as always, a stunning cover.

Finally, as before, I owe a huge debt of gratitude to the eagle-eyed Keith Sutherland, for proofreading.

Printed in Great Britain
by Amazon